FRANCESCA CATLO\ in the heart of Suffolk, Europe with her French husband and, more recently, their two young children. Of all the places she's been, it is the Greek islands that have captured her heart.

The Little Blue Door was Catlow's first novel – written during the lockdown of 2020 while feeding her newborn in the early hours. To stay up to date please visit www.francescacatlow.co.uk.

T: @francescacatlow

F: @francescacatlowofficial

I: @francescacatlowofficial

TikTok: @francescacatlow

For trigger warnings visit: francescacatlow.co.uk/trigger-warnings/

The Little Blue Door Series in order:

Book 1: The Little Blue Door (2021)

Book 2: Behind The Olive Trees (2022)

Book 3: Chasing Greek Dreams (2023)

Book 4: Found in Corfu (2024)

Standalone novels related to the series:

Greek Secret (2023)

Novellas:

For His Love of Corfu (2021)

One Corfu Summer (2022)

Greek Secret

FRANCESCA CATLOW

Gaia
Fenrir

Published in 2023 by Gaia & Fenrir Publishing

First edition

ISBN: 978-1-915208-25-5 (paperback)

ISBN 978-1-915208-26-2 (ebook)

British Library Cataloguing in Publication Data A CIP catalogue record for this book is available from the British Library.
www.gaiaandfenrirpublishing.co.uk

I dedicate this book to my children; the driving force behind everything I do.
M, you told me to hurry up and write more books...
you can't say I'm not trying.
Love you both always.

Acknowledgement

I would like to thank my good friend Brian Hawes QFSM for talking to me about his experiences.

I would like to acknowledge and thank my editor for always pushing me to be better. I'm so grateful for your insight.

I would like to thank my ARC readers, in particular Gemma, who always sends me lots of helpful feedback.

Last, but never least, my mum and my husband. I think we make a nice little team now. We still have some growing to do, but my success thus far wouldn't have happened without you working alongside me. Love always.

Chapter 1

Now

The heat in his eyes burns my skin. I glance in his direction, but he doesn't look away. Instead, he pulls his narrow glasses down his nose and continues brazenly watching me. I flick my eyes back towards the table, the last table still occupied by diners in La Salle à Manger – a man and his sad girl. My fingers link behind my back. Swaying my weight slowly, back and forth to keep my calf muscles from cramping, I pull my neck straight and tall, desperate to extend my spine and stretch without giving away my exhaustion. The dim, red-tinged lighting doesn't help. The languorous glow sucks me in and makes my eyelids feel heavier than ever. I don't mind it when I'm busy, but when it's quiet at the end of the night, the little candles flickering in their burgundy glasses mesmerise me and dull my senses.

I can feel Charles is still watching me. He's sitting at a table for two in the corner. Usually when he comes out of the kitchen on a Sunday to look over the books, he sits in the opposite corner at a big round table below a low-hanging, gold-fringed lampshade. He always sits alone, looking over his papers or his tablet, scrolling the books and bookings. Perhaps this evening he just decided to shake things up, and sit somewhere slightly different.

I do my best to keep my attention off him; to look attentively present for the couple who should have left an hour ago. The skill lies in doing this without looking like I'm desperate to kick them out. Which I am. The girl's crying. Not wailing, sniffing. Her fingers clutch at the man's hand, making her knuckles white like she's holding on for dear life on a rollercoaster. I'm pretty sure the other wait staff had laid bets earlier with each other about why she was sniffing all night. They've all gone home now though, as we stopped serving food two hours ago. Not sure if they picked a winner or not. I'm not usually involved in such games. It's pretty obvious, to me at least, that he is breaking up with her. Shitty to take her to a nice restaurant to do it. Maybe he thought she would make less of a scene. Didn't work.

Amara would normally be about until closing – along with me and Charles – but she had plans with her boyfriend and left earlier than usual. Soon it's going to be just me and Charles to lock up.

'I'm sorry,' the man snaps loudly at the petite brunette in front of him. His eyes narrow as he turns to nod at me. 'Bill?' Apparently, he's had enough of pretending to care; and doesn't know the word *please* either.

I already have the bill prepared. It's in his hand, a card beeps on the machine and he ushers the girl out in less than a minute. As I bolt the door behind them, I whisper, 'You can do better', to the girl, not that she can hear me, and even if she could, I'm quite sure she wouldn't believe me. Not yet anyway. My fingers drag down the worn red paint on the door as I remember a time I was as stupid as her. Never again.

I turn on my black high heels toward Charles. Still watching me. The corners of my lips tug into a smile, but I don't say anything. He carries on watching me as I pick up the generous cash tip the man left. Honestly, it was the least he could do. I drop it into the big fishbowl next to the till. It won't get divided up until Wednesday though.

'Ruby…' Charles's voice is strained. As my eyes meet his, he pulls off his glasses and places them on the table in front of him. He beckons me closer with an outstretched hand. His fingers retract and curl to pull me towards him. I try not to sigh or roll my eyes, but I do move towards him with a step that is heavier than normal. My shoes sound like sandpaper as they drag on the floor.

When I first began working here, Charles made it clear that he found me attractive. That was back when I was with Jonathan, and it was easy for Charles to hide his compliments with a jokey tone, saying things like, *It's a shame you're not single*, and *I chose you for your good looks, but you're the best thing I invested in*. Even when he isn't saying anything obviously flirty, I have caught him talking to my boobs at least once a week the whole time I've worked here. The only reason I put up with it is because it's a step towards my dreams and I get to work with at least one close friend.

I exhale through my teeth, lightly gritting them under a smile, and come to a standstill. As I stand over the table looking down at him, he reaches across and taps a finger in front of the chair opposite, and lifts his eyebrows. I tug my

3

white shirt at the hem and slip down into the velvet chair across from him, pulling my shoulders square, ready to cut him down if it's required. Our knees are only millimetres from each other and I can feel the shuffle of his feet close to mine.

When I first met him, I wouldn't have pegged him to be so flirty and, honestly, sleazy. At the interview he seemed so innocuous, even as far as bumbling and mildly useless. Now I just can't believe he has the nerve. He's dire. Half his clothes are corduroy, and the other half are washed out mustard; some items are both. They look like faded and shabby hand-me-downs that he has been wearing since his twenties – and he has to be in his mid fifties. He looks like the *least* intimidating man. But with that look – that heat – in his eye, I'm still uncomfortable being alone with him.

'Ruby, you know I adore you.' He places his hand flat on the table with the palm open as though I should place my hand in his. I don't.

We've been getting on well enough for such a long time and today I can feel he is about to ruin it, and possibly get a slapped cheek if he isn't careful. I'm in no mood for stupidity. Charles is closer to my dad's age than mine and even if I did like him in that way, which I don't, it would be inappropriate for him to proposition me like this.

Without tilting my head, I let my eyes lower to look at his hand, then return my gaze to his slender face. 'What is it, Charles? I'm tired and I would like to go home.'

His fingers curl back into his palm and his hand retreats back across the table.

'I really like you—'

'Yes, you've said. Look, that's very flattering, but I'm not at all interested in you like that. So please, save us both the embarrassment. I'll go home and we can forget this ever happened.'

I push my chair back along the old wooden flooring. The sound shudders through the air as I ready myself to stand.

'Actually,' he says, 'I am firing you. I had been planning on saying something about appreciating everything you've done for me, and for the restaurant, but...' He swallows and shuffles in his seat.

Shock pours over me like cold water rushing from my face down my spine to my toes. My mouth hangs ever so slightly open, and it feels like it's been stuffed with cotton. My hands find my knees and grip.

'I—'

He waves a hand dismissively, almost as though I have turned into an unpleasant smell that he is trying to waft away. 'Don't bother to say anything. But if you want a goodbye shag, then I wouldn't say no.' He smirks. 'It's not like you work here now.'

Something about hearing Charles say *shag* hits me right in the gag reflex, although I somehow manage to hold it back without flinching. His thin lips had smirked over the word. I don't break eye contact as he looks me over. Assessing me. If I say yes, then it would have been a genuine proposition, I'm sure. I don't acknowledge it. The less I say, the less satisfaction he can take. 'Joking, of course,' he continues. 'Anyway, I just can't afford you anymore, Ruby. Wish I could. But I'm not making the money I was a few years ago. I've gone over the numbers again and again. It's you or two of the other servers, and I think I can split your job as maître d' between us all, if I'm a bit more active and such. Even if I dropped your pay, I

5

would still need to get rid of someone else as well. This way you can look for a job that will be able to do you justice.'

There's a pause. Perhaps I'm supposed to fill it. I wait, because I can't think of any words that fit together.

'I really didn't want to do this,' he goes on, 'not after everything you've been thr—'

'Thank you so much for the opportunity, Charles,' I snap before he can continue. I don't want to hear another word uttered from his lips. Letting him comment on my life is a step too far. 'I've learned so much and I really appreciate it. Now, as you do not need to replace me, this will be my last shift.' Pushing my chair further back, I stand, my right hand automatically extends in front of me, ready for him to shake it. 'Thank you again.'

He gulps in surprise and stutters something before standing and weakly pumping my hand.

'Are you alright to lock up on your own? I think I'd like to go home now.'

'Ruby…'

His hand becomes firm in mine for a moment, and I snatch my fingers back from his sweaty grip. I do my best to stay looking breezy though, to smile as I back away from him. He mirrors my smile but with uncertainty. My reaction has surprised him. I've always just stayed quiet around him as best I could. He scrambles to get his glasses back on his face as I walk away from him, still talking, holding myself with perfect poise. 'I know as well as anyone that business hasn't been what it was. I wish you the best of luck and I'm sure I'll pop in when I can for Amara's delicious coq au vin.' Then I give him one last smile because I would rather smile than show any other emotion, and there have been times in the past where Charles was kind to me. But now it's time to move on. Like it or not.

Marching through the kitchen, the stainless steel reflecting the shimmering light from the dining area. In the cloakroom, I push my arms like a zombie into my sensible black coat, grab my leather backpack and step towards the service door. I tug the top bolt down and take one last look over my shoulder before leaving. My lungs feel as though they are constricted. I heave desperate breaths before being slapped by the cold March air out on the street.

This is the first time in a long time I've wished Jonathan was there to go home to. Just someone to talk to. To reassure me. The part that was my friend, my companion, I want that back the most. But that isn't going to happen.

'Shit.' I rub my hands together in the cold and mutter to myself, 'I'll never get that bloody tip now.' With a low groan under my breath, I make my way to my car.

Chapter 2

Then

'Babe, do you have some money on you? I've got to get a train to an audition.' Jonathan's hands are in his pockets and while his mouth is stuck in a wide grimace, his eyebrows are pulled together to look like a sad dog, pleading. I know the look.

'What about work?' The muscles in my shoulders tense and I take a deep breath to stay calm, or at least try to.

'Can you tell them I'm sick?' He's gathering together his things – a portfolio of headshots and the usual items he takes with him to auditions.

'They'll know that's not true, and I'm not lying for you again. Charles isn't stupid. You're the worst waiter we have.'

'Thanks, Ruby.' His voice and face crinkle at my comment, but I know he doesn't care. If he did, he wouldn't duck out at any chance he gets.

'Not the worst, but the least reliable. You can be as good as you like, but if you're not there, then it's pointless, isn't it?'

My fingernails find my waist and grip and I look him over. 'There are a lot of tables in tonight. Please come in with me.'

Jonathan turns to me and clasps his hands together as though he is about to beg, but really, I'm the one who's pleading with him. I'm the one who's embarrassed when he doesn't bother showing up to work. I'm the one forced to lie, even though I hate it.

'This isn't just a regular audition, babe.' He pulls my hands away from my hips and grips them in his own. 'This is a callback for the supporting role in a feature-length drama. For the BEE-BEE-CEE.' Jonathan draws out each letter as though it's a separate word that he is explaining to some idiot who has never heard of the BBC. Then his mouth stays hanging open, almost like he is gasping even though he isn't. This is the first time I've wanted to slap the excitement for his acting career right out of him. At thirty-one, he's a few years older than me and he still expects me to be gleeful about any audition, like there's nothing else in the world. I love him, and I've supported him, but I've definitely fallen out of love with his acting. Probably because he stops turning up to his paid job and thinks that's the best plan. It's not that I think he's a bad actor or anything like that, quite the contrary. He is a good actor, and he has the right look to fit in with Hollywood any day of the week, but this isn't exactly the first time he has ditched work for an open-call audition. Far from it. It's one of the reasons we had to leave the last restaurant – he begged and guilted me into lying, then made it pretty obvious I had, when he excitedly ran in during the shift to tell me he had got a part in a panto. My cheeks burnt with the heat of shame like I had a fever, to the point that my lips were chapped for a week after.

I swore I wouldn't do it again. I didn't want to lie and say he was ill at home ever again. But then I get sucked into it all because this is his dream and I'm the one who wants to make sure he has a stable job to help pay rent alongside dreaming. He's the artist and I should support him. It's all he's ever wanted, and after all, I knew this when I started going out with him. He uses all of this to his advantage and I always end up giving in for a quiet life. And because I love him.

We're lucky to have the job at La Salle à Manger, though. It hasn't been open all that long and a friend of mine, Amara, is the sous chef. The thought of letting her down and losing a friend over a bloody audition makes my throat go completely dry.

When my fingers hang loose in his, and I don't scream with excitement that he *has* to get a train into London, he drops my hands completely and shakes his head.

'You know how much this means to me. You've always known. This could be the one, Ruby. The. One.' His hand releases his folder as he fans out his fingers and repeats the motion for emphasis. 'The one that changes it all. Changes *our* life. Come on, just smile sweetly at Charley-boy. We all know he fancies the shit out of you. You could get away with anything.'

'I don't want to get away with anything,' I mutter, but either Jonathan doesn't hear me or he chooses to ignore me. I take a deep breath and inhale his aftershave. He's been a bit too heavy-handed with the stuff and it's gone from attractive to choking, smothering me with sweetness. After everything I've done to support him, I just want a little bit in return. This job is the first time I've been a maître d' and I don't want to lose it because he can't be bothered. 'I'm not going to lie for you. But I will tell Charles the truth and try to explain that it's a really great opportunity. He's a good man under it all. I'm sure he'll understand.'

Jonathan's face completely changes. It's almost back to the faux gasp from moments ago.

'And,' I cut across his emotions and even this word makes him take pause, 'I'm not paying for the train. We don't have the money right now. Not since we took on the rent for this place.' My hands wave towards the pristine white walls. 'We agreed that we had decided to settle things down a little bit. If I pay for your train, I can't pay my part of the rent in full and I know you can't, so—'

Before I'm even finished, his words are cutting into mine. 'Oh, for fuck's sake, Ruby. It's a great opportunity and you're only pretending to be supportive. What am I going to do? I swear you're always trying to hold me back.'

I bite back the upset of this comment. He doesn't mean it. He's angry and not thinking. 'Just call your mum. I'm sure she'll lend you the train fare.'

He slips on his coat and mutters something before he leaves, slamming the door as he goes. My fingers pinch the car keys from the bowl and toss the weight of them from one hand to the other with a satisfying clinking noise. Charles is going to be angry, but Jonathan is as aware as I am about the way Charles looks at me. Jonathan is probably right, and Charles won't be half as mad with me telling him as he might be if Jonathan called in. But it doesn't matter now. It'll be what it'll be. And for the first time, I stood up and said no to Jonathan. Well, at least half a no.

Chapter 3

Now

I didn't tell anyone last night that I had lost my job. I held it in. To contain it makes me feel safe, as though I have control over things. And if I don't tell anyone, it hasn't really happened. Keeping everything in my head until I've processed it stops it all from spilling over into directions that I might not foresee. Anyway, it was too late to call my parents by the time I got home. Not that they would have complained even if I called late, I'm sure, but it's unfair to call at midnight when it wouldn't have changed anything, anyway.

My face is buried in the new black, silk pillowcase that I recently treated myself to. Stupid frivolous purchase. Instead of scouring my phone for a new job – like I should – I consider cancelling my hair appointment that's booked for later in the week. I regret ordering myself new clothes and of course a stupid silk pillowcase from an advert I saw while scrolling my phone.

Alone in my rented mid-terrace, I'm encircled by snoozing neighbours, people I don't really know. They are invisible behind the flimsy modern walls. It feels as though I'm always surrounded by ghosts that run up flights of stairs and argue over cereal at six in the morning. And that's exactly what has woken me up today. Next door shouting up their stairs. *Cereal or toast?!* I roll over and press my duvet to my head, muffling their shrill sounds. Luckily, it's Monday, my day off. Then, the realisation that every day is now a day off stings like nettles and I squeeze my eyes shut again in an attempt to mask the pain as a dream.

When I wake up again, before I can even bring myself to sit up, my fingers begin running along my scalp, gently tugging the roots of my hair as though I'm trying to pull out sensible thoughts that will suggest a future to me that I can actually achieve, but all that remains is fog. I grab for my phone; nearly eleven. The first thing I need to do is call my mum. I can't avoid it any longer.

It doesn't ring for long before she answers.

'Hello, Ruby. We were all just talking about you.'

All? Then there's that feeling again, the anxiety glaze that coats my skin in a glassy sweat and causes a drumming in my chest, because it's just struck me exactly who *all* means. Aunt Hazel is visiting for ten days and I'm meant to be meeting them *all* at eleven thirty so that we can *all* head out to their local pub for lunch together. It's Monday. I know that, but my brain hadn't connected it to the events of the day.

'I'm running a little late.'

I spring out of bed and start to frantically open and close drawers while pinning the phone to my shoulder with my ear. My limbs dart independently in all directions as my eyes scan

13

the room looking for my fitted black jeans. Found them – a neatly folded pile of clean washing on the ornate chair on the other side of my bed. I clumsily stomp over the bed to get to it.

'That's not like you, Ruby. Is everything alright?'

I hesitate as my fingers reach for the fabric of my top. Although the reason I called was to tell her I'm now unemployed, there's no point blurting it out now when I'll see her in a matter of minutes anyway. Plus, I don't want to waste time when I need to have a shower and to do my make-up.

'I'll explain when I get to you. I'll be there soon. Love you, bye.'

'Okay, sweet pea. There's no rush. Drive safe okay. Love you too.'

After the fastest shower and hair wash of my life, I pull tops from my set of white drawers. My clothes decorate my teal duvet with an array of colours, like fallen petals, before I find a cream top with big black polka dots and long sleeves that'll go nicely with my jeans.

I hesitate over the mirror. I haven't left the house without concealer and foundation on for almost two years, but time is running low. I twist my face towards my left shoulder and examine the silver line that snakes across my chin. There is a matching line across my forehead. They aren't something I like to have on show. My fingers tug at my fringe to try to hide the scar on my forehead. Sadly, it can't cover the one on my chin, and if my hair moves it stops hiding the one on my forehead.

The scars are not a fun talking point for me. I cover them up with foundation in case some stranger decides they *have* to know where I got them from and what interesting story is attached. My hands frantically search my make-up bag. There is no time for concealer, so I need the super-thick foundation that I reserve for weddings or days when my skin is having a tantrum. I do my best to blend it out and it does its best to hide the shine of the scar, to remove its ability to catch even the most sparing of light. It's neutralised, much like everything else in my life.

The heating in the car blasts my feet and face. I try not to rush, but to utilise the time, when I stop at traffic lights, I try to tilt my head closer to the vent to dry my hair a little.

It's a bright and fresh morning. The dew glitters on spiderwebs at the side of the road, but only on the ones in the shade where the sun is yet to melt away the remnants of the cold night. Jonathan's mum used to tell him that spiderwebs on the grass are trampolines for fairies. Don't think about him. There's too much going on to reminisce about the past. My eyes latch on to the rear-view mirror to check for bikes well in advance of turning left. Instead, I catch sight of myself. I look washed-out with no blusher or bronzer, but presentable enough for lunch.

The way to my parents' place is lined with trees casting solid shadows against the beaming midday sun. My house is on the outskirts of Ipswich and my parents live in a village called Barking. It isn't too far away.

We are going to be late for our booking. As a maître d' – or, ex maître d' now, I guess – I'm not a fan of late arrivals, which puts off the timings with tables when the dining room is all booked up. Although, it has been a while since that has happened in the restaurant. My teeth find the sides of my cheeks as I wonder how long Charles has kept me on when he couldn't really afford to. It isn't something I want to admit to, but I've known for at least six months that things have been bad. Probably for longer.

My tyres crunch to a stop on the gravel of my parents' drive. Their house is an old red-brick cottage and all the windows have typical Suffolk Woolpit white bricks above them, and each corner of the house has them too. My dad always likes to point that out to people. It's a part of local heritage and history and something he thinks people would like to know.

My mum opens the front door before my engine is off and she, my dad and Aunt Hazel all come bustling out of the door. Hazel has an unseasonal glowing tan from living in Corfu. She divorced my uncle Tim almost twenty years ago now, and I haven't seen him since. When she went on holiday with some friends to Corfu about sixteen years ago, she did the cliché bit of falling in love. Hazel met Pericles, got pregnant and married him a few years later. Pericles' wife had passed away a couple of years before he met Hazel. He already had a son called Yianni, then together they had a daughter, Natalia.

Aunt Hazel's straight blonde hair is flying about her ears in the breeze and catching across her face as she races towards me, with arms and hands so forcefully stretched out that her fingers are hyperextending.

'Ruby mou!' Hazel grabs my shoulders then reels me in before squeezing me to her bomber jacket. 'Gosh, your hair is ever so wet.' She touches her cheek where she pressed herself to my hair and then nips at the ends of my sandy-coloured locks. 'It's so lovely to see your pretty little face, Ruby mou.'

'Right, you two,' Mum cuts in. 'We can all fit in one car, no need to take two.'

'I'll drive, then you lot can all have a glass of wine.' I kiss my mum and dad hello before we all pile into my Renault.

Hazel is in the front and Mum and Dad are in the back, and it is Hazel who asks the obvious question. 'How's work? Did you get in late last night?'

I snatch a breath and bite the middle of my lower lip making sure my eyes are fixed on the road. Grey and solid. Unchanging. The car gobbles up the road metre by metre just like the anxiety that is gobbling me up from my toes to my head. I hesitate, making humming noises until my mum leans forward, her mouth almost next to my ear from the passenger seat behind.

'What's wrong, sweetheart? Was it a bad night?'

'Yeah, you could say that.' My fingers drum the leather steering wheel. 'Charles took me to one side after work, and explained that he can't afford me anymore.' My shoulders lift in a shrug and I plaster a smile onto my face to hide my disappointment. 'He fired me.'

Catching sight of myself in the rear-view mirror again makes me realise I'm grimacing, not smiling.

Their questions muddle with cooing and they tell me I can do better and it will all work out. It's hard not to tell them all just to leave me well alone. Even if that's what I want. They're being kind and I don't want to be rude. But I've become so sick of people's sympathy. It isn't an emotion that comes with any productivity. It's stagnant and it lingers over situations like a smell. The smell, initially nice, always turns sour if it sticks around too long, and as resentment makes the situation go off.

I have to say something.

'Can we talk about something else? It is a job. It's not like someone died. I don't have that job anymore and I'm sure I'll find another restaurant job soon. Auntie Hazel, how is *Theios* Pericles? I haven't seen him in so many years.'

I put my indicator on to turn into the pub carpark and we all file out as Hazel tells me that my Uncle Pericles is well and how much he wishes he could have come with her on the trip. The tension that has been pressing on my rib cage lifts now that my news is out in the open.

Chapter 4

Now

A giant-size bowl of moules marinières is placed in front of me, and another in front of my dad.

'Like father like daughter. It's that French blood.' Hazel winks. 'Ruby, do you have a French passport? You're half French. Did you ever get one?'

I nod as I take a mouthful of the bread I've just dipped in the butter and parsley sauce. It's so garlicky it's almost spicy. My dad continues to answer for me, so I keep dipping my bread into the creamy sauce covering the mussels.

'We made sure to get her dual nationality when she was only a year or two, didn't we Fern?'

Dad looks and sounds typically French. I'm not one to feed into clichés, but he really does look like he should be walking around with a beret and striped T-shirt. These days he is as grey as a pigeon, but he used to have rich brown hair and deep dark eyes over a character nose. I didn't get his nose, luckily, as

I don't think it would be as attractive on a girl, but he's where my natural colouring comes from, and my hooded eyelids too. My roots, lashes and eyebrows are chocolate brown but the ends of my hair I've bleached a sandy blonde for years. I distinctly look more like my dad's side of the family. I got his bee-stung lips too. So much so that people often ask where I have my lips done, because they *look so natural.* Only for me to explain they *are* natural. My dad is exactly the same. My mum, on the other hand, doesn't look much like me. Her skin is pinched pink and she's exceptionally fair. All I got from her is my straight nose and the smattering of freckles on it that come out in the sun. Sadly, they're inevitably hidden with foundation as collateral damage when hiding my scars.

Mum agrees with Dad. 'It was back when we wanted to move to France. Never happened, of course. When Marc's dad died his mum came to live in Suffolk, didn't she? Until she passed.'

'Of course, of course.' Hazel's nodding, and a forkful of mashed potatoes dripping gravy hovers above her plate. She seems to stay like that for a moment longer than necessary, and clearly my mum has noticed too.

'Why do you ask?' Mum pushes her blonde fringe out of her eyes.

Hazel doesn't answer. Instead, she turns to look at me, her sapphire eyes wide behind her black-framed glasses. 'How about you come and work for us this summer? No need to sort a work permit. You're already European, after all. We would love to have you, and if I'm honest, we could do with some reliable hands.'

It's a sweet idea in theory but not a viable one. Even if I gave up my little house, where would I put all of my possessions? I highly doubt that Hazel and Pericles could pay me enough to cover my rent here all while feeding me, giving me lodging or enough money to also pay rent there *and* have enough money to enjoy any spare time in Corfu. To go to Corfu would be to bury my head almost literally in the sand. I need to move forwards and get my life and goals back on track.

'That's a lovely thought, but completely impractical. What would I do with my house?'

Out of the corner of my eye I sense my mum sighing and her body seems to release. I hadn't noticed her becoming tense, but the release is now obvious. I think Hazel catches it too and wants to pick at it.

'Don't you think it would be good for her, Fern? After everything she has been through—'

'Please,' I cut in, 'I'm right here, and it doesn't matter what I have or haven't been through. I'm sure it would be lovely to spend time in Corfu, but I can't. Sorry, Auntie Hazel.'

Hazel presses her lips together as though a zip has been pulled across. I hadn't meant to pull out my firm tone, the tone I use on people who are trying to pull a fast one in the restaurant or if a bloke is being a pain. It doesn't happen often, but when it does, it's often on me to smooth things out. Most of which is done with a gentle smile, but on occasion a firmer tone is required so everyone knows I mean business. And that's the tone I just dished out to Hazel. My mother uses the same tone with me sometimes and I wonder if Hazel has used a similar one with Natalia. I've never spent enough time with them to find out. One week in a year is never enough, and this time, Natalia hasn't been able to join her mother in England. Apparently, she has too much schoolwork that she just can't miss.

The subject isn't mentioned again, but I catch a look between my dad and Mum that I can't read. Hazel sidesteps into talking about how they really will need to find someone new as one of their staff members is off to uni this year. My dad's little finger strokes my mum's arm and when she glances at him, he furrows his eyebrows. It doesn't seem like he is confused or angry. Perhaps it is a look of concern? I can't be sure. Mum quickly looks away and moves her arm from the reach of his little finger. The moment passes as quickly as it arrived, and the conversation flows to a new topic.

After lunch I drop everyone back at the house and decline the offer of coming in for coffee. The thing I really need to do is speak to Amara. She is the one who got me the job at Charles's restaurant. Amara's the sous chef and we have known each other for years. As the restaurant is shut on Mondays and Tuesdays I know she isn't working, so I send her a message to see if she can come over. Luckily, she says yes, and arrives at my house shortly after.

We are so very different in almost every way. She has long flowing curls that whip freely around her back, and her spirit is just as wild. In the whole time I've known her, she's lived in more countries learning local cuisine than I can remember. La Salle à Manger is the longest she's worked anywhere and even then she went off for a month to France and called it training. I've always lived in England. Mostly Suffolk, but I did do a stint in London. That's where I met Jonathan. Amara never seems to worry about much. Not outwardly. It's not that I spend my time worrying, but that is because I try my best to keep my life in order.

I pour Amara's tea into a plain black cup and slide it to her across my oak kitchen table. I flop down at the table and drop a sugar cube into my coffee. 'Charles fired me last night. I'm going to assume you didn't know.' I take a sip of the coffee. Its bitterness mixes with the sweetness of the sugar and soothes me.

'What? I had no idea. He can't do that. We *need* you. Christ! You're the only thing holding that bloody place together.' She places her cup back on the saucer without drinking any tea and sits hunched over it before peeping up at me. 'What the hell are you going to do? Maybe I should threaten to leave unless he takes you back.'

My shoulders lift then drop down hard.

'Don't be ridiculous. There's no point in us both being in the shit. He can't afford me. Without me the restaurant has a chance. Not a bloody clue what I'll do though.' My lips round into a snigger. 'My aunt thinks I should swan off to Corfu with her for the summer.' I take another sip of the scorching coffee.

Amara sits bolt upright and taps one of her rebellious, neon fingernails on the tabletop. 'That's exciting. When do you leave?'

'I didn't say yes, Amara. Blimey. What would I do with this place?' I gesture at the room. 'The idea's completely impractical.'

Her face crumples into a frown and she takes a quiet sip of her tea.

'How's Si?'

Si is Amara's boyfriend. They've been together about eight months, which is the longest I have ever known her to stick with a guy.

'Good. Still working hard, as ever.' Amara's finger moves along the edge of her cup. 'We're thinking of moving in together. I never thought I might *want* to settle down, or at least not for years. You know me, I love my freedom.' I raise an eyebrow knowing exactly what she means as she always used to give me every little detail of it. 'But with Si, it's different. We click. I wouldn't even mind marrying this one.' As soon as she says it, her face shifts. 'Sorry. I don't mean to be rubbing my happiness in your face, with everything—'

'Don't be ridiculous. It's wonderful, and I would never want you to be anything but happy. You deserve it.'

Her face relaxes back into peachy cheeks and a soft smile. 'If you did go to Corfu…'

I can't help but roll my eyes. 'I'm not—'

'I know, but if you did. I assume you would be working?'

'Of course. In my aunt and uncle's restaurant. Greek Secret, it's called. It's traditional food and a cocktail bar too.'

'So still working in a restaurant, which is what you always seem to want.'

I nod before her eyeline drops to her teacup. She shifts her cup on the saucer, edging it around in a circle, then looks up at me. 'What if I sublet this place over the summer? You know, if you did *actually* want to go and do the Greek bit for a few months. It would give me and Si an opportunity to see if we *can* live together before signing a formal contract. If you say yes, you'd be doing me a huge favour.' Her hair falls across most of her face and her dark eyes peer out at me like a bush baby.

'I'll think about it.'

Chapter 5

Now

It takes a week of looking at dreadful job listings to tip me over the edge into a decision. So, being a good friend and a good niece, I have no choice but to go to Corfu. I have one month to prepare myself. I empty my drawers and cupboards of clothes, most of which go into my old bedroom at my parents' house, and then I pack swimwear, floaty chiffon trousers and sensible black miniskirts and shorts for work. That is it; and today I am taking a flight to Corfu where I will work from May until October.

There's a spare room waiting for me at Aunt Hazel's house. I will be living with Hazel, Pericles, his son Yianni, who is about twenty-six, and their daughter Natalia who is almost fifteen. I've only met Yianni once before, at their wedding. I was sixteen or seventeen and he would have been perhaps eleven-ish. I can't really remember him, other than being introduced. I don't think we spoke much. It was the biggest wedding I've ever been to. Hundreds of people dancing and eating. I do know Natalia at least. We've always got on well, even with the age gap.

I leave Heathrow with a light drizzle slicking the runway, and arrive in Corfu to a wall of warmth. The sun greets me as I step out of the aeroplane door and I have to lift my hand to shade my eyes. My body shivers, as though it's shaking off the cold air from the plane and welcoming in the heat of the early afternoon sun, still high in the sky.

In the tiny airport, my bags are among the first to appear on the carousel, so I make my way into the arrivals area in good time. I am faced with a small crowd of taxi drivers with names scrawled on paper. It's slow going with two suitcases and my backpack, but this gives me time to look over the faces of waiting people and their little signs. One catches my eye: *Ruby*. I know it's not for me though, as Aunt Hazel is meeting me in person. I see other names too, but it amuses me that there's another Ruby being picked up, as it isn't the most common name. Not that uncommon either, I suppose. I can't see the driver's face as his head is bowed and hidden under a mass of hair while he looks at his phone. Momentarily I glance about, wondering who this other Ruby might be.

I stand on tiptoe in my ballet pumps to see over people's heads, but there's no sign of Hazel. Thinking she might be waiting outside, I leave through the glass doors and stand on the pavement, watching taxis, minibuses and cars filter past. People casually step out in front of them, expecting that they will stop in time as they cross the road. My entire body shudders at their confidence. Even with a zebra crossing, I can't do that. Not for a long time anyway. Perhaps when I was a teen, I can't remember now. Maybe. As it is, I have to turn away and avert my eyes. I lock them on to the pavement. Focussing on the shade of grey.

Hazel still does not appear, and I start to feel a thudding in my chest as though there's a fire burning behind my ribs and my heart has been tasked with stamping it out. The flight was a little late, so she should be here by now. I glance at my phone again, but there are no messages and no missed calls coming up. Nothing.

Another fifteen minutes go by. I type out a message to Hazel to say I have arrived, and I'm worried, so I'll get a taxi and meet her at their restaurant. That way if she's forgotten me, I'm on my way, or if something worse has happened I've put forward my intentions or, if she's late she'll arrive, see my message and turn around. Hopefully. Also, my thinking is, better to be dropped in a seaside resort with tourists meandering around, because someone will be able to point me in the right direction for the restaurant. If I get dropped off in a little village with only people who *actually* live in Corfu, it might be harder to find where I need to be. Stupidly, I didn't bother to take down the address of Hazel and Pericles's house, only the name of the village. What would have been the point when Hazel was meant to be picking me up? Apparently, the point was in case I was left at the airport.

I drop my phone back into my pocket and anxiety stabs at me as my brain pulses with two little words: *what if*. What if something has happened to her on the way to the airport? What if she's stuck somewhere? Scenes of her car tumbling off the road and colliding with olive trees slide across my eyes and I can almost feel the loose items in the car bouncing around her as she falls, and hear the call of sirens when she's found. No. She must have got the time wrong or has just been held up. I've known her to be late for things, although maybe not important things. Usually she sends a message to say what's happening, but there must be a valid reason. Standing with my cases leaning against my legs, eyes still desperately scanning the face of anyone who comes near me, I circle the ring on my right hand with my right thumb. I proceed to actually cross my fingers, desperately hoping that nothing has happened to Hazel. Taking my phone out of my pocket, I punch out a message to her, hit send, and lock my phone. I keep my fingers tightly wrapped around each other for a long moment, though. This is ridiculous.

Seeing an empty taxi pull up to the kerb, I thrust my phone into my pocket and walk towards the clean-looking Mercedes. A woman gets out to help with my two large bags, and asks, 'Where you go?'

'San Stefanos, North-West. It's also called Agios Stefanos.' I smile, but only briefly as a man passing by turns abruptly. He is taller than me with a mass of wavy hair that grazes his broad shoulders, and a fine layer of stubble crosses his face.

'San Stef? North-West?' he says. 'You are Ruby?' He lifts the sign with *Ruby* scrawled on it in front of his chest, then taps it with his right index finger.

Apparently, there is no other Ruby and he really *has* been waiting for me.

Turning to the first taxi driver, I say, 'I'm so sorry. I had no idea. Thank you. *Efcharistó.*'

She shrugs and seems okay about it. The other driver, the man with all the hair, says something to her too. She replies with a smile as she unloads my bags from the boot of her car.

I follow behind him. On long legs he strides into the traffic with barely a glance, leaving me wincing and trotting to keep up with his pace.

'I was looking for my auntie. I guess she is the one that booked you. She was meant to be collecting me.'

'I know.' He yanks my luggage up onto the high kerb and keeps walking through the carpark. Sweat starts to collect on my upper lip from all the trotting.

'Well, I didn't. I saw your sign, I just thought there was another Ruby. Shame you didn't put the last name.'

He turns to me with his eyebrows hunched over his eyes.

'You didn't think it was a good idea to ask? To check?'

His grumpy face irritates me. It isn't as though I did it on purpose. 'I'm sorry, but I would have thought my aunt would text or call. You don't know her. This is very unusual.'

He pulls a set of keys from his pocket and presses the button. The indicators on a Ford Focus flash. He laughs a little. Not a big booming laugh. More like a little snort.

'That is funny. Living with someone for many years and not knowing them. I suppose it is possible.'

Now it's my turn to frown. What is he blabbering about? I watch as he lifts one suitcase into the boot then places his hands on his hips and eyes the next one. He settles on opening the rear door and shuffling it onto the back seat.

I open my mouth to speak, but I'm struck by the realisation that this car doesn't look like any of the other taxis at the airport. He turns to me, and his face lifts slightly.

'Am I missing something?' I look from the mass of wavy hair back to the car.

He points at his chest. 'Yianni. We have met. I am Hazel's stepson.'

I shake my head in disbelief. How could this tall man in tight-fitting jeans and wild almost shoulder length hair be the boy from the wedding? I can't marry the two images in my brain at all. He had short hair, maybe curly on top?

'Are you sure?' It's a ridiculous question, which I realise as I'm asking it, even before he's vaguely struck by mirth. 'No, I mean, you don't look at all how I remember you.'

'Good. You look about the same.'

'Do I?'

Yianni pushes his lips out, tilts his head and inspects me for changes before shrugging. 'Yes.' He turns towards the car. 'And she did text you – Hazel. I saw it send.'

To stop my mouth from hanging open I pull my phone from the pocket of my playsuit. 'Here.' Yianni turns to me, his face so damn smug, I thrust the phone towards it to wipe the look right off him. 'No message,' I add for good measure.

He takes the phone out of my hand and studies it. He looks at me with a raised eyebrow.

'It's still on flight mode.'

Chapter 6

Then

Jonathan's smooth cheek is pressed to mine and his fingers are running the length of my arm.

'Please don't go out tonight,' he murmurs.

Amara has invited me to go out dancing after work with her and a couple of her friends that I get on well with. Jonathan doesn't have a job anymore. He's been looking for another waiter job somewhere else since he quit working for Charles to take on some extra work when he didn't get the part in the BBC feature-length piece. The extra work pretty much only covered the costs of him getting to London and his lunch while he was there. Of course, this still means it was worthwhile to him, because *you never know who you might meet on set.*

'I've said I'll go.'

'But I'll be all alone at home.'

He's edging for an invite, but I know Amara would be

irritated if he were to be invited to a girls' night out.

'It's girls only.'

'I could dress up.'

Irritation smacks on my face before I can stop it. I do my best to rein it back in. 'I'll only have one drink and then I'll be home. Okay?' I twist to face him, hoping it'll reassure him.

Jonathan slumps down onto our sofa and kicks his feet up over the arm and begins to play with his phone. Either he's sulking or he's lost interest. Based on past experience, he's sulking. He never likes me going out without him. I get off the sofa and go to the hallway to collect my bag for work.

In moments I'm back in the room stooping down to give him a kiss before I leave.

'What's that?' He points at my leather backpack I've bunched over one shoulder.

'My handbag.'

'No, what's hanging out of it?'

I glance over my shoulder to see the sleeve of one of my dresses poking out.

'Oh, it's the dress I'm changing into for when we go out.'

'So, do you really expect me to believe you're off out for only one drink when you're getting changed to go?'

'I'm not going out in my work clothes. You have to be kidding.'

'Are you even going out with the girls? Or is it someone else? Is Charles taking you somewhere?'

His lips are locked firmly closed and his eyes are like the mouths of angry dogs ready to chew me up and spit me out. There's so much anger. It's the first time he has made such an accusation and I don't even know how to react.

'You cannot be serious.'

'Well, you didn't quit the restaurant when I did and you always seem damn cosy at that place.'

There are no words in my vocabulary to formulate an appropriate answer. None. I just stand with my mouth aghast like I've been frozen mid-sentence.

'Have fun, Ruby. But I might not be here when you get back,' he says, as I turn to walk away. His tone sounds like he has thrown a knife towards me and just missed, planting the knife straight into the doorframe instead of between my shoulder blades. A year or so ago, that knife would have hit me right in the back and reeled me in, stopping me from going out with my friends. But there's a smug note in his tone, like he knows that a strange and cryptic taunt like that will get me turning around, and it's enough to stop me from being reeled in this time.

I close the front door behind me and step out into the chill of the spring air. I haven't seen my school friends for eight months. Surely it can't be that long? It is. It was a birthday party and everyone was there. That had to be eight months ago. Last time I arranged to meet them, Jonathan took the car to an audition so I couldn't get there. He apologised profusely of course, but now I'm wondering if he even had an audition, or whether he was controlling me.

I slip inside my car and as I drive along, I think of how Jonathan has been separating me from people. I even start to think how often we see his mum versus how often we see my parents. There's more often than not a *legitimate* reason not to see my family. Plus, he always plays the *my mum is lonely from her divorce* card. Which works on me because I remember how sad Aunt Hazel was when she split from her husband.

That's it. I might love Jonathan, but I'm going to spend more time with my friends and family.

That night I don't just go for one drink. I don't actually drink anything other than water, but I stay out laughing and dancing with Amara. It's more fun than I've had in ages.

The *ting* of my key connecting with the lock is enough. The door flies out of my hand and there is Jonathan, red-faced, with every muscle in his jaw as tense as can be.

'I've been calling you,' he snaps.

'Have you? What's wrong?' I step round him and follow my usual walking in the door routine. Remove shoes, coat, wash hands. He follows me the entire time.

'Yes. Why haven't you checked your phone?'

'I did. There's nothing there. Maybe you were calling the wrong number.'

This is clearly the wrong thing to say as Jonathan's neck blazes a new shade of crimson. I go to my backpack and pull my phone out, passing it to him.

He says, 'I was worried about you. But now I think maybe I was right and you are sleeping with Charles.'

'Seriously? This again?' Pushing past him I creep up the stairs. I'm sure Jonathan's tone is loud enough to carry into the house next door and I don't want to make it worse.

'Look, seven missed calls and three texts.' He pushes the phone back at me as I arrive at our bedroom door.

I snatch the phone back and realise it was set to *Do Not Disturb* from eleven thirty onwards.

The next thirty minutes of my life are spent defending this mistake, explaining that it doesn't show on my home screen when it's set to do not disturb, so how was I to know? It's no use. We end up arguing. Crying. I'm permanently *shushing* him for the sake of our neighbours, but he doesn't listen. He layers me in accusations and shame and as the time passes, I sit and quietly take it. This is why I never see anyone. It had just been so long that I'd forgotten the guilt. Although, this is worse than ever.

Eventually we fall asleep and when we wake up, Jonathan begins to cry.

'I was just so worried about you. You know that, right? I just don't know what I would do if anything ever happened to you. No matter what, I will always love you.'

I want to tell him that loving me doesn't give him the right to get angry with me and berate me for hours for a mistake, but I don't have any energy left. So, I accept this reasoning. It's as close to an apology as I'm likely to get, and, I'll learn from it. If I go out again, I'll make sure my phone is on loud.

Chapter 7

Now

Looking out of the window of Yianni's car, I watch huge birds of prey, at times not too far overhead, as the car meanders from inland villages to mountain roads. Giant cypress trees protrude like thin green party hats on top of all the other trees and the sky is the brightest aqua blue I think I have ever seen. I want to breathe it all in, absorb it into my forever memory, because it's the most beautiful road I've ever been along. All types of trees hug the roads from olives to lemons and many I don't recognise. The landscape is scattered with darling hamlets of whitewashed buildings, all of which seem silent and still as though it's too warm out to even bother rustling the leaves in the trees.

If the journey wasn't being peppered with the awkwardness between Yianni and me, it would be idyllic. As it is, he's huffing every other moment after expressing his concern about how late I've made him. To really emphasise this fact, he angles his watch towards his face now and then too. It's the start of the season, and it *is* still quiet, but apparently, we are going to miss the start of the dinner rush and we – or at least he – is needed.

'I don't know why Hazel sends me and does not come herself to get you. I could have helped with the food.' Gripping the steering wheel with his left hand, he pushes his hair back off his face with the right.

'Look, instead of dropping me back at the house, we can go straight to the restaurant. That should catch up some time, right?'

Honestly, anything to shut him up. For someone so pretty he really can sulk his face into a heavy scowl. It isn't as if I have intentionally missed messages and calls. Of course, he was right; my phone had been left on flight mode. When he pointed it out, I remembered then that I had put my phone on flight mode before turning it off. The battery was running a little low and I had left my charger in my hold luggage, so, instead of just turning it off or using flight mode, I did both and forgot. As soon as Yianni took the phone off flight mode on my behalf, three messages came through from Hazel, plus one from Yianni and about five missed calls from him too, including voicemails. He isn't impressed with my stupidity, clearly.

Yianni looks me up and down in a nano second. I feel it. I feel the presence of his eyes flicking over me. Perhaps it's more obvious to me because his thick black eyelashes emphasise the motion.

'Are you sure?' he says, shuffling his weight back into his chair before manoeuvring a winding bend that lets me see right over the edge of wherever we are and down into the

37

sea of green below, which stretches out away from us until it merges with the sky in the curve of the earth.

'Of course,' I stifle a yawn. It's creeping into late afternoon and straddling the point of evening. I was awake half the night travelling to the airport, making sure I was dropped off by the taxi hours in advance of the flight. I gently twist my body as much as I can to ease some of my muscles. 'It'll be fine,' I confirm. 'Under one condition at least.'

'Condition?'

'Yep. No more sulking about the fact I accidentally left my phone on flight mode.' I make sure to elongate the word *accidentally,* so he can't miss its presence in the sentence.

Yianni tuts and mutters in Greek before taking a deep breath, pushing it out to vibrate his lips. His fingers fidget on the wheel. I'm starting to think I've asked the impossible here. He might never agree to the terms.

'I am not sulking. I am late for work. This is all.'

'Should I assume you're not agreeing to my terms then?'

I stop avoiding looking directly at him and shift in my seat, folding my arms over my chest, and watch him suck in his cheeks.

'How can I stop sulking, when I am not sulking? This is impossible, no?'

He glances at me, doing his best to briefly smile in my direction.

'Fine. You're not sulking. In that case can we start afresh? Can you forgive me for making you late in the first place?' There might be a slightly sarcastic tone to my voice, and at the same time I am questioning why I even agreed to move here for six months. I snatch a breath and look out the window. *You work with this knob now, Ruby,* I remind myself. At least the view out of the window is enticing, and just because we are going to be working – and living – together doesn't mean I can't ignore him. Hopefully.

I've given up on trying to please people ever since Jonathan. I learnt the hard way that it is better to just do what makes *you* happy and not worry if someone else wants to be miserable. However hard that can be.

'Fine, fine. We can go straight to the restaurant. If we make it on time, I forgive you.'

My skin prickles with bad memories. Old wounds seem to throb like they've been reopened and I wish I could be swallowed up by the pretty view and spat out at home in my bed. Then I hear Yianni exhale next to me, and he almost laughs.

'I'm sorry I seem…sulky. This season is a big deal for me. More responsibility and… You know, it doesn't matter. I'm sorry for my sulk face. We all make mistakes.' I'm completely perplexed by this shift. It's not something I'm used to seeing. I watch him as he watches the road ahead. A smile inches across his face. 'I should be used to it anyway. I didn't realise you would be as bad as Hazel. She is useless with her phone.'

I don't respond, but I do share in his smile.

Yianni pulls the car into a small dusty car park that has two other cars in it. The restaurant is almost all terrace with a wooden framework around it in lieu of solid walls. Pericles is standing at the entrance holding a menu. Above him on a metal chain is a sweeping wooden sign that reads: Greek Secret. The words are baby blue and the sign looks as traditional as it could possibly get. To the right of the restaurant there's a trellis hung with grape vines. On the left side there is a bar with high wooden stools, then at the back is the main building where the kitchen and toilets are situated.

I'm leaning towards the windscreen and taking it all in again after only having a very vague memory of being there when we visited for Hazel and Pericles' wedding. It hasn't changed much, only a fresh lick of paint perhaps.

Yianni jumps out of the car before I have even managed to undo my seatbelt.

'Bye then,' I whisper as I get out of the car.

He's jogging into the restaurant and well out of earshot. I can see that a handful of tables are already taken. Pericles grips Yianni's arm, smiling under a quiff of thick slate-grey hair that has a wave to it. I wonder if that's where Yianni got his curly hair from, or if it's from his mother's side. As I slam the car door, Pericles looks across at me and his face changes to a frown. He looks at his son then hits him on the arm with the navy leather menu. They have a heated micro conversation in Greek before Pericles turns towards the restaurant's interior and calls Hazel's name. Then he jogs down the few steps towards me with open arms.

'Ruby! It has been so long. *Kalispera.*'

Pericles is a sizeable guy, almost six feet with broad shoulders and a little too much weight balancing around his middle. His big hands grab my shoulders and he kisses my cheeks four times before releasing me. Behind him I hear a squeal and the tapping of feet running down the wooden steps as Hazel comes and embraces me too. Garlic and dill permeate the air around her, which only makes me realise how hungry I am, having not eaten since a big fried breakfast at the airport many hours ago.

'Look at you!' She cups my face with her garlicky fingers. 'I

40

am so happy you decided to come. I thought you were going straight to the house though to unpack and rest. I left food in the fridge for you.'

She puts her arm around me and begins to walk me at a quick pace towards the restaurant.

'There was a little misunderstanding. I accidently left my phone on flight mode and made us late.' I reach the steps where Yianni is standing with his feet slightly apart and his hands behind his back ready to greet anyone coming into the restaurant. His fitted black jeans and shirt are obviously his work clothes, and he looks like he was born ready to start work. 'Yianni, was very good about it though. Didn't sulk or anything.'

He looks at me from the corner of his eye as I say his name. There's perhaps a tug to the corner of his lips – is it the spasm of the ghost of a smile? Who knows?

I smile at him through pursed lips. I expect him to mirror my sarcasm, but instead his lips seem to twitch again with a suppressed smile before he returns his gaze towards the street.

'Well,' Pericles says, 'you are here now. That is what matters, yes?'

'I bet you're hungry, aren't you? Why don't you put your feet up for tonight, just as we intended. I'll get Natalia to bring you some food over. Look, there she is.' Hazel points as Natalia comes out of the kitchen balancing two huge plates with whole fish on them. As soon as she sees me a grin spreads across her face. She can't stop and say hello with her hands so full, but she mouths *Kalispera* from a distance.

Hazel disappears back into the kitchen, and I sit at a square table for two waiting to be served. At last, excitement ripples over me because I'm outside of my comfort zone and in paradise.

Chapter 8

Now

My fingers smooth the ripples out of the white paper table-cloth that has been carefully placed over a blue cloth one. I watch the other diners in the restaurant. I'm not sure what Yianni was fussing about. It isn't as though it is high season and out-of-control busy. There are only three tables with customers and all he is doing is standing at the door like a statue. Waiting.

A breeze rolls through the restaurant and I let myself take a lungful of the warm air. Greek Secret has a rustic vibe and even the smells from the kitchen are homely and welcoming. Warm bread, grilled lamb, fresh fish. All, of course, with the distinct notes of garlic and dill and thyme.

I'm relaying everything that has happened so far to my mum in a message when Natalia's bright young face appears above an enormous plate filled with a whole sea bass and roasted potatoes.

'Come here, you!' I push back my chair, and she barely has the plate out of her hands and on the table before I'm squeezing her.

'Mama says as it's not too busy I can have a break to say hello. What drink would you like?'

'Well, this is one of the few evenings I won't be working, so a glass of white wine please.'

She trots off behind the bar where Pericles is making drinks for one of the tables, and I carefully begin to fillet the fish on my plate while it eyeballs me. Over the past ten years I've spent my life circulating through every type of restaurant job. Therefore, filleting a fish isn't an issue in the slightest. Hazel hasn't mentioned what role I will take on while I'm working in Greek Secret – whether I'll be serving, in the kitchen, mixing cocktails, or playing a statue like Yianni.

Natalia makes her way back to my little table and sits down opposite me. She's somehow a plain but pretty girl. The sort of girl that anything could be moulded on to. The right makeup could make her a model, or she could be forgotten in an instant. The thing that makes her striking without effort though, is her hair. Much like Yianni's, it's a mass of curls. Only hers is much longer and in better shape. Even with it wrapped up and fastened in a big claw clip, curls playfully poke out in defiance to show the beauty of it all.

'Yamas,' we chime as my bulbous wine glass clinks against her lemonade.

There's a pause as we both sip. I close my eyes and let out an involuntary hum of satisfaction. The wine is cool on my palate, sharp and refreshing against the warmth of the evening. The temperature isn't quite sweaty-hot, but it is only a few steps away from it.

'How's school?' I slip a forkful of fish into my mouth.

Natalia lifts her eyes to the ceiling and complains that a teacher still hasn't been replaced at the school and how she can't wait to go to university in England when she is older.

'At least it's only Greek history we have no teacher for. I could not care much for the subject. And how have you been? I have not seen you since—'

I wave my hand to stop her. I can't bear to hear the end of the sentence, but I have a mouth full of lemony sea bass and can only interject with my hands.

Eventually I manage to say, 'I'm fine', before swallowing the remainder of my food. 'Seriously. Please don't pull that face at me. I don't want to see it.'

She goes from the pathetic sympathy face to opening and closing her mouth to gulp back unsaid words, or just empty air as she tries to load herself with new words. It doesn't matter which it might be – if she is trying to escape words or create them – as I continue talking to prevent her letting out any either way.

'It was a strange time, and we really don't need to talk about it. I really don't *want* to talk about it. So don't feel like you *need* to acknowledge it or even bring it up. I'm just really excited to be here and ready to learn anything and everything I can. Fresh start.'

'Learn? You have been doing this longer than me!'

I shrug as I stab my fork into a piece of potato. 'That doesn't mean I won't learn something new. I hope I get to learn something new.'

'Perhaps you can learn how to fish?'

I let out a little snort. 'I think I'll stick to filleting.'

Natalia is soon called back into the kitchen, and once I have finished my meal, I'm already itching to be useful.

As I am carrying my plate towards the kitchen door, Yianni catches my elbow.

'Where are you off to?' He is so hard to read. I can't tell if he is irritated or just curious.

'The kitchen.' I indicate with my head as my hands are full. 'I thought I would help by taking my plate back there.'

'Tonight, you are the guest. Hazel's orders. Let me take this.'

His hands edge towards the plate, but I step back, pulling it just outside of his reach.

His jaw tightens and his brow lowers, casting a shadow over his eyes, making them look like cups of black coffee – no sugar though.

'Ruby, you are our guest. Hazel's orders. Now please, come sit.'

He edges towards the plates again, but I ignore him and keep on walking towards the kitchen at the back of the restaurant. I can hear a distinct hissing sound emanating from him, but I ignore it and march on. There's no actual door to the kitchen, although there is a doorway and behind it a staggered entrance, so it isn't easy to just look into the kitchen from the restaurant. It's a good way to get some air into the room.

Everything looks modern, more so than the restaurant. In here it's all stainless steel and expanses of worktop space. The sort of kitchen that's easy to work in and keep clean.

'I brought these,' I announce, lifting my plate and glass.

Hazel's glasses are being used to push her hair back from her face and she's wrapped in a black apron. Her cheeks and chest are rosy as she gently jiggles a frying pan with eggs in it.

'You naughty thing. I told Yianni there is no work for you today. Didn't he say?'

I slip the plate down onto one of the surfaces near Natalia who is scraping a used plate over a bin. As I try to tell her that, yes, he told me, but I'm actually hoping to help, she continues, 'Yianni, you let her take her own plate. I said she isn't to do any work today.'

Hazel's lips purse and she seems to be genuinely disappointed. I turn to see Yianni looming behind me, pushing his hair back off his face. Although I can still see tension in him – even in his biceps which seem to contract under his short sleeves – he dips his head to Hazel.

'I am so sorry, Hazel. I did not catch her in time. Ruby, please.' He gestures towards the entrance of the kitchen and I apologise before stepping out ahead of him. 'Why not sit here?' He indicates the bar, and I don't argue this time. I sort of feel like I've got him in some kind of unintentional trouble. For the rest of the evening, I nurse another glass of wine and have a sensible conversation with Pericles about the business. He tells me there are two other people who work at Greek Secret on a regular basis, Nico and Gaia. The man, Nico, works behind the bar during the busier parts of the summer and the girl, Gaia, comes in once or twice a week and on themed nights to help clear plates and sometimes take dishes out to tables. Gaia's one of Natalia's best friends and is also only fifteen.

When I can, I watch Yianni. I'm not sure why. Maybe because he's a mystery. He's nothing like the boy I vaguely remember from all those years ago. And he is the only one not to give me the famous Greek welcome. I try not to dwell on it, but it nags at me. It's as though something has caught between my teeth and without anyone noticing, I have to get it out. I have to be clear of it and know what it is. What he is. I sip my now-warm wine and wonder if he'll be this enigmatic all summer.

At the end of the shift, we all sit down together to discuss the plan. The tables have been cleared and cleaned, and we sit to one side of the restaurant near the bar where it's a little more sheltered from the view of the road. Yianni and Pericles push two square tables together for us to sit round. Everyone else has either been wearing long sleeves or slipped something thin over the tops they're wearing. I guess the May evening holds a mild chill for them; to me it's delightfully warm still after the drizzle back in England.

Hazel's glasses slide down to the tip of her nose, back to where I'm so used to seeing them. Her blonde hair is tied up in a way I have never seen it before, though. I suppose I'm used to seeing the Hazel on holiday and this is work Hazel. It seems so backwards, for England to be the holiday destination when paradise is home. But I suppose it is what it is.

'As we have discussed, we will pay your wage at the end of the month and you will get free meals and have your own room in our home. Our home is your home. Now, I know you were enjoying your work as a maître d', but after lots of debate,' her eyes flick towards Yianni in a micro move that I catch none the less, 'we think perhaps you will start here with work behind the bar. If you are happy with that.'

'That's perfect. I'm just happy I can help.'

Hazel's cheeks lift; she doesn't smile as such, but she visibly relaxes. She sits back in her chair instead of having her forearms pressing into the table and the lines around her eyes soften. Perhaps she was worried I would be disappointed and that's why she distinctly wanted to talk about it before I started work. Maybe she thought I would make a fuss. When I was younger, I had a reputation for being bossy or a handful. Life can change all things. That's not to say being a maître d' didn't suit me – because I loved it – but I have had to learn to accept situations as they are. I've had to realise that I can't control everything. In fact, there's very little in life we truly have control of, if anything.

What the role is doesn't matter; I'm happy to have a job again after a month of feeling useless. The idea of munching my way through more of my savings would break me. I've already eaten into the dreams for my future much too much, one way or another. This job will tide me over and get me back on track until I can find the right thing somewhere else.

Now that the conversation is over, even Yianni seems lighter and a smile tickles his full lips more than once. He makes the odd witty remark, actually, and is sarcastically funny. Maybe he had seen me as some English threat to his job and that making him late might make him look worse. I'm not sure and anyway, I'm now at the point of being too tired to care.

It has been such a long day, since getting up early to travel. I can't suppress my yawns any longer. It's skirting midnight when Hazel says we should make a move. Everyone stands and begins to kiss Yianni goodbye. For some reason I thought he still lived in the family home. Without more than a nod to this thought, I follow suit and edge round the table to say goodnight to him.

'Thank you for picking me up from the airport today. I really am sorry for the confusion.'

He shrugs, not in the sulky way he did earlier though; he's more relaxed. Almost like he barely remembers the misunderstanding. I lean in to kiss his cheek. It's stubbled against my lips. I hadn't meant to kiss him, not really. It was going to be an air kiss, close enough to almost seem real but with no lasting sensation. Instead, my lips find his cheek and the smell of warm citrus and a note of burnt wood charm my senses. I don't want to, but something under my ribs can't help but note the feel of him. The shape of his mouth as his lips briefly imprint on my cheek. As I pull away, I smile then tuck my lower lip in. The taste of salt from his skin lingers.

My forehead buckles under the weight of my unintentional attraction and I can feel a frown crease it. Yianni's eyes sweep over me as we step back. His eyebrow arches and alarm pricks at the base of my spine that he might say something about the look on my face.

But he doesn't. He just says, 'Sleep well, Ruby. *Kalinikta.*'

'*Kalinikta*, Yianni.'

Chapter 9

Then

'Ruby, I could never love anyone the way I love you. You know that, right?'

It's Sunday morning and we're watching cartoons like we're kids. Like we used to when we first met and fell in love. He strokes the hair from my face and kisses my neck.

'Of course I know.'

When I first met Jonathan, he asked me if I was an actress. We were both working in a restaurant in London back then. A friend from college, Rob, got me a job and I was living in a flat with him and his boyfriend, Jaz. Rob's a talented chef and he knew I wanted to immerse myself in his world, and so, when a job came up, he had put me forward.

It was my first day and within the first minute Jonathan had turned and caught my eye as I put plates down on the table next to him. He followed me and whispered in my ear, 'Are you an actress?'

'No.' I remember laughing at the idea. He hadn't laughed. He had looked at me from the corner of his eye. I was still coursing with first-day nerves – first-minute almost – and he was asking what I was before he even knew who I was.

'A model then? You have to be a model. Not runway, but commercial, right?'

'No. I'm a waitress.' My hands smoothed my outfit. The outfits there were very stylised, with red shirts and black bows at the neck. The same for any gender and everyone had to gel their hair back in the same way too. 'And why not runway? Not that I think I'm any kind of model material.'

'New girl!' Rob interjected across the room.

I smiled at Rob's sweating red face and marched away from Jonathan before he could answer me. I remember not actually wanting to hear the answer anyway.

'Yes, chef.'

'Never, and I mean *never*, date an actor,' he warned as he glanced over my shoulder. 'Even if they're as tasty as this steak.' I distinctly remember him flipping a steak in a pan making fat hiss and spit. Smoke fused with steam as it filled the room with greasy air.

Moments later someone was shouting *service!* and I went back to where I was supposed to be, next to a hot bright lamp above a chrome surface that reflected the burning glare back into my eyes. Then I heard his voice at my shoulder, Jonathan's voice. Back to inform me why I couldn't do runway. 'Because you're too short. You're definitely stunning enough. Just too short for runway.' His chest skimmed my arm as he grabbed a plate from the counter and then he was gone. It wasn't long afterwards that he asked me out.

I look over at him on the sofa as he scrolls his phone.

'Jonathan?'

'Yep.'

'Do you remember what you first said to me, when we first met?'

He shifts his weight and pulls me along the sofa until I'm underneath him and between his legs.

'Did I tell you how gorgeous you were?'

'Sort of.'

'Did I let you know that you were always going to be mine and no one else's?'

Now he is kissing my jawline and down my neck. 'Love you,' he whispers.

'Love you too,' I whisper in return.

I never did ask Rob why I shouldn't date an actor.

Chapter 10

Now

It's only a short drive to the house. I do my best to consume the terrain but it's too dark to see more than a few metres ahead out of the windscreen. I'm desperate to look at more of the nature of Corfu again. Driving back from the airport was breathtaking, and I can't wait to inhale it all in the morning.

The car pulls up and we get out to the sound of cicadas. Without their song I'm sure we would be in complete silence, but they fill the air so densely it can barely carry any other sound. The house is a little out of the way, still in the village but on the edge of it. I can't see my surroundings, but I can feel the life around me in the same way I can feel the life of the air in the breeze. I tilt my head to the sky and the light of a million stars punctures the night with devastating brightness and definition. I don't have time to hover though, as everyone is making their way towards the house.

A sound manages to push against the cicadas and the

headlights of another car creep up behind me. I shade my eyes against it, and I can hear Pericles speaking in Greek with a gruff tone. He steps forwards and is in front of me, feet crunching along the ground, calling a name. *Yianni.*

He gets out, a shadow over the headlights, says something to his father, slams his door and goes to the boot. That's when it hits me. My bags. We'd forgotten to take my bags with us. My hand presses to my forehead as I make my way towards the car.

'Yianni, I'm so sorry.'

He doesn't look at me as he passes the first suitcase over to Pericles who smiles and reassures me before taking the bag inside.

'It is okay. Lucky I remembered, no?'

'I'm so sorry. Were you on your way home when you noticed? I hope you hadn't got far.'

His eyes lock onto mine and a half smile lingers on his lips. 'No,' he says slowly. 'I had not got far.' Then he swings open the back door of his car and tugs out the second suitcase.

'I'll take that. Sorry again. *Kalinikta.*'

'*Kalinikta,* Ruby. Try not to forget more of your things.' And with that he is back in his car.

After offering me drinks, more food, and pretty much every-thing under the roof, Hazel sends me off with Natalia, who shows me to my room. She flicks a switch and illuminates a room that is not what I expected. I think perhaps I was expecting something plain and spare with white walls and floral bedding. This is not that. There's a single bed with a charcoal-coloured sheet and chalk-white blanket. The furniture is plain wood and a white reading lamp is on the bedside table. But none of that really draws my attention. It exists in my view, but it's not what confuses me. It's the collage of photos hanging above the bed that draws me into the otherwise plain room. All the photos feature Yianni.

'I'm so happy you are here for the summer,' Natalia says. 'It's like I now have an older sister as well as a brother! *Kalinikta,* Ruby. Sleep well.'

I kiss Natalia on both cheeks before saying goodnight and closing the door behind me, then stand there for a moment with my back pressed against the door. Is this Yianni's old bedroom? Why would he leave all those photos behind? I creep along, glad the floor is tiled and not creaky wood. My feet make it to a shaggy black rug before I climb to stand on the bed. Although the floor isn't squeaky, the bed is. I study the pictures. I have to. Something about them is like gravity pulling me in.

There are some family photos, of Yianni holding his baby sister in the hospital for example; but most of the photos are with friends. Days at the beach, beers, smiles, topless in swim shorts, dressed up in full pirate costume and one as a princess with a wand in one hand and a beer in the other. It's the life of a vibrant twenty-something played out in thirty or so photos.

This particular room has a small en suite with a shower that has a thin curtain. It's so close to the loo that it's almost on top of it, but I like having my own space. In a daze, I get undressed and ready to sleep. I watch myself wipe away the day's makeup in the mirror over the sink, gently pulling off the black mascara from around my almost equally black eyes. My chin-length hair – slightly longer at the front than the back – is more all over the place than the style demands. I like it a little wild, but the long day has left me a complete mess.

I push my fringe to one side and edge my way back into the bedroom.

Taking one last gawp at the photos that will live above my head for the next six months, I ease myself under the sheet and the blanket. The sheets smell of Yianni's aftershave mixed with freshly washed linens. It has to be his current room, no question. Not a room he once lived in, but sheets that he has used and worn that have been washed ready for my stay. I take in another lungful of the deep citrus with that same note of pine; no, not pine, something woody though. I take one last deep breath of him before closing my eyes to a pang of guilt. It's rolling across me two-fold. Firstly, the idea that I might have kicked Yianni out of his own bed makes me wonder if that is the reason he is being stand-offish with me. Secondly, there is a feeling that I want to ignore, a feeling that has crept up on me over the afternoon and that I have intentionally refused to notice. I'm not ready to feel the heat of lust for anyone. Being alone, living alone, it's easy and pain-free. Feeling a microbe of lust for Yianni, someone who is a step away from being related to me, is just embarrassing. Everyone keeps trying to point out how much I've been through. I don't want anyone's pity; I just want to be alone. I want to move on. I want to live my life for me. Anger rises up above it all, and however much I try to ignore my feelings about my past, they collide in my mind with my present. We are all a product of the past. I hate that.

Squeezing my eyes tightly shut, I expel a small tear onto Yianni's pillow in the dark.

Chapter 11

Now

Being exhausted doesn't prevent me from being up early. I roll to the right side of the bed and sit on the edge of it. The light is already pouring under the curtains. In the dark I was aware of driving down a narrow road with shadows the shapes of trees, but I have no idea what it's really like out there. Before I wash or get myself ready for the day, I rush to peek out of the window. With great ceremony I tug the curtains open and it is all I can do not to press myself against the window.

My lips part and I whisper, 'Oh my', to the window. To the view.

Undulations of every shade of green roll in every direction. Dark points of tall trees tower above others in clusters. Olive trees are scattered about and there are runs of drying golden grasses here and there too. There's even a lemon tree not far from my window. I feel as though I have officially arrived at last. As though the day before was just a dry run for the view out of my window. It makes me want to put some trainers on and walk. I want to explore everything, to immerse myself in it all. It's so long since I've been abroad.

The last time I went away was with Jonathan, back when we were happy and life seemed to be coming together for us. We had booked a last-minute weekend to Barcelona. My feet ache just thinking about the amount of walking we did on that trip.

I snatch a deep breath, filling my lungs until they burn a little, before exhaling any thoughts of Jonathan. There's no point going over the past. There is no way I can go back and change it or improve it.

I drag myself away from the view and pull the curtains wider before washing and dressing. I run a little mousse through my damp hair and sit down on the edge of my bed. *Yianni's bed*, my brain automatically corrects. I bite my cheek at the thought of kicking him out of his own bed. I'm sure he thinks that I want to kick him out of his job too. He must resent me. All the drawers are empty, though. I need to find out if he has left because of me or if he was moving out anyway.

I make my way down the twisting, creaky stairs. The house looks very different in the light of day. It's older than I expected. The kitchen has worn pine cupboard doors that are almost amber in tone, although I doubt they started that way. The surfaces are a paler wood that doesn't compliment the cupboards at all. Little round plastic handles adorn every drawer and door about the room, and there's Hazel in the middle of it all, frying eggs on a small white oven hob. The kitchen couldn't be more different to the one in Greek Secret.

'How did you sleep?' She grins at me over her shoulder.

'Good, thanks. Where is everyone?'

I sit down on one of the four metal chairs at the round kitchen table. The room is already a bit warm – the frying eggs don't help of course. I'm glad I'm used to a hot kitchen, but wonder how I'll feel about it in August. At least I'll mostly be making cocktails, I guess.

'Pericles is collecting more eggs from the chickens. Natalia is still in bed. Coffee?'

I nod as she points at the pot.

'And eggs?'

'Please.'

I scrunch at my hair. It's drying well enough, but I'm desperate to get myself out in the sun.

'I have been thinking,' Hazel begins, 'you're not going to want to rely on us to drive you places you might want to go. You had a little scooter when you were sixteen, didn't you?'

I sit back in my chair, almost blown away at the memory. It was powder-blue and I saved up for it working in a darling little independent coffee shop washing up cups and saucers. Buzzing about on that thing gave me independence and almost gave my mother a heart attack.

'I did indeed. Feels like forever ago'

'Well, Pericles has a little bike he never uses. I spoke to him, and he is happy for you to use it over the summer. If you'd like?'

Excitement makes my fingertips tingle in the same way they do when holding the handlebars of a running motor. 'I would love that. Thank you.'

After breakfast Pericles takes me out to a little shed and shows me the motorcycle. It's a lot bigger than I expected. I think he thought I might turn it down. Maybe I'm wrong. There's just something about the twist in his lip and the sideways look he gives me as he pulls open the tall wooden door to reveal the bike that makes me question him. It doesn't matter. He's wrong. I'm more than happy to get behind the handlebars of this little red devil. He shows me how things work, but as soon as I can, I have the satnav in my earphones and a helmet on and I'm off.

I head back to San Stefanos. It makes sense to me to feel out the journey that I will be doing late at night on my own. I want to have it engrained in me as soon as I can. My sense of direction is pretty good, but I want it to be part of me.

I'm easily distracted though, as I glide along the road next to olive groves and skies that are more blue and clear than any I've ever encountered before. It's not long before I'm pulling up outside the restaurant.

The bifold doors have been pulled around the bar area side of the restaurant where there is a solid roof. All the chairs and tables that were under the terrace with the vines have been brought into that area overnight. There's also a little chain across the entrance that says, 'Closed'.

I hope to look over the stock so that I will be ready for the evening. During May, I'm only working six evenings a week. As the season progresses, I'll work lunch and dinner.

I step over the 'Closed' sign, then take a step towards the glass to press my face to it. Scanning the bottles as best I can at this distance, I make mental notes of where everything is.

'What are you here so early for? You start tonight, no?'

Yianni's voice close to my neck startles me so much I bang my forehead on the glass door. 'Shit. You frightened the life right out of me, Yianni.'

I rub my forehead and turn to look at him. He's in an unbuttoned shirt, baggy grey trousers and his lips are suppressing a laugh, presumably at my expense.

'*Sygnómi*. Sorry.'

The smell of freshly baked goodies accompanies him. He steps around me and unlocks the door. I hear him talking in Greek as he goes in. I'm not sure whether to follow him or not. A girl smartly dressed in black with silver pumps walks out and beams at me.

'*Kalimera*,' she says as she passes me, unhooking the 'Closed' sign and rehooking it once she's past. An action with no thought, as though it's been done many times before.

The door has been left open. I step towards it only for Yianni to begin the process of unfolding the doors. As I enter the bar area, he places his hand on the back of a stool and drags it back making a toe-curling grating noise. I notice that he is barefoot.

'Where are your shoes?' I stare at his feet.

Instead of replying, he stretches. Fists and arms tense, brought out wide to display his lean muscular body and golden-brown skin. I look back at the bottles behind the bar. Havana Club. Gordon's. Blue Curaçao.

'I haven't been awake long. Thought I would walk to the bakery.' He folds his arms across his chest.

Limoncello. Bacardi. Jack Daniels. Chambord. Baileys.

'Sorry if I... disturbed you.' A little laugh unintentionally pops out as I glance towards where the girl disappeared out of the taverna. 'Did you sleep here last night?' I turn to him, and my arms clamp themselves across my breasts and my eyebrows pull themselves together. I notice that I'm mirroring his body language, and now I want to switch position, but I know it would seem unnatural to do so.

'Yes.'

'Here?' My arms release to my sides.

'Yes.'

'Last night?'

'*Naí, Naí, Naí.*' He hops off the stool and makes his way round behind the bar. 'My bed is taken. This is my home for the summer.' A lock of hair drops in front of his face, and he pushes it behind his right ear. Then he disappears, ducking down behind the bar before popping up again shaking a carton of orange juice. He tilts it towards me, wordlessly offering me some of the contents. I shake my head.

I was right. I'm an unintentional usurper. I've taken his bed and I bet he thinks that next I'll be after his title at the restaurant.

'I had no idea. I thought perhaps you'd moved out or—'

'I have. To here. No worries. Why are you here? I answered your question. You still have not answered mine.'

'Oh, I want to familiarise myself with the drinks. What order they're kept in, what stock you have, what cocktails you serve. If I'd known Hazel's plan to put me behind the bar, I would have studied a bit more last night. I'll go if I'm disturbing you. Or if your friend is coming back.'

I need to stop. I don't need to know what the girl was doing here. Stupidly, it's niggling me.

Yianni smiles and casually says, 'She won't be back today.'

I'm not really sure what that means. Maybe a casual encounter? She didn't even stay for a croissant that's hanging out of the bag on the counter next to me. Perhaps I frightened her off.

'I can still leave if you want me to.'

He doesn't respond right away. Instead, he watches me while he takes a swig from his juice, then he wipes his top lip with his palm, and wipes the palm on his trouser leg. Although he is hard to read, I'm pretty sure I can give as good as I'm getting. I relax and let my face fall blank under his gaze.

Eventually, he nudges his chin upwards and says, 'You had best come here then. Better I show you, than Nico tonight.'

I hop down from my stool and walk behind the bar. Yianni picks up the croissant and takes a mouthful. My stomach is lurching with a cocktail of emotions. There's usually a feeling of comfort when I step behind a bar or into a restaurant kitchen. It's where I've spent all my working life. It has that sense of being home. But being in a confined space with Yianni is less than ideal. Not that being close to someone behind a bar would normally be something I even notice. It's second nature to skirt around people, arms becoming tendrils and slithering past each other when needed. Bodies seem to learn the dance of working behind a bar or in a kitchen. But with Yianni it's different. I'm letting myself feel a heat that I shouldn't. Maybe it's because it has been a long time since I haven't been in charge. He is in charge here. Even with Charles, I was the one making sure the place ran smoothly. Here, it's Yianni. Anyway, no need to dwell on the heat of our bodies in close proximity. Fixing my eyes on the menu he's placed in my hands helps to calm me and bring me back from the pang of emotion that being near him makes me feel. I pull my shoulders back and wait for him to continue talking me through everything. I am a professional. I repeat it in my head and add: I do not need or want a man in my life. I do not have any inappropriate feelings for my cousin's brother. Those thoughts and a snatched breath keep me together.

We spend an hour discussing cocktails, wines, prices, glasses, where things go and how important it is to keep receipts and records, as spot checks are regularly performed in Corfu and penalties are high if books aren't in order. We settle into an understanding, and it melts away some of the knot I was feeling. Only a tiny part remains. The part that irritates me the most. The part that finds him attractive. There must be something in the breeze that is messing with my head, something that smells of citrus perhaps, as well as the fragrance of vines.

Chapter 12

Then

'How was the show?' My voice is barely a croak from under the covers.

Jonathan is doing his best to sneak in, but the light from the bathroom is streaming on to my face because I forgot to fall asleep facing the other way. My eyes blur as I open them to see him wiping away makeup from his eyes. He kneels down next to the bed and looks like something from a cartoon. Thick dark makeup is being pushed around his face by the wipe in his hand, until it slowly fades into thinner and lighter lines.

'Fucking brill. This guy came up to me after, pushed his card into my pocket. Turns out he directs independent films. Knew this play was worth it. Didn't I say this would change our lives?'

I make a noise of agreement, or tiredness; either way it spurs him on.

'You won't have to work in any shitty restaurants again. No

serving people for us. We'll be going to them, not working in them, and picking anything we want to eat.'

I pull the cover a little further down and cross my arms over it, peering at him as the makeup dissipates until I can see him instead of a character he's been playing.

'But that's not my dream. I don't want to just follow you around. What would my job be then, to do what?'

'Have our gorgeous babies.'

It's too late – or early – for this. There's no point arguing or pointing out that I have ambitions and goals I've been working towards since I was a child. So I roll away and store it all up in my head. Asking questions I don't say out loud, like, why is your dream more valuable than mine? What makes you think my ultimate goal is to have *your* babies? But it's not me who's talking out loud. It's him.

'Don't be like that.'

I don't say anything.

'Fine.'

I don't say anything.

'You'll love it when I'm famous. Then all you'll want to do is have my babies.'

I don't say anything.

The door to the bathroom is pulled closed. In the dark I contemplate at what point a relationship turns from fun and hopeful into a habit. When does it go from two people enjoying each other's company to waking up next to each other and living separate lives with separate dreams? When is it that only one person learns to compromise and the other continues blindly on? Is it the same in all relationships? For all women perhaps? I don't know. I don't think so. My parents seem happy enough. I'm not one for making a mess, but since we moved in together in a *sensible* house out of London, I thought we were going to start being *sensible*, and maybe shift some of the focus on to my much more *sensible* ambitions. But instead, we have slipped into a pocket like a packet of cigarettes, and we are a habit. A habit that might kill me off if I'm not careful, so that all that's left of who I was and what I wanted to become is a shell for Jonathan to bask in.

As Jonathan slips into bed next to me, I squeeze my eyes shut because even when a habit needs to be stopped, there are always those good times together that creep in. The times when we laughed at each other's foibles or went out for romantic meals or drinking at parties. Now is the time to focus. It's not the time to look into his eyes and see their beauty. I remember a book I once bought, which has never made it back into my hands since purchasing it. It's about manifesting your future.

In the morning, I'll pick up that book and bloody well read it.

Chapter 13

Now

Four weeks slip away from me as I find a routine that suits
me. Breakfast with Hazel and Pericles. On weekdays – when
Natalia has school – she joins us. Then I'm on my bike and
at the beach. It's not too busy at eight in the morning. I park
outside a restaurant named Fantasea, which is almost as far
from Greek Secret as you can get within the resort. There's a
dusty car park opposite with a jaw dropping view across the
bay. I could park at the beach, but I prefer it here. I love the
view. The turquoise endless sea and the scattered buildings
of bars and tavernas that skirt the shore. The sun makes its
way into the sky from behind the resort and I make my way
down the slope towards the rich golden sand.

Even in the Med, the water feels fresh before the sun is high
enough to warm it. Each day I spend a moment with my toes
sinking into the wet sludgy sand on the water's edge as the
foam traces its way further up my legs, preparing me for what

is to come. I like to take a moment to breathe. Letting the salty air and subtle smell of seaweed fill my lungs before I fall deep into the reflection of my life. I spend those moments looking as far out to sea as I can, looking at that place where the sky and the sea are brought together in a thin line, at times defined and at others almost impossible to make out. The thought makes me touch the scar on my forehead. I can feel the fine ridge under my fingers. This is the only time of day I venture out without a scrap of makeup. I never speak to anyone; I never even get close to anyone. That's probably the real reason I park where I do. Yes, I love the view, but there are more people parking on the beach and more people to walk past if I stop there. I hate that scars are like writing nightmares on flesh – silver lines that represent the darkness of pain. I tell myself that they're also a representation of living, because these things go hand in hand. That one is a harder sell for me. I can only see the pain.

As my legs adjust to the temperature shift, I ponder the way the sea looks like a shadow of the sky. Or perhaps it looks like the sky's fallen comrade. I spend so much time considering the colours, why they are the way they are and why life is the way it is; why we have to endure pain and scars. I think about how I love it in Corfu but also feel myself slipping into thoughts I know I shouldn't dwell on. It is too easy for me to put up my social front here, that is, to spend time chatting and laughing, making friends with customers who are at the restaurant for one meal or one drink then never to be seen again. I'm used to it. Used to only having some friends for a matter of hours. Micro friendships where I hope I've done well enough in their company to gain a tip. That thought isn't a fun one. I think I need the grounding of my parents and my friends at home. Amara's a good one for that. She gets it.

One of the reasons I love working in hospitality is people. Hearing stories, watching people laugh with their friends and loved ones. But lately I feel like something that has slipped down the crack in the sofa like spare change. It is only a job after all.

I do spend time with Natalia, Hazel and Pericles at least, and it is refreshing to have people around me when I wake up and not just faceless figures running up and down stairs waking me up but not talking to me because they're behind a wall. Chatting over breakfast or sharing a smile to say goodnight has been something I hadn't realised I missed since living alone for so long. I don't know what's missing, what's dropped me into this little pit that seems to underpin my days.

I haven't spent any real time with Yianni other than processing drinks orders. *One Sexy Greek, one Sex on the Beach, one beer and a dark rum and Coke.* That's usually it. I've spent a small amount of time with Gaia, Natalia's friend who seems hard-working and full of questions – not quite to the point of an interrogation, but she isn't afraid to say what is in her head, and I respect that. And, of course, I work next to the other bartender, Nico. After five minutes I understood why Yianni thought it was better I learnt from him and not Nico. Nico is almost the opposite of Yianni and would flirt with a tea towel if he was bored. Other than the girl I saw that one morning, I haven't seen Yianni take much interest in anyone. Nico is nice enough though, and honestly, I think he might just be lonely. That or I'm reflecting myself into his eyes. He loves to chat to everyone and often stays late to help if it's needed. I do think Hazel or Pericles must have warned him off me though. After offering to show me around the island, he has never set a time or day or even ever mentioned the subject again. I brought it up and he skimmed over it. Maybe he has decided I'm too dull to show around.

Once I'm done considering how strangely disjointed my life is, between the quiet mornings of reflection and the constant chatter of nights, and after my daily comparison of my life and my scars to the line of the blues of the sea and the sky, it is time to swim.

Each day, I wade in with my hair in a tiny knot and goggles pulled over my face. Then I put my face in the water until the salt makes my skin feel as taut as the strings of a violin. I float along, catching sight of silvery fish darting about around me, carrying on until my shoulders and buttocks are warm with exertion. When I'm done swimming, I lie on the beach reading, mostly books about manifesting my dreams. The dreams I haven't told anyone about – apart from Jonathan. The ones he kept with him; I have to give him that at least. They are still there inside me though, burning just as hot as my muscles and my skin in the sun.

After my mornings of tanning, I go home, have lunch and ready myself to work from six often until midnight. But all of that is about to change. As June is edging forwards, so are the numbers of people in the resort. People want to have a little drink or a meal in the afternoon. Beach bars are more popular for lunch of course, or places with swimming pools. Greek Secret doesn't possess either of those attractions, but it is situated on a road near hotels that are a little further out of the resort. This means people are starting to pop in for a drink on their walk back from the beach, or they are venturing a few more steps from the pool for lunch. I haven't eaten anywhere except for Greek Secret or home, but every person visiting says that they've never had a bad meal in San Stefanos, and one of the reasons they return year after year is the standard of the food. Hopefully, I'll find out sooner or later if that's true. Although, I know time isn't really the issue. When I do have a whole day off, all of twice so far, I've taken the bike around the island, along the meandering roads and through the olive groves. I've loved it.

But now, it's midday and I'm already in my long, tailored black shorts and a black three-quarter-length shirt standing behind the bar polishing glasses with a tea towel. It's still quiet, but me being there means that Pericles is free to help in the kitchen or run errands as required.

Yianni comes over to the bar, and lightly taps it, saying 'Two vanilla milkshakes', before he turns to walk away. Pericles potters around in the background. I make the milkshakes and walk around the bar to take them to the table. There are only two tables of customers, one with five people whose drinks I've already made, and another with two girls, a blonde and a brunette, perhaps in their twenties.

'Here.' Yianni walks towards me and puts his hands out to take the glasses from me. 'I can take them.'

As I pass them to him, one slips through his hand and shatters on my foot, slicing it open. Greek words swirl out of Yianni's mouth and around my head as my entire body goes tense. For a moment I don't even look down. My jaw locks. My fingernails penetrate the skin on the heel of my hand before a thin whisper slips out of my lips.

'Fuck.'

Then, as a deep pain ripples up through my body, I twist to hop towards the bar and away from the pool of milkshake that's curdling with my blood on the floor, scooping to clutch my left foot in the process. I don't mean to, but French pours out between my teeth, literally, not just "excuse my French" but the rich and potent force of it. '*Ai! Putain d'enculer de bâtard! Putain de merde!*' For some reason French swearing always comes more naturally to me than English when I'm in real pain or a temper.

Yianni momentarily stops talking to tilt his head and open his mouth as though he might ask what the hell I'm saying, but I bare my teeth at him and growl, 'Please get a cloth before I bleed out on the floor.'

'I am so sorry, Ruby.'

I can't reply. Yianni calls his dad and tells him to make fresh milkshakes, and to clear the mess. Or I assume that's what he is saying as Pericles starts bustling around us.

'Come. I need to get you to the back,' Yianni says, then slides his arm around my ribs to get me to lean on him instead of the bar stool. I hobble for a step or two before Yianni gives up, and instead scoops me up like I'm made of cloth and marches me and my dripping foot towards a side room.

It's his bedroom.

I'm torn between my interest in looking around the room and my throbbing foot, which seems to ooze more blood with each and every pulse of pain. The foot wins of course. Yianni presses a cloth carefully to the wound, making me scrabble away from him.

It's my left foot and my left hand has been clutching it since moments after it happened; subsequently my fingers are covered in blood. Yianni grabs what I assume is a cloth and presses it to my foot. Hazel bursts in like a police officer called to an ongoing crime with all guns blazing.

'What happened? Oh my god, Ruby. Let me see.' She drops

to her knees next to the bed and Yianni quickly moves out of her way as she bustles past him. Hazel carefully lifts the cloth and her eyes bulge before she firmly presses it back into my foot making me gasp. 'What happened?' she repeats.

Yianni steps forwards. 'A milkshake glass. I dropped it onto her foot.' He paces the room. 'It is the bloody…' He clicks his fingers to draw the English word out of his Greek mind. '…the bloody condensation. It was wet and it slipped.'

I squirm a little as I try to blow the pain out with each breath before giving up and pressing my lips so tightly together I'm sure they've completely disappeared in on themselves.

Hazel pulls her glasses off her face and rubs one eye with the back of her hand before replacing them. 'I'll have to take you to the health centre or something, Ruby. I can't put a plaster on it, it's much too big, and what if there's glass in it? I saw the mess on the floor.'

'No.' Yianni interrupts the plan, making my face screw up even tighter than it already is. If he says I need to keep working and put up with it I'm going to bloody well slap him with the back of my hand. 'I will take her. If we get stuck waiting or get sent to hospital, you, Papa, Natalia and Nico will make it work this evening. Get Natalia to ask Gaia if she can work today too.'

And with that, I'm scooped up by Yianni again who has paid me more attention in the past few minutes than he has in the past month.

Chapter 14

Now

We're in Yianni's car heading to the health centre. He was gunning it until I snapped for him to drive sensibly. I'm not going to die from a glass to the foot, but a car is a lethal weapon.

I have my knee pulled up to my chest and my foot between my hands, firmly knotted in the cloth Yianni has given me. The one that was white, but is slowly making its way to red. It's a really long time before anything is said. He's gripping the steering wheel so hard it looks like he might break it, and his eyes keep darting towards my foot. As if spurred on by his glances, the urge to look at it again takes over me. I peel back the cloth to see the narrow gash running along the middle to the side of my foot. I snatch a sharp inhale through my teeth at the sight of it. I can almost taste the sweet vanilla from the milkshake residue as I do. My swelling flesh screams with anger at having the pressure taken off it. It is enough to make me momentarily hold my breath while I wrap it back up. I think the bleeding is slowing at least.

'Oh shit!' I exhale my words as I press the cloth back down.

'What? Is it worse?' Yianni's head keeps skipping between me and the road.

'Please keep your eyes on the road. You're making me nervous. And no, it's not worse. I said shit because I just realised, this is a T-shirt. I thought it was a cloth. Is it yours?'

An audible exhale falls from his lips and amusement lingers. This time he doesn't turn to look at me but keeps his eyes locked on the road as I've instructed.

'You can keep it. I am not into tie-dye.' He briefly glances at me and smiles. 'How is it feeling?'

'Rubbish. I can't believe it's this bad.'

'I cannot believe it cut you at all. I have dropped a glass on my foot before. I've never been cut.'

'Mmm. You wear trainers to work. I don't even want to think about it.' I push my weight further back into my chair. Every position is uncomfortable. 'Remind me not to wear flip-flops to work again. Trainers only from now on.'

'Yes. Agreed.'

We pull up at the health centre. It's pretty small, smaller than I expect it to be anyway. I let Yianni do all the talking, for obvious reasons. I zone out and watch the ceiling and imagine I'm looking at the line where the sea and the sky come together. The haze. The complexity of life drawn in pale blue lines and where they begin and where they end. I probably won't be doing that as much until my foot heals. There's no way I want to get sand in this cut.

As the wound is being cleaned with some kind of antiseptic, my mind bursts back into my body with a hiss and my hands fumble for something to grab onto and find the corner of Yianni's shirt.

'You owe me a drink for this,' I say through gritted teeth.

Four steri-strips, some gauze and a bandage later, and we are on our way back. Still in silence.

Now my foot just throbs in the same way my pulse does. I know the wound is clean and there's nothing left that I can do outside of feeling pissed off. So, I try to enjoy the view again – the million shades of green and the sun bouncing off people's swimming pools. I even like the look of the half-finished buildings with their rebar and concrete platforms. I like to imagine how they'll eventually look or whether they've just been abandoned. When I see people behind rusty gates kicking balls or being chased by puppies I smile against my pain. Those little snapshots into someone else's world are always entertaining and absorbing. It makes me feel more human to silently witness someone else's life and world when they don't know I'm watching. It's one of the reasons I fell in love with working in bars, restaurants and cafés. I get to be a part of so many lives. Getting to see the happy moments over a celebratory dinner or serving a glass before it's raised to a smiling face has kept me going. Many years ago, working in a café I was consumed by peoples stories. The things they would tell each other over a coffee... I'm still amazed to this day the things we all talk about in public forgetting hospitality staff are always nearby.

Yianni breaks the spell of silence. 'What were you saying? When you hurt your foot?'

His voice is like a doorbell at my brain, trying to rouse me into a response, but I can't understand what the question is that's being asked.

'When?'

'You went into a different language. French, no?'

'Yeah. I'm half French. I mostly know how to swear and order food, a little conversation too.' I don't like to make a big deal out of speaking French; it's nowhere near as complicated as Greek.

Yianni pushes out his bottom lip and bounces his head in thought.

'Of course, your father. That makes sense to me. These are the most important of subjects. To show anger and passion and to fill your belly. Sensible.'

'Something like that.'

A smile tugs at the corner of my mouth at his appreciation of my language skills.

'What did you say? In French?'

I know what I said. I know exactly. But I feel a little stupid translating my outburst so instead I repeat it in the original language.

'*Putain d'enculer de bâtard. Putain de merde.*' I say it quickly with as little emphasis as I can. Almost like it's only one long fluid word sliding along like treacle.

'In English.' Then he quickly adds, 'Or Greek.' And glances at me with a tickle in his tone and a glint in his eye. I'm not sure I've seen his eyes glint like that, not in my direction anyway.

I cough, as though taking ceremony in what I'm about to say. 'Roughly, I said, *Whore of a fucker of a bastard. Whore of shit.* It sounds better in French, obviously.' As soon as the words leave my mouth, I nibble back my bottom lip and my hand finds my forehead to partially cover my face. I'm not embarrassed as such, but a certain level of cringe washes over me.

Yianni, on the other hand, is laughing. His ribcage contracts as he struggles for air. 'Good to know the French like to swear as much as the Greeks.'

'Oh, really?' I lower my hand a little off my face.

'If you had dropped the glass on me, I would say: *gamó ti poutána mou.*'

'Do I dare ask what that means?'

'It is not worse than you: *fuck my whore.*'

'I honestly feel disappointed. I thought that Greek was the origin of basically everything. Surely it's more colourful than that?'

'If you drop a glass on my foot, I guess we will find out.'

We chortle along together before silence falls over us again, but this time with a smile lingering between us. It hovers there for a long moment. I relax and turn back to the window, but Yianni continues, albeit with a new subject. 'I will take you back to the house. You must not work this week. Not until you have some rest.'

Within a few minutes we are back at the house to the chorus of cicadas and I quickly get out of the car before Yianni can get to my door and scoop me up again like I'm some kind of ice cream. It's a struggle so I let him take my elbow and hand to rest my weight over his fingers.

'I think you should lie down. Come on.' He keeps hold of me and walks me in the direction of the stairs as soon as we are in the house.

I sort of want to argue; I feel strange about him taking me up to his bed with no one else here. This is one of only a handful of times I've actually seen him in the house. I know he has been in every day over the last few weeks, but our paths don't cross all that much. He comes back for showers and some meals, but apparently not when I'm about.

After sitting me on the bed, he leaves the room and returns with pillows to put under my foot. He hesitates. His arms cross over his chest making his short-sleeve black shirt constrict around his biceps. Perhaps he wants to say something. His lips look poised to speak, but something is stopping him. Maybe he feels he shouldn't leave me alone, or perhaps he is desperate to leave and doesn't want to say. I really don't feel like being completely alone right now. Ever since Jonathan, I have become a complete queen at filling my time. Work, gym, friends, family, and if I'm at home, I pick up any book or binge-watch TV programmes I've seen a thousand times before, all to the sounds of the neighbours which makes it feel like someone is there. Even here in Corfu, when I'm alone on the beach, I'm not really. There are people readying themselves for the day and a few early sun worshippers already adorning the sand. Luckily, there is always a space carved out for me far away from anyone else and I distract myself with the view and the fish that like to swim along with me. But when this house is empty, it's really empty.

'Does it seem strange? Me settled into your room as though it's mine?' I'm fed up with him wanting to say something and not opening his mouth and saying it. Plus, asking questions will keep him here longer, otherwise I will have to silently look at the ceiling or my phone, because I left my book at the restaurant.

He shrugs. 'Yes. But I don't want you to feel like I want you out.'

'You do though, don't you? I know I pissed you off with the

whole taxi thing—'

'Not this again.' His eyes almost disappear into the back of his head, but there's a lightness in his tone that makes me think twice. He sits himself down next to me on the bed. The edge of his leg presses against mine and I'm as aware of it as I would be if someone pressed the cold, flat edge of a blade against my leg.

'Oh, shut up. You almost broke my foot this afternoon. I think it's high time you start being nice to me.'

'When am I not nice?' He clicks his tongue. 'Well, I suppose I will be covering many of your shifts behind the bar now, so, I think this is punishment enough.'

'Oh, seriously? Shut up. I've seen you! You bloody love it. The girls only come in to chat to you and Nico.' I shake my head and catch sight of the smug look on his face. Before he can open his mouth, I know what he wants to say and correct myself before he can. 'Not that Hazel's food isn't brilliant, it is. Of course people come to the restaurant for that, and my cocktails too.' I suppress a smile. 'But you *do* seem to have a high percentage of women who come back at any excuse to linger at the bar for a chat. You and Nico are like some sort of bloody…tag team. You smile and chat them up over dinner and he takes over when it's time for a cocktail.'

Throughout my little rant he is pouting under furrowed brows. Now he can't resist a chuckle. He tries to deny my allegation, of course, but the chuckle turns into laughter and he stops trying to hide his knowledge of such an obvious fact. He says, 'I do not know what you are talking about', without conviction.

'Really?'

'Really?' He mocks, pressing one hand into the mattress and

leaning a little closer to me. It's my turn to fold my arms across my chest. I put on my best tell-tale voice. That annoying little know-it-all tone that rattles around primary schools.

'So, you're telling me, that my poor little foot *didn't* come about because you wanted to be the one to go to the table and chat to those two girls?' I lower one eyebrow and raise the other as much as I can, and as he suppresses laughter – poorly – I add a *hmm?* for good measure. That last sound tips him over the edge, again.

'*Nai*, yes! You caught me. I think I will get better tips than if you take the drinks. Okay?'

My cheeks are starting to ache from smiling. There's lift in his cheekbones too. It's emphasised by the neatly thought-out stubble that defines his jaw and his cheekbones perfectly at all times. The way his face transforms under the helium-like lift of laughter is almost elegant. I really need to tell him to leave, before I make this more awkward in my head.

The light in the room shifts to a burnt golden glow as the sun hangs lower in the sky outside the window. I think Yianni must have noticed too, because he exhales the last of his laughter and glances towards the window with a slight squint.

'I should get back to the restaurant.'

'They don't expect you to come back.' As soon as I say it, I know it's an obvious invitation and I feel the prick of regret stab at the back of my throat. It's been so long since I've spent time with a man and liked him in any way like this. He is my cousin's brother, so what does that make him to me? I'm going to go ahead and guess that I'm not someone he would see himself taking out on a date. And I don't want him to. I don't. Plus, he is, what, maybe five years younger than me, and a silly sod.

His eyes flick back to mine, and we look at each other for a moment longer than is natural in the middle of a silent room. At the same moment, we break apart, shattering the silence with motion.

He stands, and says in a husky monotone, 'I best go.'

As soon as Yianni leaves the room, I feel about for my phone in my pocket and start messaging two people about what has happened. It's the best way to keep my mind off this stupid attraction I have. First off is my mum. Fortunately, Hazel hasn't already messaged her about my foot, or there would be a blizzard of worried texts from my her. Ever since Jonathan, and living on my own, Mum's done her best to silently check up on me. I like to see it as low-key parental stalking of the sort that fourteen-year-olds have to endure when they leave the house. I put up with it because I can see it's from a place of love and it doesn't bother me to be loved. There are times when she can get a little overbearing and that's usually when something with any edge of drama actually manifests. Luckily, those times have been pretty rare so far. Then there is the person I'm going to tell every stupid girly detail to: Amara.

Amara has been loving living in my house with her boyfriend, Si, and even after only a couple of weeks has decided I should live in Corfu full-time so she can have free holidays visiting me, and she and Si can continue living in my little house for the foreseeable future.

Amara and I are in the middle of sending a million quick-fire messages back and forth when there's a little knock on my door. An involuntary gasp makes me drop my phone on to my chest with a painful slap. I pull myself further back on the bed, my attempt at moving further from the door.

'Who is it?'

'Yianni.'

Yianni? What the hell is he doing knocking at the door? I thought he was long gone.

'Oh. Come in.' Although *come in* is a statement, it comes off more like a question, because really I want to ask if he has been standing outside my door for the past fifteen minutes or so.

'I know it is not much, but, as you know, we mostly eat dinner at the restaurant, so there is less food here.' He passes me a tray with a small salad and a massive slab of feta in the middle with a can of lemonade on the side. '*Kalinikta,* Ruby.'

Then he is walking away, and I'm stunned and calling in his wake, 'Thank you, *efcharistó.* Have a nice evening.' Before whispering, '*Kalinikta,* Yianni. You enigma.'

Chapter 15

Now

I don't do much for a few days because my foot is puffed up. I think the bone is bruised or something, as well as the cut, because when I stand the blood rushes to my foot, and it starts to throb again like my heart has fallen down my trouser leg. The whole thing has turned delightful shades of lilac and black and I couldn't put my trainer on if I wanted to.

It isn't long before I resent lying in the garden, however tranquil it is to watch enormous butterflies with wings of all shapes and sizes dance with bees and beetles. Yes, I adore the shade of the olive trees in the garden which shelter me from the thirty-degree heat in the afternoon, but I'm sick of my bruised bone and of being alone. So, I tell Hazel I'm coming in and if I have to sit on a chair to prep vegetables to keep myself busy, then so be it.

As it turns out, I mostly get in the way in the kitchen and Yianni eventually gives me the role of sitting on a chair next to the till. I'm now officially in charge of all the bills and receipts. Nico is in, and keeping me company, although, Yianni has told him what I said and he is finding any opportunity to bring it up.

'I'm thinking do you think I am only meat to these girls? No?'

Nico tries his best to look sad through his doe eyes. Pressing his fingers to his lips, he tries to look dramatic and hurt at the idea of being a piece of meat. Then he begins to press the back of his hand to his forehead like he might faint, before he moves around the bar as though the wind is blowing and he is caught in the breeze. It's a rather strange but comical skit. It's only after some tutting from me that he breaks character and laughs at himself as he tosses a glass in the air with one hand and watches it somersault into the other.

'Please don't keep doing that near me.' I flap my hands at him. 'I'm still traumatised from Yianni dropping that bloody great milkshake on me. I don't need you chucking one at me too, thanks.'

'Poor Ruby. Do you need a cuddle?'

Nico puts the glass down on the bar and walks towards me with his arms outstretched.

'Nico.' Yianni elongates the O of Nico as he places his hands on the other side of the bar. 'Leave the poor girl alone. She might think the girls are only here for our good looks, but that does not mean you should be terrorising her.' He leans forwards and hisses, 'Save that for the customers. We need money in the tip jar, not Ruby crying on your shoulder. It is not good for business.'

'At least that's something we can agree on.' I give Nico a look that's just shy of poking my tongue out at him in triumph.

It's nice to just be an employee again and not worry that I'm having to set an example to other staff members. It's a completely different atmosphere here than being a maître d' for Charles.

Yianni and I smile at each other. It's the first night of seeing each other since the glass incident. He has messaged to check on me, but they were all sort of formal, checking how I was healing. It's been nice so far, but it makes my body and my heart ache. Part of me wishes we could go back to being quiet and efficient work colleagues. Our eyes are still locked as Nico begins to chat again.

'*Nai, nai,* Yianni. You made this clear to me weeks ago. I know, I am not allowed to talk too much with Ruby. Not too cosy.' Nico wags his finger at Yianni playfully, but Yianni's eyes have shifted and I get the impression he is biting his jaw down hard even under the strange smile he's plastered to his face.

I tilt my head and look between the two of them. 'What?'

'Yianni, he says, *Nico, you are being too mutz saying you will take her places. You can't date staff...* Blah, blah, blah.' Nico's hands circle around the space near his head as though showing me a reel of words.

Was it really Yianni who warned Nico off me then, and not Hazel after all? Why would he do that?

'Is that why I'm still waiting for that date?' I blurt out.

Their heads whip around to look at me. Nico is grinning and throws the glass from the bar in the air again, this time catching it behind his back.

'I am sorry, Ruby. It is not meant to be for us. Yianni say it is so. Don't you, Yianni?'

'I just know what you are like, Nico, and I need the staff.'

I catch sight of a girl sitting taller in her chair glancing about looking for someone to call over.

'Yianni,' I say, and nod towards her table. Then he is gone and so is the moment. When he comes back it is with a list of drinks. I add them to the bill and Nico tosses glasses before filling them.

It's a busy and late night. A few different people gather at the bar to stay and chat. Everyone else has left, apart from me, Yianni and Nico. Hazel told me to leave hours before, but I didn't really want to. It's been hellish sitting about with my feet up and nothing to do. I'm enjoying being part of the furniture here instead. There's more enjoyment to making sure every bill and receipt is in order, than lying in bed. It helps that Yianni pushed a beer towards me – and one to Nico too – about twenty minutes ago.

The group at the bar are quite drunk, but in a fun and excitable way. It's the first night of their holiday and although they'd had every intention of an early night, excitement has taken hold. So, here they are, almost one in the morning, and still sipping tequila.

Nico is doing most of the entertaining, making jokes, being charming, catching flying glasses. As Yianni hovers over me to check the books, I can smell the sweet scent that I inhaled that first night on my sheets. The sheets smell like me now and therefore, to *my* nose at least, of nothing. Slowly I inhale a lung full of him. The heat from his body is like a radiator. As if it isn't hot enough in Corfu. My thighs keep sticking to the stool as it is. The breeze that sporadically appears isn't cutting it. If I could easily get up and walk away without making it obvious, I would, because sucking all the air into my lungs to absorb Yianni's scent is making me lightheaded.

'This all looks good,' Yianni turns to face me.

'Of course. I *have* been doing this sort of stuff longer than you.' I flick the hair from my sticky neck and I'm glad it isn't longer than it is.

'No, no. I'm born and then I'm working for my father. Learning how it all works.'

'Come on, how old were you really?' I fold my arms and jut out my chin, knowing it can't exactly be *that* young.

He bends down and opens the chiller, not far from my feet, then stands up with two more bottles of beer. His eyes focus on a far-off point while his hands smoothly pick up the bottle opener and pops off both lids, all without looking down. I gaze towards where his eyes are looking. It's too dark to see much that's outside of the chairs and tables or the fruit hanging from the trellis.

'Not long after my mother died I had to learn more...' He slides a beer towards me but doesn't meet my gaze.

Anything he wants to say is interrupted by a chorus of *good night, kalinikta, see ya soon, bye, sleep well* among other pleasantries from the gang of smiling holidaymakers who have decided it really *is* time to call it a night now.

Nico moves across the bar towards us and says, 'Now who is cosy?' Half his face pulls into a cheeky smile. 'I am going to Athens Bar. You two coming?'

'I'm in.' I hop off my chair with genuine excitement about being invited somewhere outside of Greek Secret, only to screw my face up at the vibrations running across my foot. '*Putain!*'

'French is such a beautiful language.' Yianni grins, but I can only return a grimace.

Nico slings a tea towel over his shoulder and furrows his brow at us.

'I thought you are English. Where are you from?' Nico's face is so perplexed he almost looks concerned.

'My dad is French. I am English, mostly. I'm from a place called Suffolk. You won't have heard of it, no one ever has.'

'You are wrong.' Nico pulls the towel off his shoulder, picks up a glass and slowly twists the edge around in the towel. 'I knew a girl from there once. Her name is Alice.'

'You remember a girl's name?' Yianni feigns surprise. Nico responds by whipping the towel at him, only missing because Yianni anticipates the movement and pulls away.

'I do have girlfriends, sometimes. There are more than the ones who throw themselves at me.' Nico continues cleaning the already clean glass. 'I'm going to go now. I say I would meet some of the others when they are off work. See you down there?' Nico places the glass back under the bar on the shelf, and the towel neatly on the bar. We both nod and off he goes down the road.

'So, what's left to do before we go?' I'm still clutching the bar and gently letting the blood get used to my foot moving again after a night full of sitting.

'Finish our beers. Lock the doors.'

I reach forwards to grab the beer, sipping at the light golden hops.

'You got any spare lime?'

It's as though I've asked for saffron. Yianni makes a *tss* sound and steps away. He grabs a lime from the bowl of fruit behind the bar. 'Last one.' He shakes his head as though he is disappointed in me before picking up the knife and board that are there for the fruit needed in some cocktails. The lime also hisses in protest as Yianni cuts into it, and a mist fills the air with its sharp and sweet scent. Instead of passing me the wedge, he leans forwards and places it in the top of my bottle.

'Who said it was for my drink?' I lower my chin and peep out from the depths of my fringe.

Yianni twists on his heels and his hands slap down on his thighs. 'There is no pleasing some people.'

I shrug and push the lime all the way into the bottle. Yianni busies himself putting away the remaining lime in the fridge, taking the knife and board to the kitchen among other tasks. Then he sits himself on the other side of the bar as though he is just another customer, before standing up again, reaching over the bar for his beer and flopping back down.

'How old were you when your mum died?' The question has floated in and out of my mind many times and this time it floats out of my mouth with complete ease.

Yianni smooths his thick hair in his hands; pulling it like he's about to tie it into a low ponytail at the nape of his neck. Then he releases it again, the curls rebounding around his face. He glances at me and answers, 'Eight.'

He takes another swig of beer. Deeper than before, with tension rippling over his face, as though drinking is suddenly hard work.

'I'm really sorry. I know loss is really hard. I can't imagine being so young and losing your mum.' I think back to the start of his sentence that was left unfinished and add, 'If you ever want to talk about her, you can.'

People pass by the bar, probably heading towards Perros Hotel or Jasmine Hotel. They're quietly laughing as they meander along the road. Even with the narrow car park at the front, the restaurant is still open to the road. Yianni hops down from his stool, dragging his hand along the wood of the bar as he goes. With a little bit of fiddling, he begins to tug on the bifold doors to lock up the bar area.

'Sorry, if I shouldn't have asked.'

'You lost your job, I lost my mum. It is all in the past.'

I tilt my head and narrow my eyes. Slowly, he makes his way around the doors, closing us in. I'm still waiting for the laugh, or a hint of irony or something about his comment, because that is an insane comparison. There's nothing.

'Seriously? You're going to compare me losing my job to you losing your mum? And...' I stop myself. I've changed my mind about how much I want to divulge, although surely he knows everything about me. But then, I guess, I don't really know all that much about him. Everything I know from Hazel is the crust, but I'm sure there's a whole lot of burning magma underneath that surface. Something about Yianni says that his interior is just waiting, shifting the plates ready for an earthquake. Unless, of course, I'm reflecting my own fears about storing things up on to him. Impossible to say really.

After falling in on myself as I so often do, I look up. He must have sensed my hesitation or my internal exploration, because he's watching me intently as he makes his way back to the bar.

All he says though is, 'Almost finished?' Before he points towards my bottle.

'Almost.' I lift it and slosh the contents a little making the lime look like a very poor attempt at a miniature boat in a bottle.

Silence again.

I wonder if he feels awkward in these moments. I'm hit and miss. Silence doesn't usually make me feel uncomfortable and this one isn't bothering me. But there are times around Yianni that it feels like the tip of my nose is itchy and there is no way to scratch it. I get too aware of myself and too aware of his good looks. It was easier when I thought he hated me. Maybe he still does, but he feels bad about my foot and has to be okay with me now from the pull of shame.

'What did you nearly say? Are you going to ask another question about my mother? People often ask questions.'

'They do, but no. I wasn't. She is yours. It's up to you what you want to tell me. And anyone else for that matter. It's no one else's business but yours. From how you feel to who you tell. It's your life. Your journey.'

His stubbled chin dips in a concise nod. Then he rolls his bottle between the flat palms of his hands, making a damp mark from condensation on the otherwise clean surface. 'And?' he says, looking at me, watching me. Releasing the bottle, it's as though he wants to take hold of me instead. He presses his elbows into the bar and balances his slightly square chin on his fists.

'And?' I pout, as though I'm oblivious to anything he might be asking. Because frankly, I am.

'What were you going to say?'

I exhale hard through my nose and my incisors nip at the inside of my cheeks. 'I guess I just assumed Hazel had told you more about me. I know you're not on socials or anything like that. It's not like we've ever properly spoken in the past. It's been, what? Ten? Fifteen years since your dad and Hazel got married? But Hazel is always giving me those sympathetic looks. She's not subtle. I guess I'm surprised she hasn't said anything. Although I guess she's a bit more like me and she isn't a blab like my mum.' I take a sip of my drink before looking him right in the eyes. His thick black eyebrows are pulled tightly together. His face is still and perfectly balanced on his fists. Waiting.

I don't really want to, but I feel like I've got no other way out, so I begin to talk, 'I had this boyfriend. We'd been together for years. I always thought he was the one.' I air-quote "the one", and as I talk, I can feel myself using my hands more than normal. Maybe if I wave them about enough, Yianni won't notice it's me talking behind them. 'He was an actor. Good-looking, talented. All the clichés. We met in London. Working.'

'And it all fell apart?'

My hands lose all momentum, and so do I. Yianni removes his chin from his knuckles and glances towards the door. My story is too predictable to hold his attention. He works in a restaurant, and when the food service is done, he works behind the bar listening to inebriated people tell him every story and problem under the bright Corfiot sun. I'm just another woman with baggage. With a boring story about a boring boyfriend.

'Yeah. Something like that.'

'Sorry it didn't work out.'

I twist the ring on my right ring finger under the bar and look down at the golden band and tiny row of stones.

'Yeah,' I say, 'me too.' And I mean it.

Chapter 16

Now

I can't shake the feeling of Jonathan, and of how things had been between us before there was no more us. The pain of it all. I make my excuses to Yianni and head off to get my helmet. I have only had two small bottles of beer across the whole evening, and I feel fine to ride my bike home.

I'm not sure if Yianni is disappointed or surprised. His fingers stretch out as though he might catch my arm, but then he thinks twice about it and withdraws his hand.

'Nico will wonder why you have not come for another drink.' There's a playful note in his voice, yet it falls flat. Like it was never there in the first place.

'I'll see him tomorrow.' And with that, I put my helmet on and drive out of the village and up towards the house.

I skim past the now empty restaurants and glowing bars. As I pass Athens Bar with its low slung, cream deck chairs and short tables, I look for Nico. I catch sight of him inside at the bar. His head thrown back in laughter. Soon Yianni will be with him and laughing. I'm better off going home alone than bringing the mood down. I shouldn't dwell on the past, but sometimes it feels so close. Like things were moments ago, not years.

As the road takes me away from the streetlight, the stars become overwhelmingly distracting. Mesmerising. Points of light so piercing that calling them diamonds seems ridiculous, because I have never been as consumed by a diamond as I am by the vast array of stars that weigh down the deep navy of the night sky. I have to consciously avoid looking at them too much and keep my eyes on the road.

When I pull into the driveway at the house, I don't want to go inside. It's a warm evening and I'm not ready to leave the cocoon of the cicadas and the stars – although I could do without the mosquitos. I meander into the garden and sit in the dark on a sunlounger. The rhythmic two notes of an owl's call sound not too far from me over the thrum of the cicadas and multitude of other insects. I watch a satellite skirt the night sky and wonder about Jonathan.

Most days I don't let myself think about him. What's the point? Everything that could have gone wrong, went wrong. I can't go back and change anything. Wishing it had all worked out differently consumed me for a long time, and when I think about what happened, there's a distinct feeling of suffocating myself. My oesophagus seems to close, in an attempt at holding everything in. There never seems to be an easy way to move on. I didn't want to be with him, but I didn't completely stop loving him either. Emotions aren't like hitting the brakes on a car. There's no sudden stop. Even when everything ends the feelings carry on. Like it or not, it takes time to heal. It doesn't matter if things end well or not. Pain lingers either way.

It doesn't matter whether I'm thinking about the good times or the bad times, it's all like a torture. Like I'm having my fingernails pulled out. Sometimes I let myself relax into thoughts of the early days when we were happy. He had a job in a touring theatre company going round schools. I was so sad I couldn't watch him in that play. I can't even think what it was now, one of Shakespeare's but modernised to make it accessible for kids. Oh, that's right. It was A Midsummer Night's Dream, of course. He loved telling me about it on my night off while we ate takeaway pizza and chatted on the floor of his room. He only had a mattress back then and not a bed. Even that memory stings now though, since I found out he was sleeping with the girl who played Titania.

I'm glad Yianni didn't press me to talk about Jonathan. There isn't a sensible start point, and certainly no ending I want to talk about. Yianni. He's like a stone that I keep tripping over. My mind trips on his name. Yianni. As I hold his name there in the same breath as Jonathan's name, guilt traces spindly fingers along my spine. There is no reason to feel guilty. Not unless it's because Hazel is Yianni's stepmother, or because Yianni is that little bit younger than me, and of course the fact he has shown absolutely no interest in me whatsoever. Actually, that's not strictly true. He has possibly warned Nico off me and looked almost sad I didn't go with him tonight. That might mean something. And also… I let myself remember the way he looked at me for a moment there at the bar.

The door to the house creaks softly open, but it's enough to make me sit bolt upright.

'Ruby?' Hazel's stage whisper cuts through the dark.

'Over here. On the sunbed,' I return in an equally forced tone.

I scoot along, nearly tipping the whole thing up but save myself and stand at the last moment before hobbling towards the shadow that is Hazel.

'Why are you on a sunbed when it's dark?'

I can distinctly hear a sing-song laugh in her voice underneath the whisper and the shroud of night. 'I made the mistake of overthinking.'

'Uh-huh…' I know she knows straightaway that I'm either overthinking Jonathan or the loss of my job. 'Do you want to talk about it?' I can see her silhouette clearly. Her head tilts sympathetically.

'I'm okay, really. Why are you up anyway?'

'I heard the bike pull up, but then I didn't hear the door go. I started to wonder where you'd got to.'

'Shit, I'm so sorry if I woke you.'

Her hand finds my elbow, then slips through the crook of my arm to link hers with mine. Together we slowly walk into the house, and away from the million glaring thoughts shining down at me from the ceiling of the earth.

'Don't be silly. I was still awake.' Hazel gives my arm another little squeeze.

I'm sure this is a lie. She's as bad as my mum under it all, worrying about people and soaking up their problems the way other people drink water. That's why I'm here after all, because she wants to help. Unless July and August change things drastically, or Greek Secret magically gains a swimming pool, there is no way they need me at lunch. In the evening, fine, yes, we get busy, but I'm sure adding me into the lunch rotation was just another layer of Hazel's pity and desire to make everything *right* by distracting me. Maybe she can tell I've been falling more and more into the mist of my own thoughts.

As we step into the kitchen she switches on the light. I almost want to shade my eyes against the trio of hanging lights above the table. The glare from their frosted glass is too much after the soft brilliance of the stars.

'Water?' Hazel wrinkles her forehead in question and readjusts her cotton dressing gown while turning towards the cupboard where the glasses live.

I nod, 'Please.'

'Yianni is feeling ever so guilty about your foot, you know.'

'Is he?'

I pull out one of the chairs at the kitchen table and place myself down, pressing the palm of my hand under my fringe and into my forehead. Letting the weight of my head and my thoughts be supported by my fist and my arm. Although he has been a little softer with me, Yianni isn't overtly acting as though he feels particularly guilty. He clearly felt sorry at the time, and he has shifted his manner, but he hasn't continued to make a fuss about it. Unless he has conveyed something to Hazel that I don't know about.

'Maybe on Monday he can take you somewhere to say sorry. Maybe a trip to somewhere you'd like to see. I think it might do you both some good to take a day off.'

'How? I mean, one of us taking the day off, maybe, but both?'

'I'm sure I can find someone for a day, don't you worry.'

I pull my feet back from under the table and stand in front of Hazel as she passes me a glass of water.

'Honestly, Hazel, I think you might be overestimating how guilty Yianni feels. And really, he has nothing to feel guilty for. It was an accident. My foot's a lot better today, just tender, really.'

'We can talk about it tomorrow. Right, you should get off to bed. Goodnight.' And with that, she leans forwards to kiss my cheek. Her night cream smells of lavender, just like my mum's. A pang of longing for the comfort of my mum passes through me like the striking of a chime.

'Night, Hazel.' I quickly depart the kitchen, taking my water with me.

Hazel quietly calls after me. 'Sleep well. I'm always here if you need me.'

Chapter 17

Now

Apparently Yianni *does* want to take me out. Either that or Hazel talked him into wanting to take me out. I text this news to Amara, I'm not sure why. Maybe I want her to think that I'm having a good time and not isolating myself completely. I know she thinks that's the case, and it's been hard to deny completely. Before Monday lands at my feet, I muddle along at work, which involves another day of me sitting and doing the till before I'm on my feet more. My foot's still badly bruised and standing on it for too long makes it swell up a little. I think it is more to do with the heat than anything. My body is used to standing about for work but not normally in sweltering heat that exceeds that of a normal kitchen. Plus, I haven't actually worked inside the heat of the kitchen for quite some years. Only walking in and out of them, organising. I did a stint as a commis chef many years ago to try it out. Same as I have with every role hospitality has to offer. All in my attempt to understand every minute detail of how a restaurant works and runs when the kitchen and front-of-house teams are in perfect harmony.

It's Sunday evening, and things are starting to quieten down. I nestle myself in a corner table with a plate of food, away from the people still finishing their meals. There is a real selection on my plate. I wonder what I'll eat tomorrow with Yianni. Apprehension niggles as I take my first bite of Hazel's garlic-laden tzatziki.

The screen of my phone lights up.

'Hey you,' I smile as I press the phone to my face. 'How's the life of pretending to be married?'

'Urgh. It's all gone to shit and I nearly kicked him out.' Amara exhales and I can hear the banging of things in the background of our call.

'Are you still at work?' I ask, before taking a mouthful of my tender porkchop.

'Yep. It's been so quiet though. Good ol' Charles said I could knock off early. Thank god.'

I swallow my food, wishing I could enjoy the tang from the garlic, mint and dill in the tzatziki for a moment longer, but I need to open my mouth to ask questions.

'Last time we spoke, you two were all loved up. What the hell happened?'

'What? Me and Charles?'

'No, you fool, not Charles. Si.'

I balance the phone between my shoulder and my ear so I can devour the rest of my meal – the pile of salty purple olives and the entirety of the chop – as Amara explains that Si has just started to get on her last nerve. He leaves his socks all over the place and wants to play on his Xbox a little too much.

'None of this sounds like a good reason to end a good thing. These are little niggles you've had before. Am I missing something?'

'Well, I haven't ended it. I threatened it, that's all. I just can't be bothered with him messing everything up all the time. You know? Didn't you ever feel like that with Jonathan? It can't have always been perfect.'

I know she isn't trying to be inconsiderate, and I don't want to become overly sensitive, but I have just taken a bite of pita piled with feta and swallowing now feels like I'm trying to gulp down a balloon.

'No, it wasn't perfect, and you more than anyone know that very well. We argued, mostly about money and the future. But it was a very different situation.'

I've never gone into detail even with Amara about my internal turmoil around Jonathan. How it took me so long to see the pattern, the ridge formed by manipulation I'd slipped deep down in to. How there was never any obvious abuse; in fact, I'm loathe to think of it as abuse, more that the relationship soured over time. He soured. He became too possessive, too controlling.

I change from my left ear to my right. My appetite is completely diminished, which is good as I'm also full and that will stop me eyeing up a bowl of ice cream. I'm still impressed at how I'm now completely full and utterly empty, simultaneously. I suppose because one is physical and the other is emotional. Amara is apologising, agreeing, talking over herself, stopping and starting and restarting sentences. '

'Let's change the subject.' I push my plate away from me. 'Are you outside now?'

'Uh huh. Now heading to my car. Are you excited about the date tomorrow? What are you doing again?'

'Please stop calling it that. He is a step away from being my cousin.'

'He isn't your cousin though. He is no relation at all, and he is taking you for a full day of just the two of you. Sounds like a damn date to me.'

'I have to get back to work. Unlike some, there's no getting out early for me. Keep me updated about you and Si, okay?'

'Shall do. Have a nice date.'

'Night.'

I relax back into my chair and scan the room. People are enjoying their food in a dreamy Greek setting. The restaurant is just the right balance of authentic and holiday cliché; with everyone sitting in the shade of the grapevines. The room is starting to empty and the tables that are left are mostly on to desserts. There's a hum like the background sound of the cicadas, only this is the consistent murmur of human interaction – people sharing stories, food, drinks and excitement for the rest of their time on the island. Some people are taking it all in, eyes scanning every inch of the restaurant – the way mine are – and they're relaxing into the atmosphere. There is even traditional Greek music playing underneath it all. I turn my head sharply to the bar. I want to check if it's busy, if I need to hurry up with my dinner. But instead, I catch Yianni watching me. I caught him just before he managed to divert his eyes. He just wasn't quite quick enough.

The rest of the night is busy to say the least. Hazel says I should leave when she does, and let the boys entertain for the last few hours behind the bar. There is no argument from me.

I want to curl up in bed and sleep. Not that it works quite like that. The nights are sweaty and all I have for relief from the heat is one of those lights with a built-in fan. The house does have air conditioning, but not in every room. It does keep it cooler than it otherwise would be, but once my door is closed my body heat seems to ignite and if it wasn't for the overwhelming exhaustion some nights, I'm not sure I would sleep much at all.

Even with the mixed feeling about the day ahead with Yianni, I actually managed to get some rest last night. Stuffing my black leather backpack with anything and everything I can think of, I dart downstairs. I'm no sooner at the bottom of the stairs when his car pulls up. I feel like a teenager again, back when I didn't want to introduce my date to my dad, so I'd run outside and jump in their car as fast as I could. The difference is, this is Pericles' son, Aunt Hazel's stepson. He is seen as my cousin. My family. I'm grateful that at least he doesn't call Hazel *Mum*. It is always *Hazel*. Always.

As I pass through the kitchen, I wash the room with pleasantries and manoeuvre around the chairs. Pericles makes it to the door first and swings it open before I can get there. Yianni's casually walking towards the house. He doesn't seem the least bit awkward or abashed. He comes in and kisses everyone's cheeks, including mine. In French it is called *la bise*. The two bland kisses to each cheek, as robotic and unwavering as a handshake or even just a verbal *hello*. He isn't looking at me or talking to me. It calms me. He isn't chasing me. Instead, he's saying something to Natalia, his half-sister. My cousin. I need to keep repeating this because the stupidity inside me isn't going anywhere.

'No, sorry little one.'

I had tuned out the conversation by accident, and instead I was focusing on my own thoughts. I really need to stop doing that.

'Ruby wouldn't mind. Would you Ruby?'

My mouth drops open, hoping to find an answer to an unknown question. Luckily Hazel saves me.

'You still have to work, Natalia. Perhaps you can show Ruby around more places another day.' Hazel lifts her eyebrows high above the frames of her glasses. Without words her body language shifts and she manages to hurry us out of the door seamlessly. She's so much like Mum sometimes.

Only once my bum makes it onto the seat of Yianni's car do I ask what on earth we are going to be doing.

'Well,' he begins, 'I am surprised not to have you ask me this sooner.'

Momentarily he falls silent as he turns the car around, shunting it a little forwards, a little backwards, until it's facing the right way, and making me wait even longer to know. He's right though. I could've asked at work, pushed him more. I asked once and he replied with, *I'm not sure yet*, and I left it at that.

'Well,' he starts over, 'I asked Hazel what you have been doing. In the mornings. And what you like to do. She tells me before you hurt your foot, you went swimming, so I went to speak to a good friend and I have hired us a boat.'

At first, I'm not sure what to say. There's a tickle inside of me at the thought that he's actually gone to the trouble of asking a question about me. Maybe he really does feel guilty about my foot. Before I can formulate a response, he continues. 'How is your foot now?'

I shrug. 'A lot better than it was. I'm not sure if I should go swimming yet though.'

He makes a sound like opening a can by way of disagreement. 'The sea will keep it clean and heal the bruises. You'll be fine.'

It's not long until we're parked on the beach. A place I wouldn't normally park as it's too central and I'd have to pass too many people without my makeup on in the mornings. But today I'm wearing all my normal evening coverage. It's also not as early as my usual beach trips, and people are already in rows on beach beds. One whole row is nothing but bodies with open books for faces.

It is going to be a very hot and muggy day. I can tell because the line between the sea and the sky is almost invisible. It's a cornflower-blue haze that ripples between the two. Lines are blurred. Everything is one and the same now. The distant islands are a confusion, almost as though they are being absorbed into a cloud. In my limited experience of being in San Stefanos so far, that view means the weather will be uncomfortably hot. Hopefully there'll be a breeze out on the sea at least.

After a brief – almost non-existent – introduction to Yianni's friend, who has other people waiting for boats, he points us towards a small white one with a thin aqua-blue line running all the way around the hull. Poles support a matching blue awning that shades about half of the boat from the sun. The boat is barely even bobbing. The air is still and so is the water. It gently caresses the sand, lapping slowly at our toes. There is no sign of angry froth or foam, only the sensation of comfort.

Following Yianni, I remove my bag from my back, tossing

it on deck along with my flip-flops and climb aboard. Yianni starts the engine, and we pull away towards the haze. The air rushes past, making my hair sauté and pirouette around my face.

My fingers skim the surface of the water, which is so clear I can see the stones, fish and shapes on the seabed. Then I turn my attention to the island – Corfu Island – while my fingers continue bouncing and gliding along like a fin in the sea. To my side, jutting rocks with layers of trees carpet every available surface. Then there are the surfaces that have been stolen from nature but are somehow just as beautiful. Some are whitewashed buildings, others are pale yellow with sunshine-coloured doors. My favourites have traditional blue doors and look like they were made to be photographed for postcards. All have flat roofs and windows that are like eyes looking out to sea, watching boats go by. Watching us, as we're watching them. Or I do anyway; Yianni is looking where he is going. I break my eye contact with the shore and gaze at him. He continues to look straight ahead. His hair, much longer than mine, dances even more wildly around his face. I don't know how he knows I'm looking at him, but it's as though it has initiated a cue for him to speak to me.

'Do you know why Greeks call Corfu Kerkyra?'

I shake my head and as I edge round to face him more, I gently lift and lower the ring on my right hand as I wait to find out the answer.

'Kerkyra was a nymph. Poseidon fell in love with her and they had many children called Phaeacians, who were accomplished sailors. These sailors, they helped Odysseus on his journey to Ithaka, but there was a shipwreck and Odysseus turned up at Palaiokastritsa, not far from here. He was then

109

gifted a boat, but Poseidon, he was angry at him and turns it to stone.'

'Why was Poseidon angry with Odysseus? What had he done to annoy him?'

'I forget this part.' Yianni shrugs and a brief smile crosses his lips as he lifts his arm to sweep his hair back to one side. I take a deep lungful of the salty air and bite my lips at the view, which now also contains Yianni. His muscular frame beneath his clothing... I really need to stop having these thoughts. I have an urge to put my head underwater and scream at the fish, but instead I turn away to watch the cliff and coves gliding past.

'Corfu is also where Hercules partied with Melite and – what do you English say? –knocked her up.'

I slowly turn my head back to look at Yianni. He has a grin plastered on his face. When he said, *knocked her up*, he had put on his best cockney accent. He has never been silly like this with me before. I've seen him laugh and joke with Nico and Natalia, but not really with me. Delayed laughter splutters from my lips.

'What? These are the most random Greek myths I have ever heard. Are you just making them up?'

'Maybe. I was not so much interested in Greek history at school.'

'Natalia said the same thing.'

The mention of his sister's name brings softness to his face.

More than I expected to, and more than I want to, I feel completely relaxed in Yianni's company.

Chapter 18

Now

We carry on skirting the island. Fawn-and-cream-coloured cliff edges bite down into the sea most of the way. The salts and the shingle have dug away small alcoves, caves and notches over time as well as bays. Squinting, I try to see into the darkness of one or two caves. It feels magical enough to believe there is treasure hiding in there. Our boat is buzzing along now, cutting through the water which protests with a rhythmic *ch-ch-ch* underneath us. Since Hazel and Pericles' wedding in Corfu, I had only made it as far as Spain – most of my money had gone on rent and not on holidays abroad. I have never hired a boat like this before. I can taste the fine salt spray tracing my lips, and it tastes a lot like freedom.

The boat comes to a gentle stop and Yianni nods towards the beach, perhaps fifty or so metres away. 'Paradise Beach.' His dark eyes hold the view of the shore. 'Locals call it Chomoi.'

The sand is so white I have to squint to look at it, and the rippling water around us is like glass. In fact, even with ripples it is clearer than the glass in a bathroom mirror. Fish are darting about, some almost looking like they are nibbling at the hull.

'This is as far as we go. The rest of the way, we swim.' He hesitates. I haven't really seen him hesitate. 'If... if you want to. If not, we can keep moving.'

I shrug, smiling over at him before thinking about all our belongings on the boat.

'What about the bags?' I point at the two bags and the shoes under the awning, but when I look up, Yianni is already unbuttoning his shirt to reveal his firm, almost hair-free chest. It's the richest gold tan I've ever seen, as though his skin has been painted in a dark brandy. 'So, leave them here then, I guess.'

'It is up to you. I need a swim, either way.'

He turns to face me, steps backwards onto the edge of the boat and holding his body completely rigid, lets himself fall backwards into the sea. It's as though a bucket of water has been thrown in my direction. Even though I turned my face at the last possible moment – if I could have believed what he was doing, I might have looked away sooner – water still slaps along my ear and my chest.

After the initial gasp that automatically shot into my chest, I mutter, 'You shit,' and start pulling my celadon-green smock over my head. I'm wearing a much darker green swimsuit underneath with high legs and cut-out sides. It's my favourite. I don't wear bikinis anymore. I have this, a plain black one and one with flamingos all over it that my mum got me before I left.

I dive in after him. Without even thinking to tie my hair

into its usual little ponytail, or even considering my makeup, I dive in, skimming along the sea, not down into it. It isn't really deep enough for that. Or maybe it is. These things can be so deceptive that I wasn't going to risk it. Instead, my aim now is to catch up with Yianni who, after his insane backwards fall into the sea, has started swimming to shore. He is dawdling though, and swimming is one of my favourite things to do. Not that I have had much opportunity in the past few years. Sometimes I get up early in the summer and force myself into the freezing sea at Felixstowe. At home it's more a game of sprinting in and swimming as fast as humanly possible. Here, it's a pleasure – other than today, as now I want to prove some pointless point to Yianni. Even as I edge towards him, I wonder what the point is. But somewhere deep inside me there is a naughty little laugh wanting to escape, as though getting ahead of him is the funniest thing in the world.

Soon it's too shallow to kick but I'm ahead and smiling to myself. As water drips off the tip of my nose, I desperately want to touch my face, wipe it away. But I can't. The tingle of the saltwater makes me feel fresh and clean, other than on my face, which is itching underneath my foundation. Of course – I have put on concealing makeup that holds up against sweat and splashing, but I've never tried it fully submerged in the sea before. There's nothing I can do now though. If my scars are on show, so be it. He's a bloke, and not just any bloke, but Yianni. He likely won't notice and even if he does, what's it to him? I know deep down it's nothing to anyone but me.

My fingers rake the ends of my hair and my bangs press like limp seaweed on my forehead. Wet strands of hair saturated with saltwater weigh on my skin, hopefully covering the scar there. All of this thinking has wiped the smile from my face and washed it away and I wish I could sink back into the water and swim away from myself. As long as I don't touch my face, it'll probably be fine. I need to stop thinking.

As I make my way out of the shallows, the hot sand sticks to my feet in clumps like powdered sugar on butter. The sticky strips holding my foot together are allowing my body to form yet another scar inflicted by someone else. My flesh is safely working its healing magic under the wrap provided at the health centre. I'm unsure how much longer the bandage will last, though. It's almost time to expose the wound to the world now anyway. To give it fresh air to heal more quickly.

I turn to Yianni who is equally caked in pale sugary sand.

'Now what?' I say, my hands gripping my hips. The sun is steaming the water from Yianni's body, leaving it glittering with lines of fine, white salt crystals.

'We swim?' He takes a breath then continues. 'There are,' he waves his hand in front of his face, 'snorkels in the boat. Or we can relax on the beach. Hazel says I should treat you like you are on holiday. This is what people on holiday do.'

He's right. If my phone hadn't been in the boat, I would have been taking a photo and sending it to everyone I know back home, just to show them how gorgeous it all is. It's no wonder it has the nickname of Paradise Beach.

'Well, do you want to swim, or stay on the beach? Or I can take you somewhere less beautiful in the boat.' He smiles at me. Straight white teeth, definitely from braces. Surely no one is born with such perfect teeth. Yianni pushes back his black curls that are dripping onto his shoulders and squeezes water from them.

'Your hair is actually a lot longer than I thought.'

Turning back to me he throws his head forwards and then,

much like a mermaid might, he whips his head backwards making a stream of water droplets dive from the tips of each strand of hair. He then poses like a model. Not a good model though. It's exceptionally exaggerated. Poking out his bottom lip a little too far and looking off into the distance through lightly squinting eyes. I think the look is meant to be smouldering, but it's overtly camp instead.

'Do you like it?' he says, still posing like a statue.

Laughter that I've been storing up inside me since he fell off the boat rolls out, tickling my sides as it flows up from low in my abdomen. 'Very nice. You're the perfect gay icon.'

His body relaxes back into its normal frame. 'I take that as a compliment. Gay men always have good taste, no?' He winks at me, a super-cheesy wink.

My forehead wrinkles, but laughter is still slipping off my tongue. 'Who even are you and what have you done with the miserable sod I work with?'

I stomp past him into the sea. It's late in the morning now and there isn't enough breeze to be standing around under the full power of the sun. I need the relief of the sea to cool me off. Yianni follows me and keeps pace. He is making some kind of *uh-uh-uh* sound. I'm not looking at him, but I imagine he is shaking his head. I release my body back to the sea where I'm sure it belongs. It's only deep enough that it comes up to my neck while sitting though. But it feels like cool silk on my burning skin.

'I am no *miserable sod.* I just like to get my work done. I am hard-working, this is all.' His fingers curl around the words *miserable sod*, as well as exaggerating them verbally.

'Maybe it's just me then. You've been better since smashing that thick milkshake glass on my foot, but before that I felt like you were avoiding me. At best.'

Yianni flops down opposite me in the water, so he is facing out to sea. There's a pause. His hairy knees poke out above the water and his arms loosely wrap around them, with his fingers linked together, using his arms to hold everything in place. I'm more free, leaning my weight back on my hands and letting the slow rocking of the sea do what it wants with me. This is how I want to be. How I've always wanted to be.

'Yes, I will admit. I'm not a fan of these overly pretty girls who don't eat food. Their minds are only on the next photo for Instagram.' My eyebrows lift so quickly I can feel the hair that was stuck to my forehead abruptly peel off. 'This is who I thought you are at the airport. I come out and there you are looking at your phone, not seeing me. Living in some daydream. Not thinking that *your* name on paper could mean *you*. Now, I think maybe I'm wrong. Maybe I judged you too soon.'

'Are you saying you thought I was pretty and now maybe you don't?'

'Yes. This is exactly what I meant. I am glad I made myself clear.'

'It's the scar, isn't it?'

His face changes and the joke and laughter jars to a stop. I don't even know why I said it. That unconscious self-doubt crept out into the open and mocked itself publicly. I suppose because the past is always there in the back of my head. Lurking. Never wanting me to fully let go. Never letting me relax with someone I might like. Not that I want to like Yianni, but he's making it almost impossible not to today.

'What scar?' His head tilts and his eyes narrow on me.

I shift and mirror his body language, pulling myself in and

116

wrapping my arms around my knees then habitually pulling at the ring on my right hand. Slipping it up and down, twirling it around.

When I don't answer, he asks again. 'What scar? The one on your foot? I am sorry. I do feel bad for hurting you.'

'No. I'm being silly. I'm just not used to you being so friendly.'

'Do not get used to it.' He laughs and in one quick motion, flicks water at my face. My jaw drops open.

'You're such a shit, Yianni.' I don't mean it, of course. It is obvious to anyone that I'm laughing under my words. 'And, I'll have you know, that the first time I saw you, you were looking at your phone. So, who is addicted to their screen *really?*'

'I was checking my messages from Hazel. It's a big shame you couldn't do the same.'

I press my lips tightly shut. There's not much I can say about that.

'And, Ruby, you are wrong. That is not the first time you saw me. The first time was the morning before my papa and Hazel were married. You came to our old house with your mother and father and we all had drinks and English biscuits.' He looks past me towards the boat, then back to look me in the eye. 'You drank tea.'

'I'm sorry.' I don't want to be sorry so I continue searching the files of memories in my mind. 'I don't remember that at all.'

'You spent a lot of time on your phone. Your hair was long and dark.'

Any skin that's not submerged burns in the sun overhead, or that's how it feels, because it seems like Yianni hasn't blinked in a while. Maybe he has, but there's something so intense about this memory that he's projecting onto me. Intense for him, it seems, anyway. I can barely remember being in their house. And he is younger than me. He was the kid.

'It was a long time ago,' he continues. 'Would you like to snorkel?'

Of course, the answer is yes. We spend the next hour snorkelling, watching fish of different shapes and sizes. It's so peaceful, even though there's a handful of other people on the beach and in their boats, or like us in the water, it's still like no one else is around.

Everyone wants to maintain the gentle peace, so, it doesn't really matter that they are there. At times, it's almost like being completely alone even without Yianni. The difference is the comfort of knowing someone *is* here, experiencing it all with me. Someone *is* here if I have something to say or want to point something out. He is here, just because I'm here. He is here completely for me. I haven't had that feeling since Jonathan. And even then, it felt different to this. With Jonathan, it was always the other way around. I felt like I was there for him. I was the warm-up act and he was the main attraction. It rarely felt balanced. The thought settles somewhere in the depths of my head. It's something I normally get a tinge of guilt for thinking, but I don't let it in. I let myself be consumed by the sea and all of its beauty and wonder. And anyway, Yianni is just a friend.

Chapter 19

Now

It's only when it feels as though hungry fingers are grabbing hold of my stomach that we get back in the boat. There's nothing much on Paradise Beach. Yianni explained to me while we were bobbing about in the water that people are warned not to walk on the beach. Those who do, do so at their own risk, as stones and rocks often fall down from the cliff face which lines the narrow strip of sand. If it hadn't been for this piece of information, I might have gone exploring in some of the little alcoves on the beach, but it doesn't seem like the smartest idea, given the facts. My foot injury is enough to last me for a little while.

'We can sail somewhere else for lunch, or...' Yianni reaches behind where I'm sitting and taps something with his open palm. I turn to see a cool box.

'Ohh!' My eyes grow wide and Yianni playfully sniggers at my reaction before standing to pick the box up and place it in front of us. 'I asked my friend to stock it for us.'

Pulling off the lid, his hand disappears into the box and comes back out with two bottles of Corfu beer. This is met with an applause *and* a small cheer from me. I gladly take a bottle of beer from him then put it down to dig into my own bag.

'Ah ha!' I pull out my keys, which are actually Pericles' keys for the bike and the house on one key ring.

Yianni reaches out to briefly touch the key ring. 'I got this for my mother on a school trip many years ago.'

It's a flip-flop that doubles as a bottle opener on a key ring. I use it to open my bottle and then pass it to him. His thumb runs along the shiny surface of the flip-flop before using it to open his bottle with a hiss, then he carefully hands it back. I give it one last look with a new interest, before placing it more carefully back in my bag.

'Nice that you got your mum such a useful gift.'

'The trip was on her name day. We are big on name days here. I do not know if you know this. We do name days and not so much birthdays.'

I nod. I'm aware because of Natalia. She likes to celebrate both and when she was very small, she liked to tell me about how important her name day was.

'I had got her something already, but on the trip I wanted to get her another gift. I see this,' he points towards my bag, 'and it's the only thing she might like. I used the money Papa gave me for lunch to get it for her.'

'So, it turns out, you're a thoughtful one when you want to be.'

He doesn't respond. Instead, his hand dives back into the cool box to pull out more items – a small loaf of bread, a tub of tzatziki, a tub of another dip that I don't recognise, and a big bag of crisps.

'We can eat on the boat, or I can take us somewhere.'

'Here's good.'

I slap my hands on to my thighs and my cheeks are painfully tense from grinning.

While we eat, we talk. As we dip our bread into the pots, we compare childhoods and I get to ask lots of the questions I've been storing up. Like, does he get on well enough with Hazel? He says he does. And, why doesn't he come to England? He tells me they can't always afford it and he wasn't bothered about going, preferring to spend time with his dad instead. This surprises me.

'The restaurant does well. It is doing better now I am taking over and changing things. But we only make money half of the year. Money is also being saved for Natalia to go to university in England.'

'And what about you? Did you go to uni?'

'I studied business in Athens. You?'

'Same, business studies. Not in Athens though.'

'No, your Greek is…not so good. How long have you been working in bars?'

'How do you know my Greek isn't so good?'

'An boreíte na to katalávete aftó. Syngnómi.'

I study his face before saying, 'I forgive you.'

Yianni almost spits out the bread he has just put in his mouth. His eyebrows shoot upwards and he searches my face for answers. There's no way I can suppress the giggle a moment longer so I let it all out. 'All I understood was *sorry. Syngnómi.'*

His entire body relaxes now he is safe in the knowledge that

I truly don't speak Greek, and anything he has said in Greek near me has indeed gone by me.

I say, 'To answer your question…' He gives me a confused look before the memory of asking me a question slaps him round his face and makes him nod. 'All my life I've worked in hospitality, one way or the other. Cafés, bars, restaurants, pubs, tavernas.' As I say the last one, half my face twists into a smile, which he catches and mirrors back at me. 'I've always wanted to own my own restaurant. To run it how I want and put the food I want on the menu. Every time I save some money towards my dream, I've had to spend it. Rent, Christmas…a new car.' I take a sip of my beer. The liquid is quickly warming up even though it's in the shade. 'You know, I've only ever told two people that.'

'I am honoured.'

I haven't even told my parents my dream. They've always wanted me to do something more than working in hospitality. To try something else.

There is peace in the air, a calm where the only sounds are tiny creaks from the boat, a wild goat occasionally bleating near the edge of the cliff, and some people laughing in the distance on one of the other boats. The haze over the sea isn't letting up. It's cocooning everything. Maybe it's all that mist that's fogging my brain and making it open up for a change.

'What about you? Are you happy? Do you have dreams of somewhere that isn't Corfu?'

'No. I would like to travel more, but when your home is this,' he gestures towards the cliffs and out to sea with his bottle, 'then there is no reason to find a new home.'

I agree. Who wouldn't want to live here? It's paradise for god's sake. Even though I miss my family and my friends back home, Corfu is already holding me tightly in her grasp. As though the lush greenery is growing over me and pulling me into it.

Without thinking, I let my fingers glide through my hair, momentarily pushing the hair off my face before the sticky, salted strands fall back down, and I sip at the last of my beer.

Yianni's hand meets my face. At first, I recoil, yanking the bottle from my lips to glare at him. He lifts his eyebrows gently at me. There is a softness about his face that makes mine relax too. I let him push the hair away from my forehead again. My throat is now unbelievably dry and I can't swallow; there seems to be nothing left to swallow. His index finger traces down my right eyebrow, sliding down my cheekbone and comes to rest along with his thumb on my chin. Carefully he lifts my face towards the sun.

'This is the scar you meant, *nai?*'

Chapter 20

Now

My pulse is raging, but I manage to maintain a steady breath. I don't want Yianni to know that the combination of his fingers on my skin and the revelation of my scar under the pressure of his gaze are causing me to tip over into somewhere I don't want to go. A small rock tumbles down the edge of the nearby cliff, and I feel like my heart's gone with it. Out of control, with gravity pulling it away from everything it knows.

'Yeah.' My voice is a gravelly whisper. 'It was the scar I meant.'

Yianni's eyes meet mine and he releases me from his gentle grip. I take a deep breath and it catches in my chest, the way it might if I'd spent the last hour crying instead of swimming.

'How did it happen?'

I lick my lips and snatch my eyes back to a piece of bread. It's already curling in the heat, but I press it into the last of the tzatziki anyway and thrust it into my mouth.

Then I answer through my mouthful, 'Car accident.'

I look at him. Waiting for the usual concerned look. It's there of course. His brows are furrowed and he's now leaning a little closer to me. He's not concerned that he hasn't been able to make out what I said. His body contracts slightly to indicate his lack of comprehension. I swallow my mouthful of food, and say again, 'Car accident.'

'*Gromoto.* Are you okay?'

'I'm here, aren't I?' My tone is further from playfully sarcastic and closer to shitty than it should be or than I meant it to be. Quietly I add, 'Yeah. I'm fine. Did have to buy a new car though.'

'When?'

'A few years back. It's fine, I'm fine.' I smile at him. 'These things happen, don't they? Everyone tells me I'm very lucky. I am. I'm very lucky. Not something everyone gets to walk away from. It's not something I exactly look back on fondly though, or talk about much. What about you? You don't seem to have a mark on you, not even a birthmark.' I pull my fringe back into place and press my lips together in an attempt at a smile while I wait for him to list scars or injuries to prove he isn't so perfect. That isn't what I get.

'You have been noticing me.' A smile glides over his lips and in spite of myself the muscles in my cheekbones respond by lifting too.

'I thought you were an arrogant shit, with all of your pretty thick hair, and it turns out I'm right.'

We laugh together, but the air seems to shift around us. I don't feel comfortable anymore. My swimsuit suddenly feels too tight, like I'm being strangled by it. I want to get back and maybe to get changed too.

'Would you like to go somewhere else or to go back to San Stefanos?'

'I think I'd like to go home.'

'I don't have enough fuel for England. Maybe just San Stefanos?' He doesn't flinch, as though his answer was the most sensible response and the only one I should have expected.

'Okay, I suppose that will have to do then.'

He packs the cool box away, then we are off skimming the surface of the water again, edging around the island and around the mass of my past in the process. I spend my time questioning everything in a way that I know I shouldn't. I can't even concentrate on the colours of the sea to mask what I'm really thinking and feeling. Instead, everything seems to be pulsing through me along with my blood. Pain, passion, scars. Then the engine cuts out.

'Ruby, quickly, look.' Yianni pulls at my arm, tugging me up to standing. He's frantically pointing further out to sea.

'What? What am I looking at?'

He stands behind me, pressing his body into my back before reaching his arm over my shoulder and pointing out to sea, lining it up so I can follow his arm. That's when I see it – or not it, them. Something out of the water. His arm drops but we stay stuck together for a few moments, both of us in awe of the creatures breaking through the surface of the waves.

When Yianni pulls away it's like pulling off a plaster. I can still feel the pressure of him on my skin. I feel raw and vulnerable without him. It's been so long since I've had anyone pressed against me. But now he's groping under things on the boat, pulling open places I didn't expect would open until he finds a pair of binoculars.

He stares out through them for a moment, then passes them to me.

'What are they?' In the binoculars the creatures look much bigger than dolphins, but with sort of similar noses.

'Whales.' The click of his phone taking pictures snaps next to me.

'I thought you didn't do Instagram?'

'I don't.'

Then comes the distinctive beep from his phone as he starts to film them. The whales are actually not that far away, but with binoculars it's like I could touch them. They're all marked with jagged scars and lines – like me. War wounds covering their bodies. They're strangely beautiful.

I pull the binoculars from my face and pass them back to Yianni as he lowers his phone.

'What sort of whale are they?'

'*Zifiós.*'

'English?'

Yianni lowers the binoculars leaving us both squinting. The whales seem to have vanished for good under the surface.

'I'm not sure. Beaknose whale? We must report this to the research institute. They will need these photos and videos too.'

'Do you know all the different types of whales and dolphins?'

He starts up the engine and we head off again.

'Some. The *Zifiós* are rare, but one washed up into Arillas not so long ago. Oil companies have been using *seismikós* sounds. It's thought this harms much of the sea life. Disorientating them, killing them…' He trails off in a soft tone, but his entire body is taut.

Arillas is the next village down from San Stefanos. It's not far at all.

'Did you see it? The beached whale?'

He shakes his head. 'No. There were enough people to help, and I didn't know until later. It is very sad to waste life in this way.'

I couldn't agree more.

By the time we reach San Stefanos, it's mid-afternoon, and the journey back has given me time to cool off, helped by the distraction of the whales and the conversations they brought on. And not helped by the lingering sensation of Yianni's firm chest pressed against me. I took the time to step back from my feelings as best I could and to let in the calm of the water; to let the breeze take the hurt away with it. It's always hard to think about how much I've been through because of that accident. I've rarely spoken about it to anyone, even when it happened. My mum had wanted me to see a therapist because I refused to talk to her about it. I didn't go. There would be no point paying someone just to hear my silence on the subject. It's the only way I could process the lack of control I have over my life. To be inward and quiet is all I have. That's all anyone has. Or maybe not. I guess other people like the idea of a problem shared being a problem halved. It's just not me. Having others appraise my pain and compare it to their own makes me shut down. I'm more than happy to listen to people tell me about themselves and their problems. It's one of the things I like about working behind a bar or in hospitality. I can listen to people and help people. It's all about being there for people to make them happy. The focus is as far away from me as it gets even when they're looking right at me. People aren't judging the validity of my issues or poking at my weaknesses. I'm just there to bring them happiness in the form of good food and scrummy drinks. I love that. I can still remember the first time I played restaurant with my parents. I made a menu and cooked everything on it from scratch. I must have been eight or nine. They were so happy and I knew then I wanted to see more people smiling like that. Food is a place where people come together.

My mum actually tried to use food to get me to talk about the accident. She made all my favourites and all the comforting puddings imaginable. Eventually I did talk to her a little about it. I'm sure she knew that pressing me too hard would never work to get to me open up. It didn't work when I was a child, and it wouldn't work now. I guess that's why she spent weeks making all my favourite foods.

When we stop and get out of the boat, I don't fancy people staring at my scars and I don't want to seem vain by getting my mirror out to see what I actually look like. I wish I didn't care. I don't want to care. I wish I could forget they were there and feel confident that no one would stare or ask questions I don't want to answer. So instead of going along the beach with Yianni to talk to his friend, like he wants me to, I wave at him from a distance and wait at the edge of the sea while they chat. I look away again and out to sea to catch my breath as I try to shake off the feeling that swirls around me. Instead, I close my eyes and take in the smell of seaweed that lingers around me and fuses with the smoky smell pooling down from one of the beach bars or restaurants just past Yianni. It's delightful. It takes my mind off myself and back to the charming island that I'm lucky enough to be calling home this summer.

A child, maybe five or six years old, stomps into the sea next to me with a bright red bucket, scooping up as much water as he can before splashing away again. He probably has a moat that needs filling. I lie back with my calves and feet in the water and my head resting on the sand. The desire to close my eyes and nap catches me off guard. My mind is drifting off when a voice makes me jolt back into reality.

'You will have a strange tan in that swimsuit. With those holes.'

Yianni stands over me, hands linked behind his back in the same way he stands in the entrance of Greek Secret. He's close enough that I can almost see up his khaki swim shorts.

'Well, I can see up your shorts and I'm not impressed.'

I can't *actually* see anything. Not because it isn't there, I'm sure, but because of the angle. It is enough to make him step back, though. And shut him up, which is the whole point.

'Do you want me to take you back to the house to get washed and dressed for tonight? Or are you sleeping on the beach?'

He sits behind me on the mound of sand that's been pushed there by the sea. I roll onto my belly to face him, lifting my feet out of the water to prevent getting sand in the bandage on my foot.

'I don't mind sleeping here if you'd rather spend the rest of your day off with your friends, you know. It's kind of you to hire a boat and to take me out, but you really don't have to spend your time with me.'

He watches over me for a moment before stretching his legs out and digging his heels into the sand.

'Why do you think I do not want to spend my time with you?'

'I just meant, you have a life here and probably have better things to do.'

'No. All my friends are working. I am stuck with you.'

'You could always go into work.'

I press my top teeth into the middle of my lower lip waiting for a response. He subtly rolls his eyes and turns his attention to his bag, pulling out a towel and spreading it neatly on the sand.

'Drink?' He stands over me again.

'Water, please. I can see up your shorts again.'

'Lucky you.' He pulls a wallet out of the bag and stalks up the beach.

My forehead presses into my arms and my skin itches and prickles with sand and salt. My scalp and hair are caked with the stuff. I love it and hate it in equal measure. Like a painful exfoliation that's oddly satisfying. I even take pleasure in the sun wickedly trying to set my skin on fire. Then the waves crawl up my legs to put it out.

I close my eyes to it all. I can hear people playing, a baby screaming, distant chatter, but I let the sea swallow it all up and drown it all until all I can focus on is Yianni. How he makes me laugh. How he has been so thoughtful. Against my better judgement, he's making a mark on me that goes deeper than the scars on my face.

Chapter 21

Then

'Jonathan?'

'Yes, Ruby.'

We're walking through the centre of Ipswich with rows of modern shopfronts hiding beautiful old buildings either side of us, and it's coming up to my birthday. People move around us like we have a bubble holding us together. Things have been good for a few months, and although I had previously been lining up ways to break up with him without making him homeless, it's sort of fallen by the wayside. I've settled back into the rhythm of us, because it's us and it's easy. My hand feels comfortable in his. It's so damn simple. He's actually taken on a job working for a theatre company – directing a children's production of an original script – as well as making it to auditions. He might be taking life seriously at last.

'Where are we going?' I look up at him and a smile lifts my face, as I study his blonde mop of hair and his pale blue eyes.

'To that funny little vintage shop. You love that place. Let's see if we can get you some vintage furniture for your birthday.'

'What?' I stop walking. 'I used to love that place, but the owner was really rude to my mum. Remember?'

I can tell by the way he wrinkles his nose that he doesn't remember, but he is going to try to pretend he does.

'Oh shit, yeah. Must have been getting it confused with a different shop. Let's go to a different shop then.'

'Seriously, Jonathan. You can't remember me telling you, can you? Bloody hell, she cried about it, they were so rude. You said we would never go there again. You don't remember at all, do you?'

He drops my hand and tilts his head towards the fluffy clouds drifting way above us, exhaling hard.

'No. I'm sorry, babe. I don't remember. I'm sure it was important to you, but it can't be that bad if I don't even remember.'

He starts walking and, in a daze, I follow, while thinking that he isn't the same person I met years ago. The person I shared my secrets and dreams with. Was he always this self-obsessed? I was charmed by his confidence and utter enthusiasm. He pursued me like no other man had, and I liked it. Sometimes it's like I never even knew who he was, let alone who he is now. It's all just a grey area.

The fact he doesn't remember me telling him about my mum and the shop hurts me as badly as an open wound, and I feel that anything that touches me, even my clothes, is only causing more pain. I was with my mum in the shop, when the owner was rude. She was more than rude if I'm honest. Mum's shoe caught on the floor, the rubber sole sticking, making her ankle twist and she fell to the ground like a sack of spuds. Instead of coming over and checking on my mum, the lady accused her of falling on purpose and said she couldn't sue her when she *clearly fell on purpose.* It was the most bizarre reaction. My mum actually apologised to the owner! Which in hindsight neither of us could quite believe. I went on and on about what had happened to anyone who would listen. Clearly, Jonathan wasn't listening. Clearly, he doesn't care about me or my mum.

'Come on, let's go to your favourite shop. You lead the way,' he says, and changes direction.

I stand still in the middle of the street making someone behind me almost walk right into my back. 'What's my favourite shop, Jonathan?'

His fists turn into rocks by his sides and his nose does that thing again, crinkling up. Under his breath, he says, 'I don't know Ruby. One with shoes?'

I shake my head. 'It's the bookshop.'

My arms lock together in front of my chest and we start weaving through the streets of Ipswich again, only now our bubble has well and truly popped.

'Hold on, Rubes. I need to get you more than just a book for your birthday. If that's all I get it doesn't look great, does it?'

I don't even bother to stop walking. I don't even bother to think of a response. It's all about what it looks like to other people. That's all he cares about. Not me. He doesn't know me; he hasn't got me anything for my birthday. I'm going to have to pick a present and likely pay for it. Probably a good thing, because when he does surprise me, the surprise is, it's something completely inappropriate or random. I exhale through my teeth. It's hard to manifest positivity when my lungs feel like they've shattered along the lines of their alveoli, making it impossible to breathe. I hold my breath to keep the waves of emotion in check. I can't let this get out. Not now, not yet. Soon. Next week, after the party my mum has organised. I'll tell him then.

Chapter 22

Now

Apparently while I was asleep, Yianni tried to put more sun lotion on me, spritzing me with it. But overall, he's right. I've been left with a strange tan with circles on my sides. Although the tan is a little redder than I'd like to admit.

Yianni is in Natalia's room getting himself ready for the evening. She's already at work for the night. We're the only ones in the house. I can hear him moving from place to place, and I wonder if I should invite him to chat to me while I redo my makeup. He's already seen my scars after all. Chances are, he won't ask any more questions about them. Although, he might. Maybe I won't ask him in.

I've just finished getting ready, deciding on a pair of mint-green linen shorts and a white top paired with white criss-crossing sandals. It was hard to pick anything out, because I don't want to look like I'm trying too hard, but it's nice to go out in the evening wearing something other than a black skirt or black shorts for work.

With one last glance at myself, one last scrunch to the roots of my hair and ruffle of my fringe, I step out of his door only for him to be stepping out of Natalia's at the same time. He's sprayed some aftershave and I can smell the masculinity nipping at me, the same fragrance that lingered on his sheets when I first came to live here. Citrus undertones, *mmm*. I catch myself because I nearly make the noise out loud.

Turning the creepy noise into words, I squeeze out, 'You look nice,' and smile a little too hard to cover the contented look that has drifted over my face. What I want to do is text Amara and say, *Dear god why does he have to be so hot? I can't bear to be around this man. He's so good-looking I want to cry.*

He's wearing fitted denim shorts that are almost down to his knees, but not quite, with a white shirt with a few buttons undone displaying a black chain necklace. There's nothing particularly fancy. He doesn't need bells and whistles to look good. He returns my smile and looks me over with a flash of his thick eyelashes.

'You look good too. But this is normal for you.'

A choke of air escapes my chest before I pull myself together and say thank you. Lowering my eyeline, I desperately hope he hasn't noticed my second momentary lapse. As we make our way down the stairs and into his car, I stay in his shadow. I have to, because I'm physically shaking my head to scatter any thoughts of him that might border on sexual.

I find a new mantra: *He is your cousin's half-brother. He is your cousin's half-brother. He is years younger than you. He is your cousin's half-brother.*

We drive back into San Stefanos to the sound of the radio quietly playing. I clear my mind by staring into the vast expanse of green utopia. I even catch sight of a few lizards basking in the last of the evening sun. It's the perfect way to ease my mind.

We go to a place called Manthos. To say it has a romantic atmosphere is a massive understatement. I step under a white archway into the open-air restaurant. The view across the beach and sea almost takes my breath away. I hesitate while taking it in, giving Yianni's hand the opportunity to find the small of my back, ushering me forward. In this one little movement, he snatches my attention back momentarily. He introduces me to people, but I'm still dazzled by my surroundings, and by him.

It looks like the sun is about to go for a leisurely dip in the sea. It's illuminating everything in burnt sienna with flecks of gold rippling along towards us on the waves. The entire sky is alight. No longer blue. No longer am I looking at the line where the sea meets the sky. Now the line is clear. The horizon is ablaze and the sea is beginning to turn purple under the golden glitter swaying on its surface. No more haze. In this present, there's only clarity.

By contrast, everything in the restaurant is fresh with clean sharp lines. White and pale blue engulf every surface, including the uniforms. Everything is just so. There's even a couple of swinging chairs made of wicker, shaped like eggs, white with pale-blue cushions. I want to ask Yianni to take my photo in one but I'm pretty sure he would mock me. Although, I've already decided it's worth the risk. It would be a great photo to send my parents and Amara, and I don't care what he thinks, or what anyone thinks. Two years ago, I decided I was never going to live a life for anyone but myself. I won't divert my life, my plans, my goals for anyone. Never again.

I follow Yianni to a table for two with a perfect view across the sea. The sun dips further down into its nightly bath, letting the sea put the fire out for the day. Yianni pulls my chair out for me and I can feel myself heat up, not just because of the sun – although it still holds a sharp heat even as it disappears – but because this feels like a romantic date. Even though Yianni is undeniably gorgeous with his swimmer physique, designer stubble, thick beachy hair, eyes so dark they are like sinkholes – I could go on – I don't *want* to date him. I don't *want* to fall into his sinkhole eyes. I'm still not ready for anything like that. I'm going to treat him like Amara. Take a breath. Relax. Talk to him like a friend and nothing more. Because that's what he is, after all.

'Would you like some water for the table?' The waitress's tone is as relaxed as the breeze.

Yianni nods and begins to chat. Then she asks if we know what we would like to drink other than water. Yianni asks for a Corfu beer. *What would I have if I was with Amara for a girly meal or a night out?*

'Spiced rum and Coke, please.'

Yianni raises both eyebrows. 'I changed my mind,' he says. 'I will have the same.'

As the waitress goes off with our drinks order, Yianni's eyes stay on his menu, but even without looking at him, I get the sense that he wants to say something. Maybe it's the way his eyes don't look like they are reading anything, as though the menu he has is completely blank. Or maybe it's something on a molecular level that's sending me signals that allude to the fact he has something he wants to say or do.

Eventually he comes out with it. 'You surprise me.' His eyes stay fixed on the menu as he turns the page.

'Or, you don't really know me.'

I don't look up from my menu either. My peripherals are on point from working in restaurants. I can watch patrons without them knowing, just in case they need me, or when I think they might raise a hand for the bill. No one likes to feel like they're being watched, but staff are also meant to be attentive. I suspect that Yianni has the same skill.

'You are right.' He lets his menu slap to the table so he can look at me without pretending he isn't. 'Tonight, this will change.'

'Oh, will it?'

'*Nai*. Yes.'

'Good luck with that.'

I look him right in the eye, letting a small smile bestow my lips. His face screws up and he mumbles in Greek as he turns back to his menu. I can still see the smile that's tugging at his lips even though he's trying his best to hide it in a language I can't understand.

'If we're both drinking, how am I getting home tonight?'

'I won't drink much, but there is always someone driving back to the village if this changes. It's nothing to worry about here.' I know he's right. People are always happy to give a lift. I've seen Yianni and Nico both give lifts to customers who didn't even have that far to go.

'Would you take my picture in one of those egg things?' I know he'll tell me he was right, and I am one of the girls who just wants to take photos of themselves. I brace myself for it, holding my breath.

'Sure. It would make a beautiful photo.' His eyes flick to mine then back to the menu.

I don't want to admit it as I exhale, but now we're even. We've already both surprised each other and the night is only just beginning.

Chapter 23

Now

The food at Manthos is incredible. Succulent and fragrant, rich and smooth. I can't fault it. I would never admit it out loud, but it's a good step above Hazel's at Greek Secret. It's the best meal I've had in ages. Perfectly cooked buttery sea bass followed by a Baileys chocolate fondue. Delicious. It's the sort of place I would love to own. A dream location on the beach with well presented staff and a great menu. One day it'll happen. I know it will.

After our meal, Yianni starts taking me places for drinks. Correction, one drink in as many places as we can fit in. At first I think it's a bar crawl. I've never been on a bar crawl before, so I thought this was one, as he says we have to have one drink in every bar. But now we are halfway round I've started to notice a theme. He isn't worried about what we drink. Although he did have a cocktail in Nafsika, he had a frappe in a place called Silver Star and water in Little

Prince. It's in a place called Cicala, as he walks me straight to introduce me to another lovely family that I realise… he seems more interested in people meeting me than drinking. Yianni carries on pushing me to the front and telling people about me in more places than I can count. We've been to Silver Moon, Barras, Condor, Bar 38, Athens Bar, Aquarius, Three W's and so many others.

It's nice to meet people. To chat and hear stories about Yianni, or Hazel and Pericles. Some people share stories about the history of the island or of the village, how it started out with just Waves Taverna for the fishermen, and now it's grown into a thriving hub of activity during the summer months. Yianni beams as I chat to people he has known his whole life. In Bar 38 an elegant older couple clad in vibrant prints comes over to chat to us. I've seen them in the restaurant before, but not spoken to them. The lovely holiday makers want to tell me stories of how much Yianni has changed from the shy teen to the man he is today. They seem proud of him. Seeing him grow and change on their annual visit has made him as integrated with their happiest times as the beach or the salty taste of feta. I mull over how fascinating the connection is as they continue to gush about how much they love San Stef and how much it's changed in the years they've been coming here.

By the time we make it back to Greek Secret, my face aches from smiling and the taverna is dark and empty.

'One last drink for the road. This one is on me.' He gets a key out and unlocks the door, unfolding it partway open. 'Last drink is always tequila. You know that. Chocolate or regular?'

'Seriously?'

143

He hops over the bar and starts juggling two bottles, somersaulting them in the air. 'Stop showboating.'

'What?' He doesn't stop. His mouth hangs a little open in concentration as the bottles whizz in front of his face

I press my hands into cool wood of the bar and lean forwards, then slowly repeat, 'Stop showboating.'

'I don't know this one.'

I exhale and walk away from the bar. 'It means stop showing off. I don't want you dropping anything on my other foot.'

I smile as I walk towards a table not far from the bar. It has something akin to oversized deckchairs around one side, and a bench against the wall. I slump onto the bench. The look of the plump blue cushions reels me in, and I have no willpower to refuse. I swat away a mosquito and relax with a sleepy haze falling over me.

Yianni brings two shot glasses and a bottle of tequila to the table. He pours tequila into the glasses, then slides one towards me before sitting down next to me.

'*Yamas.*' Yianni clinks my glass, even though it's still on the table untouched. Then he takes the shot with ease.

I pick up the glass, lift it in Yianni's direction and sip at it. Chocolate.

'*Yamas.*'

For a moment we both study our glasses, then I finish my shot and bang the glass down.

Yianni says, 'What made you come here to Corfu? Yes, you lost your job, but there must be other jobs in England.'

My left hand gravitates to my right, my fingers automatically ready to pull at my ring.

It's gone.

There is no ring on my right hand.

I look down in astonishment, mouth open but with no words to say.

My posture suddenly becomes perfectly straight and my feet – which had been resting on tiptoes – plant themselves on the ground as though I am ready to run.

'My ring's gone,' I blurt out, almost spitting at Yianni.

'What ring?'

'This one.' I aggressively point at my right ring finger as though he should know the ring I'm talking about. '*Merde*! No! It's a diamond ring. Shit!'

I can feel my eyes beginning to sting and my throat closing up. Yianni lines up a row of cliché questions that no one wants to answer when they've lost something and they're desperate to have it back.

'When did you last see it? What does it look like? Could you have left it somewhere?'

I bristle under his interrogation.

'It's a bloody diamond ring, Yianni. I don't remember when I last had it. It's one of those things I don't even really notice anymore. It's like skin. Fuck! And no, I couldn't have left it anywhere. I never take it off.' I get up and start looking around. Maybe I've been sitting on it, or I've dropped it on the floor. I pace a little around the bar and Yianni gets up to look about with me. 'I'd been meaning to have it resized since it was given to me. It's only a little bit too big though. Since being here, and, well, it's so hot all the time, I actually thought it was fitting a little bit better. I know I play with it, slide it up and down my finger now and then. Shit. I've lost it, haven't I? That's it. I've lost it.' I shrug and slap my hands down against my body. It's gone. There's not much chance that it's hanging around here in the bar.

There, in the middle of the taverna, I press my hands to shelter my face. My body is rigid as I try to hold in the tears swelling under my eyelids. That ring was all I really had left of my relationship with Jonathan. The good and the bad. I'd been using it as a symbol of something for such a long time. A symbol of what, I'm not sure. Of change or hope? What I do and don't want in life? I've wanted to take it off so many times. I even tried to give it back in the first place. There's no way I wanted it – or even thought I should have it – after everything we went through. Who else would want it when it was bought for me? I gave in and kept it. I felt obligated to wear it. Over the past two years it's became a part of me – a gold band lined with tiny diamonds. It sparkled at all angles. Not anymore. Not on my hand anyway.

Yianni's arms engulf me. Nothing is said. A minute, maybe more, passes by with me silently crying in his arms. Luckily a breeze rolls in from the open door, otherwise the embrace would be ruined by sweat. As it is, the warmth of his skin pressing on mine is a comfort. His lips find the side of my head and he gently presses against it.

'I'm sorry,' I begin, 'it's just, well, that ring meant a lot to me.' I quietly sniff under my hands, because I don't want to uncover my face yet. 'Jonathan, he... he bought it for me.'

That is enough to set me off again. I haven't cried like this in a long time. In fact, I think I'm bloody marvellous at suppressing negative emotions these days and manifesting the positive. Yianni starts shushing me and then leads me towards his room. For this I do uncover my face as tears dribble down and drop from the scar on my chin to the floor.

He turns on a little white reading lamp in his room, and stretches out his arm to indicate the single bed. We both sit down next to each other. He stands again and leaves the room. Moments later he's back with a loo roll tucked under his arm, the two glasses in one hand and the bottle of tequila in the other. Taking some tissue from him, I blow my nose and dab around my cheeks and chin to remove the tears stinging my face.

'Tomorrow I will ask everywhere we have been if they have seen it.'

I shake my head and my posture crumples in on itself.

'No. I bet it's in the sea. Shit, what am I going to tell Sue. *Merde*.'

'Who is Sue?'

'It doesn't matter now. I've fucked up.'

'He pours me a drink and I hold the tiny glass in my hand and instead of taking it as a shot, I sip the liquid slowly. It's sweet and it trickles down my throat warming me in an already sweaty-hot box room.

As though he is reading my thoughts, Yianni reaches over to the set of drawers next to the bed and turns on a fan. It comes alive to whirl and creak, slowly rotating to move air around every inch of the room. Then he props the door open with a shoe to let in the cooler night air. It's enough.

'Why are you still wearing this boy's ring? You are not together. You broke up.'

Another little sniff gives me a moment to think what I want to tell him about Jonathan. Yes, we broke up, but there is more to it than that. Much more, but my heart is still raw from losing the ring. I'm not sure I want to tell him all about my painful past. I look into his face and it's lined with questions and concern. His skin looks even more golden in the orange glow of the lamp and the full waves of his hair cast shadows, making him look so damn intense. He needs a slice of the truth, but I can't bear to relay any of the details of it.

'Yeah. We broke up a long time ago, but that doesn't mean I just stopped loving him. It doesn't always matter if you want to be with someone, or if they don't want to be with you. Love doesn't always just end. Yes, I broke up with him. But I... Don't you have an ex?'

Yianni slips his shoes off and unbuttons his shirt. My eyebrows knit together, but he doesn't seem to notice my confusion. Instead, he shuffles onto the bed and props the pillow up to lean it on the wall. Folding his arms over his almost completely bare chest, he exhales in thought.

'Yes. I have many ex-girlfriends. None have my rings though. A few have necklaces.' His lips downturn at the memory of them, or perhaps the thought of girls walking around with necklaces he got them.

'Well maybe they wear them, and maybe they love those silly necklaces. And maybe if they lost them, they would cry, even though they might not want you anymore.'

'I do not think so.'

I groan in protest. 'We're all different, okay?'

'This, I can agree with.' He looks at me with his rich eyes and a gaze that is so intense I have to look away for fear he might see all my deepest secrets. 'I am sorry you lost the ring.' His voice is almost a whisper.

'Me too.'

I lift the glass still cupped in my hands and sip the last little bit. I try to recall the last time Jonathan and I had a drink together. I can't remember. It was a lifetime ago.

'It's late. Do you want me to drive you home?'

My head snaps round to him so fast, the ends of my hair

nearly catch me in the eyes.

'What? No. You've been drinking.'

'Not that much. I feel fine.'

'No.' I lower my voice and my chin tucks itself into my chest. I need him to know that I don't find this acceptable, even if some of his drinks were just Cokes, like me. I know he has had rum and at least two tequila shots. I feel fine too, but I don't think I should be driving.

'You will be sleeping here, with me, then?'

'No, you said that someone would be able to give me a lift back. There's only one bed here.' I say this as though he doesn't already have this information to hand. As though he isn't sitting on and now shuffling off the bed in question. He removes his shirt completely and turns to face me.

'It's much later than I thought. It's okay, I trust you.' A smile glides over his lips. 'Would you like to borrow a T-shirt?'

Chapter 24

Now

I have to leave my mascara on. It's waterproof and there is nothing to remove it with, unless I painfully try to pick it off. No. I don't need sharp shards of mascara making my eyes hurt along with everything else my body seems to be feeling. There's a dreadful mix of my painful past and Yianni looking much too appealing without his damn shirt on.

Heading to the public loos in the restaurant, I wash my face, exposing my scars in their entirety. I can see them in the mirror. Having them on my face is torture in itself, a constant reminder of everything I want to forget. There's no point dwelling on them, staring at them, wishing them gone. Those silvery lines are as much a part of me now as my liver or my lungs. Like it or not.

Stretching the T-shirt Yianni has given me out at arms-length, I inspect it. One of his very own T-shirts. Plain white. I pull it into my nose and take a deep breath. It smells like

Hazel's washing powder with a hint of Yianni underneath. Masculine and citrusy. I bite my bottom lip then press it under my nose again for another deep inhale of his scent. Exactly the same as my bed on my first night in Corfu.

I strip down and pull it over my head. I'd have liked something baggier, or at least longer. Yianni isn't exactly the sort of person to wear baggy or ill-fitting clothes, though. Everything I've seen him wearing is fitted with sleek lines. This thing's just about long enough to cover my knickers, and it's a bit tight over my chest.

I'm tugging the hem of the T-shirt as I skulk back into the side room that is his bedroom. Yianni is lying on his bed with his hands behind his head and his legs crossed at the ankles. As I come in, he abruptly sits up.

'I am thinking, I will sleep on the floor.' Yianni begins to shuffle along the bed until his feet meet the cool tiles. His Greek accent has popped up a little. It's not the strongest accent, it's not as strong as Nico's, I guess because Yianni's stepmum, Hazel, is English.

I look down towards my feet at the hard tiles to consider his idea. At least he would be cool enough down there.

'Do you have any spare bedding?'

'No. I have a jumper I can use for a pillow. It is fine.'

'That's not enough. Don't you have anything else?'

He shakes his head and begins to ball up the jumper. I can't let him sleep on the floor. Not really. It'd be more comfortable to sleep on the beach.

'Don't be silly. We're both adults. Move over.' I flick my hands towards him to usher him along.

Stepping back, he sits back down and moves towards the wall. Shuffling forwards, I lie down next to him. The lamp is

151

still on. My left shoulder is pressing against his right as we both stare up at the ceiling completely still. The only sound is the hum of the fan. I turn my head away from him, followed by my whole body. The little room is a strange mixture of busy and empty. There's the set of drawers, the bed and a wooden chair and an old cupboard near the end of the bed. That's it. The chair has a pile of clothes on it and the drawers are piled with everything from books to aftershave.

'Was this an office before I arrived?'

As I'm scanning the room and the clothes on the chair his voice appears in my ear, low, almost as simple as a vibration in his chest.

'No. It always has a bed here.'

I roll to face him, shifting around while trying to keep my T-shirt in place. I place my cheek on my hand against the pillow.

'Why?'

'Really?' His brows furrow because we both know it's a silly question. It's obvious why. He works late, maybe has a drink or three and doesn't want to drive home. It makes sense to have this little space hiding in plain sight. 'Can we swap? I don't like to be near to the wall. If something happened, I can't protect you.'

'Protect me? From what?'

'There's nothing. But I like to, what's the phrase, *be on the safe side.*'

I smile up at him as he lifts his weight onto his right elbow. I don't agree, or go to move. We just spend a moment studying each other. Perhaps he's waiting for me to move. I don't. This is San Stefanos, I'm not worried about anything more than Hazel and Pericles bursting through the door in the morning and getting the wrong end of the stick.

Yianni's left index finger runs the length of my jaw and comes to rest on the scar on my chin.

I roll away – as best I can – turning myself to face the pile of clothes on the chair again. As soon as his fingers touched me, I could feel the quickening of my blood pulsating around my body. The heat inside me seems to gravitate to certain areas more than others. I close my eyes tightly shut. In my mind's eye I see the sea and the sky. Not the distant pinprick line I so often see in the morning, but the blaze of this evening.

'Please, can we swap?'

'Fine.'

This time I turn and scoot to sit up on the pillow, pulling my knees in. He lifts himself up, reaches his left arm over me and he climbs past, his face close to mine. He has plenty of space not to get so close to me. I can almost feel the warmth of his breath. We settle ourselves down on the thin sheet of the bed and this time Yianni switches off the light.

Moonlight gives enough illumination to see shapes in the black of the room.

I like sleeping on my right side, so I'm left facing him. His weight shifts and moves before settling. I'm quite sure his face is only inches from mine. I close my eyes.

'*Kalinikta*, Ruby.'

Then his lips find mine. I don't know if he meant to kiss me right on the mouth or, if he was aiming for my cheek and misplaced himself. Either way, we've collided, and I can't bring myself to pull back. He presses more firmly into me when I don't move away. His fingers slip around my waist and carefully grip *his* T-shirt that's wrapped around *my* body.

His lips were no accident.

153

Or if they were, he isn't regretting them falling on mine. His mouth parts and mine follows, our bodies press together. My fingers slide into his curls and our tongues slip over each other's and soon I'm burning hot and gasping for air.

My mantra comes storming into my head. *He is your cousin's half-brother.* This time I add, *If you fuck this up, you'll have to go home.* I break the spell. I pull away.

'*Kalanikta,* Yianni.'

I roll over and clamp my eyes tightly shut. What the hell just happened? How? Why? Thoughts scramble over me like insects, until I trap one in a web and latch onto it. I need to steady my breathing. I can hear his too as he turns to face away from me.

I'd forgotten what it felt like to have someone else's heat pressed against me like that. To have their breath burning my skin and entering my lungs as mine. What the hell just happened? It's a bit undeniable now that Yianni does like me too.

I need to sleep, to do my best to act as though that passionate kiss never happened. As though my blood doesn't feel like lava is coursing through my veins right now, and as though I hadn't noticed his desire pressing against me when we were kissing.

The sound of the fan is like a lullaby, but a rush of heat pulls me out of a fever dream in the very early hours. I'm in an embrace with Yianni and his face is pressed against my chest. I wonder if I *was* dreaming. He's gently snoring. My eyes adjust to the dark, or maybe it's soon to be dawn and this part of the earth is getting a little lighter. Either way, I can see a little more than shapes. Notes of colour are edging back

154

into life. Before trying to pull myself free, I keep wondering how we ended up like this. If in our sleep and our dreams, we have just carried on with our desire. I wanted to. I still want to. I've wanted to touch him from the moment he spoke to me at the airport. It was easier to focus on him being in a grump – even when he probably wasn't – because I don't want a relationship. Particularly not with my *cousin's half-brother*.

Carefully I prise us apart. I'm glad I'm the first one to wake up and find our entanglement, and that he doesn't know about it. In part because my T-shirt has shifted to be halfway around my waist.

Slowly I reposition us, but before I roll away from him to face the other, I watch his breathing. The inhale and exhale. Steady and strong. It reminds me of watching the sea in the mornings. Rolling in and out. Strong yet peaceful. His dark eyebrows over his hooded lids and thick black lashes like a frill on his eyes. He is so peaceful that he makes me feel peaceful. Carefully, I run my finger along his eyebrow. I desperately want to kiss his velvety lips again. Instead, I lightly skirt the line of his bottom lip with my index finger. It folds in on itself and he turns his face to the fan again. Reining in the urge to touch him more, I turn over and squeeze my eyes tightly shut until I manage to drift back into sleep.

A tickling sensation on my stomach rouses me again, then frightens me, making me throw myself forwards in the bed with a gasp, nearly knocking Yianni straight out of it.

Another scar. He found another one of my scars and decided he could touch it the way he had with the ones on my face.

'What do you think you're doing, Yianni?'

'I am sorry. I— This scar, it surprises me. Is it from

155

the accident?'

I answer with a sharp nod. 'That doesn't give you the right to poke at me, you know.'

Then I remember touching him in the middle of the night and wonder if he really *was* asleep. Surely he was. A flush of guilt prickles my skin. This is also the first time we are eye to eye after our kiss.

'I am sorry. I didn't mean to wake you.'

'Did you lift my top up?'

'Fuck, no, Ruby! It was up, I just saw the scar. I...'

As a blush runs over his cheeks, I'm positive he is telling the truth. I know from the middle of the night that the T-shirt has a mind of its own. I want to tell him off, but I can't. I suppose I don't really want to tell him off. The feminist in me wants to tell him he should keep his hands to himself unless I say it's okay, but the other half of me wants to tell him it's okay to touch me whenever and wherever he wants to. Plus, I was poking at him in his sleep, so fair is fair. Perhaps if I hadn't done the same in the night, then I would have told him off more. But as it is, I'm equally in the wrong. So, instead, I pull down my T-shirt to cover my abdomen again and scoot along to the end of the bed then edge my way off it.

'I need to get back to the house.'

Chapter 25

Now

Almost a week evaporates. The restaurant is busier than it has been, particularly the evening service. My foot has healed up nicely and Yianni and I have gone back into our pattern of work. Occasionally I catch him watching me – or vice versa – and a smile is shared between us. Sometimes we have micro conversations and one night I even stayed and went to Athens Bar after work with him and Nico when there was live music on. The most that has happened since our kiss is his fingers grazing mine while passing drinks over the bar. Overall, it's work as usual, with me going home at the same time as Hazel, Pericles and Natalia, leaving Yianni and Nico working behind the bar. I don't want Hazel to cotton on to my attraction, so I've been carrying on in much the same way as I had before our one and only day together. Luckily, there was barely a question about me staying with him that one night. We're friends. Cousins. No one has really questioned it. Pericles only comment was that he hoped Yianni didn't make me sleep on the floor. We all laughed and Yianni said he had given me his bed. I got the impression he didn't want to lie. Although I'm also sure he didn't want to advertise the fact we were both in the same bed either and no one suggested he might be in there too. I've spoken to my mum about losing the ring. She said all the right things to try to make me feel better about it. It's something I can never replace, and every time I get a little anxious or starts to miss home my fingers go to fidget with it, and each time I feel heat flood through my chest as though I've lost it all over again.

This morning, before work, Yianni came to the house to have a shower. This is pretty common unless he showers at the gym. Now I can hear him chatting to Hazel in Greek downstairs. I don't really want to interrupt them as they aren't speaking English. I stay in my room messaging Amara. She has been under the weather and hasn't been into La Salle à Manger for a few days, but she is starting to feel better. Poor girl. She has had some kind of migraine, headaches and a churning stomach, she thinks perhaps it's something she caught when she was babysitting her niece.

When it's almost time to leave for my pre-work walk, I emerge from my bedroom. That's when I notice the volume of the two voices has changed. They're talking in hushed tones. I'm quite sure it's still Yianni and Hazel, but they are no longer chatting in a normal way about everyday things. Now that their voices have lowered, the whole house feels dark, as though the sun has hidden itself behind some dark clouds. My phone loudly pings in my hand, alerting them that I'm hovering near the top of the stairs. Clearly, they both have heard it as they stop talking immediately. Pretending I haven't noticed their shift in tone, I plod down the stairs with my bare feet audible to anyone in the house.

'Kalimera.' My voice is as bright and natural as I can conjure.

Hazel's neck and chest are a little flushed, but she smiles at me. They both greet me in an even tone, but Yianni's tugging his hair behind his ears and doesn't look at me for more than a fraction of a second.

'I'm going for a walk along the beach before work. See you both later.' With that I leave the house, jump on my bike and head off to the beach at San Stefanos.

There is no time to swim. I only manage to squeeze that in every other day at best, as I keep sleeping in. The whole way there I wish I could speak Greek so that I could have understood what Hazel and Yianni were talking about. He seemed irritated, but I couldn't tell if he was irritated at Hazel, at me or at something else. Something I can't guess at because I can't speak Greek. Hazel looked like she was trying too hard to plaster on a smile and her skin was pink under her tan.

I march along adjacent to the sea, kicking up damp sand. I don't know why I'm steaming along like this. I meant to have a relaxing walk to absorb the sea air and to admire the line between the sea and the sky as I like to do, but now I feel that the irritation I sensed in Yianni has glued itself to my skin like a rash.

During the lunch and evening service I'm sure that Yianni's attitude towards me is off, almost as though he's intentionally not looking at me, which is the complete opposite of our normal dance. It makes me realise just how often we spend time trying to catch glimpses of each other.

'Have you upset the little boss?' Nico stands so close to

me our arms are almost touching. He's holding a glass and rubbing a tea towel around the rim.

I glance up at him. 'Don't know what you mean.'

'Yianni.' Nico places the glass under the bar and then leans on the bar top with his elbow, twisting his body to face me. 'Even I notice he is not looking at you. Usually he watches you more than he stands at the door.' He leans even closer to my face. 'I think he likes you,' he whispers, then winks before settling back onto his elbow.

'Apparently not today.' Behind Yianni, someone else catches my eye. 'Holy shit, who is that?'

Nico turns to follow my eyeline towards the entrance then starts to laugh. 'This is Gaia's parents, Melodie and Anton.'

'Wow, what are they? Retired supermodels? Blimey.'

Still laughing at me, Nico walks around the bar towards the most beautiful and ridiculously tall couple I have ever seen. No, she is tall, but he is a giant with broad shoulders and sharp emerald eyes just like Natalia's friend and fellow kitchen helper, Gaia. Nico walks over and kisses Gaia's mum's cheeks, and scoops the baby she is holding right out of her arms. It is a tiny thing, perhaps only a month or two old. He cradles and bounces the baby in his arms as he shows the couple to a table, before handing the baby back to its mother. Yianni walks up and touches the baby's head. He's laughing with them both. Although it can't be *that* long since the woman gave birth, she looks elegant in a loose-fitting button-down dress. I hope that if I ever have kids, I look that good afterwards.

Gaia comes out to kiss her parents and at different intervals so do Natalia, Hazel and Pericles. Everyone's like family or old friends, without exception. So often people arrive at the restaurant who have been coming on holiday here since before Greek Secret was even open, and everyone hugs hello and goodbye. Although Hazel is my aunt, and I am actually part of her family, there are times that I feel like *I'm* the odd one out and *I'm* the one who doesn't know anyone.

While Hazel is chatting to the striking pair, she turns and waves me over. I finish putting the drinks order together that I'm working on and bring it to a nearby table before stepping towards them.

'This is my niece, Ruby. This is Melodie and Anton, oh, and I must not forget baby Lily, Gaia's new sister.'

'Lovely to meet you both. Gaia is such a great girl. A real straight talker.'

Their faces lift at the mention of Gaia and Anton's lips shift into a joking smirk.

'Yes, sorry about that.' A low rumbling laugh emanates from him. It's almost intimidating.

'Nice to meet you too,' Melodie says. 'Hazel said you'd be coming to work here over the summer. Are you enjoying it so far?'

'Love it. What's not to love?' I narrow my eyes at her, staring at the structure of her face. 'I have to say you're such a beautiful family. You must get that all the time. I can see the resemblance. You and Gaia are both stunning.'

'I love that, and I do wish it could be true, but she's not my birth daughter. I'm very proud of her nonetheless.'

Baby Lily wriggles in her arms, and Melodie lowers her chin to appease her while I stutter, 'I'm so sorry.' Melodie and Anton both graciously shrug off my mistake.

Yianni appears at my elbow with their starter, and we leave them to eat. My cheeks feel hot as I meander back behind the bar. As soon as I get the chance, I stick my elbow into Nico's ribs.

'You told me they are Gaia's parents, you shit.'

'Yes, they are.'

'Melodie isn't.'

'She is adopting her.'

'Fine, but I still feel like a bloody idiot for saying that Gaia looks like Melodie.'

Nico's face lifts into a lopsided boyish smile. He has a nice smile, youthful and wide. He's the sort of guy that girls don't often take seriously though. I'm still trying to work out if that's the façade he has built up to protect himself or whether he really is the kind of guy who shouldn't be taken too seriously, and will never have a long-term relationship with anyone.

'Nico, how come you don't have a girlfriend?'

A subdued voice comes from behind me. 'I need two pints of Mythos, draft. For table four.'

I spin around to see Yianni, he has an almost purple tone skimming the surface of his cheeks. He turns away before I can say anything more.

'I do not think Yianni liked that you want to know about my love life,' Nico says. He picks up a pint glass and spins it on the palm of his hand before tilting it under the tap. Keeping his chin down, he looks up from under his eyebrows at Yianni as he fills glasses with Mythos. Yianni's handing out menus to a large party that have just walked in. As usual he is greeting them as though he knows them, which he probably does. 'Forget my love life,' Nico continues. 'What is happening with you and Yianni?'

'Me and Yianni? *Pfft*.' As soon as the dismissive sound is

out of my mouth, I know I've overplayed it. Nico looks at me from the corner of his eye and that's enough to break down my defences. 'I have no clue. We had fun last week, a lot of fun. But now I think he's in a mood with me. *Shh*, here he comes.' I flap my fingers at Nico, and he laughs and puts another beer on a tray as Yianni approaches.

'For you, Yianni.'

Yianni reels off the next orders. 'One bottle of house red, two cola, one apple juice and water for the table. You take it over.' Without even glancing in my direction, he gently taps the bar before walking away with his tray of beers.

'Wait,' I call after him. He turns and meets my eyes. There might be a glimpse of hope, or a spark, or something, and now I feel like complete dirt because I'm about to ruin that hopeful softness drawn on his face. 'You didn't say how many wine glasses.'

His lips press together, pulling his lips into a thin line. 'Four.' He turns and walks away.

I exhale and Nico glances at me before sniggering and collecting glasses for the next order. Nothing more is said as we work around each other. He knows I'll collect the bottle of wine and I know he'll do the soft drinks. I don't usually drink while I'm working, but I pick up a beer and snap it open on the opener attached to the back of the bar. I'm hot – and clearly bothered – and I want a cold drink to take the edge off my growing mood.

'That bad?' Nico says as he picks up the tray of drinks to walk to the table.

'I'm just thirsty.'

Even though we've only been working together for a short while, Nico and I have spent enough time together to get to know each other. But as for Yianni – do I know enough about him to potentially shock and upset our family? He seems to be back to square one with the moodiness that he had when we first met, and it makes me question everything that happened between us. There's no way at all I want to be with someone who can't communicate or someone whose negative attitude is destructive in any way.

Stop it.

I can't keep thinking in these terms. Particularly when it's massively hypocritical of me. It's so easy for me to hold everything in and the hardest thing in the world to let secrets out. Communication isn't exactly my strong point either. Anyway, I can't keep wondering whether there's something more to my relationship with Yianni. It's making me slip into an emotional headspace that I don't want to be in anymore.

Chapter 26

Then

'A guy tried to grab me at work today.' The words are out of my mouth before my keys hit the sideboard.

'Hey, look at this,' Jonathan calls from the living room. The TV is blaring. He hasn't even turned to look at me as I appear in the doorway of the lounge.

'A guy grabbed me tonight.'

He snatches up the remote, turns the tele off and twists to face me. 'They did what?' He arches one eyebrow at me and points the remote at me too as though he could use it to play the information right out of me.

'There were two men. They were drinking a lot after their meal. I was trying to be pleasant, but also move them along. You know how it is. But, then, one grabbed me as I was showing them out. I only went to the door with them because they were last out, and I was going to lock up. It was lucky Charles came out of the kitchen to sit and look over his papers the way he always does.' My throat feels like it's closing up.

I snap my jaw shut, unable to tell Jonathan that one of the men pinned me to the wall and tried to put his tongue down my throat while the other bloke laughed and said *my turn next.* Outrage burns in my core and goosebumps rise on my forearms like angry volcanos.

'What did they look like? I'll deal with them. I'll make them regret ever touching you.'

'It's over now. You're not going to manage to Facebook-stalk them when I don't even know their names now, are you? Don't be silly.'

'I'm not being silly, Ruby. It's important to protect what's mine.' He jumps up from the chair and walks over to put his arms around me. My face presses against his chest, but I don't feel in the slightest bit comforted. *Mine.* I'm my own. I don't want to emasculate him, but I don't even want to be with him, let alone be spoken of like all I am is a chain around his neck, there to be looked at and possessed.

I turn my face away from the crush of his embrace and let my thoughts trickle out. 'I know it's my birthday tomorrow and we said we would get breakfast together before work, but Amara goes to a self-defence and mixed martial arts class. I want to go with her.'

He pulls away and looks down at me, gripping my shoulders. His big hands digging into my flesh nudge in thoughts of the lecherous man at the restaurant.

'You don't need that. You have me to protect you.'

'You won't always be here, Jonathan.'

Quizzical eyes search my face and confusion seems to fill his features before he finds words. 'What's that supposed to mean?'

I twist out of his grasp and move back into the hall towards the stairs. Maybe something in my tone has given away the reality lying beneath the surface, the reality that in a matter of days he'll be packing his bags and we'll both be able to move on with our lives. I'd do it now, tell him now that we are over, but he would then create pain and drama on my birthday and I'd have to spend my entire party explaining to everyone why he wasn't there. Everyone loves him. He's always the life and soul of a party. He can tell any story. It doesn't matter whether it's true, a complete fabrication or whether he's telling a story that is actually mine. He sells it and they all lap it up. I just don't want to spend the whole time trying to avoid putting him down while everyone – except me – thinks it's so sad we're no longer together.

'Nothing. I just mean, you weren't there tonight, were you?'

My feet slap against the first two steps up to our bedroom before I catch myself and tiptoe the rest of the way, trying to be considerate of the neighbours.

'Maybe I should pick you up from work.' He has followed me into the bedroom.

'Don't be ridiculous. We have one car. *My* car. I want to go to this class with Amara.'

'What's the point? You're meant to be going out with me in the morning. It's bad enough you're working on your birthday. This incident… I bet it wasn't even that bad.'

I glare at him, biting back the words that want to jump out of my mouth to choke him. I don't tell him he is wrong, or that he is sort of right, but only because Charles shouted, *Get the fuck out or I'll call the police.* I have no idea what would have happened otherwise. I was crushed against a wall trying to duck down but failing. There's no way I want to feel so

167

helpless again. I had no idea how to react. Not really.

'We can celebrate at the party.'

'Seriously? That's days away and it was organised by your mum. What are you, twelve?'

Needles walk along my flesh, dancing over each nerve and my fists contract. I snatch a breath and take my time over the exhale. He wants an argument, but if I let myself get dragged into it, he'll twist it around until I'm the bad guy.

'I just wanted to spend some time with you, Rubes. I feel like I hardly ever see you. You're always working. Now this class. When will you have any time for me?'

And here it is. I'm the bitch. Some prick tries to – god knows what he was really trying to do – kiss me or something and *I'm* the one with a problem.

'Look, it's been a really shitty night. I'm going to sleep now. Amara's coming to get me in the morning. We'll just have to do lunch another time.'

'Breakfast.'

'Yes, that's what I meant.'

'See, our plans mean so little to you, you don't even know what they are.' He storms out of the bedroom, slamming the door. A baby starts to cry and I whisper *sorry* to the neighbours.

Chapter 27

Now

I'm back to swimming in the sea alone in the mornings, except for the couple of times that Natalia came with me. That's when she saw my scars more clearly and asked more questions. I didn't mind. She knows most of the story anyway. She told me I was brave, and it must have been dreadful, and it was all so sad. All the normal things people say.

It's August now, and everywhere is busy all the time. Early morning is still the quietest time, and I go to the furthest point of the beach to start swimming. But August brings so many people, everywhere is full of life and laughter and music. They blend seamlessly together and form an atmosphere that has a comforting glow.

Yianni's still doing his best to keep his distance from me. He's been looking at me more though, and I can't help but look at him, even though I don't want to. Maybe he thinks I should ask what's wrong, but I'm not chasing anyone. I'm okay with holding everything in and letting everyone else just get on with their own lives. Either I'm factored in or I'm not. It's that straightforward.

Tonight has been no different. Even though the restaurant is heaving, I caught him looking at me at least three times. It's so busy we've had people waiting at the bar for a table.

Things are beginning to relax a little now. It's getting late and the kitchen closes soon. Nico's chatting to a cluster of girls whose sole reason for coming to our restaurant is to get Yianni to serve them food and Nico to serve them drinks after. They're having a rainbow of cocktails and laughing at any charming or joking comment Nico can give them. He loves it.

A group of blokes comes in. Youngish. They walk straight to the bar.

'We all want chips and beers, thanks love,' a skinny boy with freckles announces in my direction, before tapping his fist on the bar.

'I'll sort the drinks first and then we can sort food. Draft or bottles?'

'Draft.'

The conversation between them concerns their wanting to be moved to a different resort, one with nightclubs. One of them, a shorter guy with spiked hair and a twisted nose is getting the blame. They're all quite pale still, but with a pink glow, which leads me to believe this is their first night here.

I can almost feel Yianni and Nico prickle at them as they talk and demand things of me. Not that anyone else would know or sense this from them; they're smiling enough. Yianni manages to herd the blokes to a free table that's safely away from the people who are still sitting and enjoying the last of their meals. Alongside the cluster of girls in front of Nico at the bar, there is a couple having *one for the road*. Before the group of boys arrived, they were telling me lots of fun things to do in Corfu. Now though, I'm pulling the pints for the boys' table and the couple's eyes keep flicking in their direction.

Yianni's watching me as I come round the bar and pick up the tray. He isn't making his usual sidelong glances; he is actively watching me while noting down another table's dessert order. Even Pericles, who is at present chatting to a table in the far corner, seems to be keeping tabs on me. Having an audience is making me a little paranoid that I might drop the tray.

For the past few weeks, I've either been wearing reasonably short black shorts or a fitted black miniskirt because it's been too warm to wear anything else. As I walk along, I can feel my skirt riding up a little, although not much. Maybe it's something I don't normally notice because I don't normally have an audience, but as I approach the boys' table, I can see an elbow being poked into ribs and they all look up at me simultaneously and fall silent. I've worked in this industry my entire life. Not much fazes me. I think my heart is only beating harder because of Yianni's eyes tracking me.

'Here you go, lads.' I carefully walk around the table, placing down all five beers one by one.

'What's your name?' I look over to see a man in a black polo shirt talking to my boobs across the table. I have a strong urge to say something sarcastic like, *Which one are you asking and I'll tell you?* or *I haven't actually named them, but they like to be treated as individuals.* I refrain, and instead maintain the smile on my face.

'It's Ruby. Just let me know if you need anything else.'

'Three plates of chips, thanks love,' another one says and they all laugh as I walk away, inching the hem of my skirt down with my fingertips. I'm not sure what's so damn funny.

Yianni rounds some tables and walks next to me. I look up at him and say, 'Do you have a drinks order for me?' It feels nice to have him so close to me again. I can feel his warmth and smell his delightful masculine scent. Something inside me that has been quietly lying dormant for the past few weeks feels like it's just kicked me in the throat.

'No, it's for the kitchen. Desserts. Tell me if they bother you, yes?'

'Don't be silly. They're harmless. I have an order for the kitchen too, three plates of chips.' I get myself back behind the bar and Yianni makes his way into the kitchen with the dessert order and the order for chips. It'll likely be the last one of the night. He comes back out moments later with bowls of chips, and takes them to the table of guys. There's the sound of tipsy laughter and I'm sure they're all looking towards the bar. As Yianni walks away from them, he has that purple glaze on his face and his lips are tightly pursed.

Nico is shaking cocktails again as Yianni comes over to the bar.

'Two more beers. Let me know when they are ready, I can take them.'

'Draft?'

He nods and turns back towards the restaurant. His fingers are digging so hard into his hips that they are crinkling up his shirt. A customer nods at Yianni, obviously wanting to get the bill. He walks over and chats to them a little while I'm pouring. I finish and he is still talking. What's two beers? I'm perfectly capable and I don't need Yianni or anyone else to walk them over to a group of boys for me. I pick them up and they feel delightfully cold in my hands. I wish I could press them to my body without getting funny looks because it would feel so nice.

As I lean forwards to set them down on the table, one of the guys taps me on the bottom. I can feel the tension ripple over me.

'Please don't do that.' I try to sound casual, but my teeth are a little more gritted than I first intended. The lads are young, maybe in their very early twenties or late teens. Perhaps it's their first holiday without their parents. I use these thoughts to curb my irritation at their excitement. Post alcohol they're basically toddlers who have no idea what they're touching.

I straighten up and turn to look down at the short one on my right. He puts his hands up like my eyes are guns and he's looking down the barrel. The smile is still etched on my face, as best I can manage. As I turn to head back to the bar, the shitbag on my left grabs my left hand with his, and pulls me on to his lap. They're all hooting and for a moment I'm taken aback. Within a split second my instincts kick in. Still holding his left hand in mine, I twist his under as I come between him and the table to stand by his left side. Bending his hand back on itself and with his arm straight to the point of hyperextending. I lean into him as his friends mostly fall silent. Apart from one who can't stop sniggering, writhing about to control laughter that wants to burst out. The one I'm holding tries to edge away, but it only forces his face closer to the table in front of us.

'We have a look but don't touch policy here,' I say, then look up. 'I think it would be good if you all remember to respect other people's personal space before you hurt yourselves.'

I drop his arm just as Yianni, Nico and Pericles appear behind me. As I turn to face them, it's Yianni's expression that catches me off guard. His cheekbones are higher on his face than I've seen them in days. There's a micro movement, an upwards twitch of his eyebrows. I think perhaps he was impressed. The expression is so brief it's hard to say. It shifts into asking the guys in the nicest possible way to pay up and leave. They just loudly say how they don't want to be in our stinking restaurant anyway and other nonsense, but the girls at the bar applaud me when I return. My fingers creep back to where my ring used to be, but there's nothing there to remind me.

Once they leave, and only once Hazel has checked on me and Nico is deep in thought over some cocktail, does Yianni come up to me.

'I hope you are okay?' He leans his folded arms into the other side of the bar making his shirt go taut around his arms and it's hard to keep my eyes on him without sighing. At least I can keep my hands to myself unless invited. The memory of touching his silky lips ripples over me and a mixture of pleasure and guilt curdle inside me.

'I'm fine, thanks. How are you?'

Yianni opens up to me with a smile. A real one that is beautiful and charming and everything I've missed seeing.

'You're impressive.' He hesitates and takes his arms off the bar. 'Can we talk?'

'Now?'

'No. Maybe after work. Tonight?'

'Sure.' I smile at him, but he doesn't look up to notice it. Instead, he turns and heads in the direction of the kitchen.

Chapter 28

Then

'It's not really a party, it's a gathering. Anyway, it's nice. We haven't exactly been able to do anything for the past couple of years.' I hook a pair of diamante earrings in my earlobes and watch Jonathan pull up his jeans in the mirror.

'Yeah, I know, I know. I just prefer it when it's just us.' Under his breath he adds, 'But we didn't even get to do that on the big day, did we?'

He has brought up the fact that I chose going to a class with Amara over a cheap fry-up with him at least three times a day from then to now.

'You went out with your friends on *my* birthday.' This has become my standard counter argument since finding out through a mutual friend that he was out dancing with groups of girls while I was serving people dinner.

'Come on, we've been over this. You didn't want to be with *me*.' I can't deny that part. 'I needed a couple of beers with my mates. What was I going to do? Wait at home and watch crappy TV?'

I don't rise to it. Part of me wants to point out that one minute he wants to pick me up from work and the next he's out without me on my birthday. It's just another nail in the coffin of us. Another step down the funeral aisle. Tomorrow morning I'll explain it all to him. I'll tell him that it hasn't been working, and that I need to focus on myself, because no one else can or does. He certainly doesn't, and I'm getting lost. No. I'm not getting lost. I *was* lost, but lately I've been finding myself and I'm not going to play his games anymore.

I nod my head to the girl in the mirror. *You're strong. It's not unkind to leave someone when you don't love them anymore. It would be unkind to carry on. You are brave and strong.*

'What you smiling at?'

His voice behind me slaps the smile off my face and guilt at being pleased to be free pours over me. I can't hate him. A part of me still loves him. But I think I'm in love with the idea and the memories of good times, and not the person behind me in the mirror. I know being alone and gaining space is what I need now.

'Nothing. I'm just looking forward to the party.' I pick up my perfume and spritz a cloud of coconut and pear before swiftly walking through it.

'God, do you have to do it like that?' Jonathan frantically waves his hand in front of his face, squinting deep creases around his eyes. 'I don't fancy smelling like a fruit salad, thanks.'

He squares his shoulders and storms past me and down the stairs.

'It's what you got me for my birthday actually,' I whisper.

'Nice to know you chose it with love…' He got me two books that I picked out and this perfume. He said he needed some new razorheads and sprinted back to the shop while I was heading to the car. The bottle that contains the fruit salad is very attractive, and to be honest I don't mind the smell, but I know he just saw a pretty container and didn't really care about the contents. Maybe that's what I am to him. I know the rest of his life is about show. About what people see and what people think.

I hang my head in frustration. I wish I could do it now, break up with him now, but the performance would be unbearable. The *show*. I would never make it to my own birthday party.

Chapter 29

Now

'We're off now. Are you coming?' Hazel leans across the bar and cups my face in her hand.

'I think it's still busy enough that I'll stay and help the boys for a bit. Yianni mentioned having a drink after too.' My left hand covers her hand on my cheek. 'Don't wait up.'

As she walks away, I blow a kiss at Natalia who is waving and yawning. Then the two of them depart behind Pericles and it's only me, the boys and a handful of customers.

Nico and Yianni slip into Greek. I'm not sure who initiates it but soon after Nico is telling me to have a nice night and is leaving too, much to the dismay of our lovely customers. The people left at the bar are fun and chatty. Normally they would be perfect for creating a fun night while I'm working, but tonight, even though I'm laughing about the fact they've known Yianni since he was a sulky teen, I can feel time slowly dripping away and it feels like Chinese water torture.

It's past midnight when they leave. We wave. We smile. Then it's just Yianni and me. I almost hear my heart beating to the sound of the music that's playing around the empty restaurant. Yianni pulls the fold-out shutter partway across to make it clear we aren't open, even though a light is still on.

'Beer?' Yianni doesn't look at me. He just makes his way back around the bar.

'Rum and Coke.'

'Yes, I suppose you did almost break a man's arm today. I think you need a good drink after that.' I catch the smug look on his face. Not that he's looking at me. He's grabbing two glasses and the bottle of rum from the shelf behind his head.

'I didn't almost break his arm. I just… caught him off guard. But he caught me off guard first, so it's only fair.'

This makes Yianni chuckle to himself and the sound – even though it's low and quiet – fills me. My entire face shifts to reflect the weight being discarded from my body.

'Where did you learn how to do this?' Yianni proceeds to sort of act out the moves, twisting up his arms.

'Me and my friend Amara have been going to different classes for a couple of years.'

Yianni passes me a short tumbler and I raise it briefly in his direction before taking a deep sip of the sweet vanilla-laced drink. I make my way from behind the bar and to the same place we were sitting together only a few weeks ago. It's as though things have happened between us since then, but they're all unspoken and I'm in the dark as to what they are. It's not the sort of game I'm used to playing. With Jonathan it was emotional blackmail and guilt trips overlaid with a slick charm. Albeit the charm only appeared when he wanted something or when other people were about. With Yianni it's thoughtful gestures or radio silence and nothing in-between. Perhaps he came to the conclusion the kiss was a bad idea and that's all there is to it. Perhaps his quiet little chat with Hazel was nothing to do with me.

Yianni sits down next to me on the pale blue cushions of the bench and we both study our glasses for a moment. Then, like buses, it all happens at once, and we both go to speak at the same time, then awkwardly laugh. Our eyes meet in the middle of it all, and we're left with hints of smiles on our lips, but something far from laughter in our eyes.

I let Yianni go first, and he says, 'Why didn't you tell me? About Jonathan?'

So that's what this has all been about. Jonathan. *That's* what Hazel had been whispering with him about. I shrug. It's not as though I open up to many people anyway, and I don't know why he would expect me to just spill my whole life out in his direction now. Even when I thought I might, he didn't make it that easy.

His silence lingers. Yianni could patiently wait for decades for an answer. At first, I think I can wait him out, but then I cave. 'I started to tell you, months ago, but you thought you knew it all, and that was that. It's not important anyway.'

'You said to me that you broke up.'

'I did say that.'

'Hazel tells me that is not true.'

'Well, I guess Hazel knows everything then.' I pick up my glass and sip before putting it down a little harder than intended. 'It's not like you've been open and chatty about your life.' I shift to face him a little better on the bench and he automatically slides away an inch or two. 'You've never told me much about your mum, or what it was like when you

180

gained a stepmum. One minute you're ignoring me, the next you're kissing me in the dark and then you're back to ignoring me again. I don't get it.'

His mouth opens then slams shut again as though his teeth were made of magnets.

'After what Hazel tells me, I didn't know how to talk to you. I felt like you lied to me. Or that you don't want to talk to me. Then tonight, I see the way you are. I see more of who you are, and I know I *do* want to talk to you. I do want to know you more.' Music's still quietly playing all around us. It's a song I don't really know, but it is painfully positive to the point of being sickly and I wonder if it's irritating Yianni too. He's so still, like a carefully crafted statue, one that comes back to life as he makes eye contact with me.

'What do you mean' he says, 'about Hazel knowing everything?'

'I was being sarcastic. Not everything is always as simple as it seems. Life is a lot more complicated than the bullet points someone tells you about someone else's life. Surely you know that? Surely, you've gone through some kind of shit in your life?'

'Then tell me what it *really* is. Not the bullet points. Tell me what is truly in your mind.'

'No.'

'No?'

'No.'

Yianni exhales hard and slides his legs out straight, crossing his ankles as well as his arms. He completely locks himself off in thought. He stays that way for the longest minute to the point where I get up, make us some more drinks and come back with them. When I arrive back from the bar, he has changed position and has both elbows on the table and his chin resting on his fists.

'What if I tell you about me. Things I don't tell anyone. Would you tell me things then?'

I push his drink towards him on the table then sip mine as I think about this proposition. I do want to know more about Yianni. So far, the things I know are all in the present. How he can be deeply thoughtful, perhaps to the point of overthinking, but I have no idea what has made him the man he is.

'Maybe.' My eyes flick to his to gauge his response.

He exhales with a shake of his head making his hair gently sway around his ears.

'I will take your maybe. You want to know about my mother. Well, she was the Greek Hazel.' This brings a smile to both our faces. 'She was kind and efficient but also fun and passionate about many things. Food, painting. She was never afraid of anything.' Yianni pauses before continuing. 'Not even at the end.'

'How did she...' For some reason I can't bring myself to actually say the word *die* out loud. It seems so harsh. I sort of know the answer already anyway. She went into a coma and died. I think she had some kind of surgery, and it went wrong. Something like that.

'She was hit by a car.' I didn't expect him to say that. 'She seemed fine. She was shaken, but she was walking and talking like nothing happened. Everyone tells her she must go to hospital to be looked over. She was smiling and hardly a mark on her, only bruises. She kept saying there was too much to do at the restaurant. Mama could wrap Papa around her finger. He looked so worried, almost green. I held her hand and begged her to go. She agreed. On the way to the hospital, she started to repeat herself and slur like she had been drinking. She started saying she was tired. Everything was, *I'm tired, why am I so tired?* The last thing she said translates like, *You be good, Yianni, Mama needs a sleep.* We tried to keep her awake, but we couldn't. She went into a coma and never came out.'

I audibly swallow, trying to push down the emotions that are threatening to overflow.

'I'm so sorry.' My voice is so quiet I'm not sure Yianni even heard me. He looks so vulnerable as he picks up his drink and holds it a centimetre from his lips. I've never felt obliged to tell anyone anything much before, but I open my mouth prepared to at least give him something, but then he continues.

'We had to go on as though she is nothing. Papa was so broken he couldn't even speak to me. I am lucky, everyone here is family. I have cousins and uncles – you know, you've met them.' I nod and he nods to acknowledge me. 'But my mother was the one to hold us together. I understand why he fell in love with Hazel. I think my mother sent her to us, but I still find it hard how similar they can be. Hazel never pushed me to love her, she was patient when I hated her. And I did.' He chuckles and leans his forearms on the table, elongating his body over it slightly and twirling his glass in his fingers. 'I put them both through hell with my silence when I was younger, but they are hard to hate, and I love my little sister. Even when she is so annoying.' Grinning, he takes a deep breath then sits up in his chair again before turning to face me, still cupping but not actually drinking his rum and Coke. The laughter rolls along with him as he continues, 'I also had a batshit crazy girlfriend at uni. She was controlling and always saying she will kill herself if I don't stay with her, but I don't

find that as hard to talk about. Talking about my mother...'
He tilts his head and sips his drink as though his actions are
the ends of the sentence and words aren't possible.

'I understand. I mean, I understand that it's hard to talk
about things.'

Our eyes are locked together. I tuck my lips in because I
know he is going to say it's my turn to tell painful truths and
I really don't want to.

'You don't have to tell me things, Ruby.' His hand reaches
across the table and rests on top of mine. The heat of his skin
permeates mine and I let his fingers knot around hand.

My heart's bounding like the bass of the music that's still
droning on around our bubble. I can feel it in my chest, but
I can't unpick the reasons why. Is it because I want to tell
Yianni everything that happened? Or because we are now
holding hands?

'The problem is,' I begin, 'there are things I haven't told
anyone. Whenever I've opened my mouth to tell anyone, I
just can't bring myself to continue. I'm not good at opening
up.'

His face changes but not in the way I expect. Instead of
shock, fear, or intrigue, he seems to soften. His deep chocolate
eyes melt me down and I start to wonder if I could tell him
at least part of the story. I grit my teeth and close my eyes
remembering that night.

'How about you just tell me what you would tell anyone?
Or what you have told people so far? If you do not want to, I
understand.'

I take a deep breath through my nose and inhale the
comforting scent of Yianni next to me. I open my eyes. I
fix them on his and warmth spreads through my chest in the

same way a shot would at the end of the night. I try to think where to start.

'So, you know you said about your girlfriend? The one who was always saying she would hurt herself if you left? Well, Jonathan was more subtle than that, but over the years I started to see that he was controlling every part of our life. *My* life with him. He was the only person I've ever told that I wanted to own my own restaurant—'

'He was the only other person you told? Now me.' His full lips hint at a smile and his eyes gleefully narrow on mine.

'Yeah.' I didn't mean to let that one slip again, and I make a note in the back of my mind to tell him not to tell Hazel, if he hasn't already. That's for me to achieve on my own one day. To see my ideas come to life and to run a restaurant how I want to run it. To serve the food I think people will like. 'Anyway,' I continue, ignoring his gleeful face, 'Jonathan was always putting his acting career before everything else and making *me* pay all the bills, so I could never save up for my dreams. Then he started making it hard for me to see friends and family, then I had fewer and fewer people to talk to. It sounds silly now, but it was everything layering on top of me constantly. He was so different when people were there compared to when we were alone. Charming one minute, shouting at me the next. I started to see who he really was and...' My breath catches. I haven't even said this much to my mum or dad, or anyone. I never wanted people to think less of Jonathan, or less of me for staying with him for so long. If they caught a glimpse of what our relationship had really degraded into, what would they think? '...and I knew I had to break up with him. The problem was, he had nothing. No money of his own and his mum had downsized to a place with no spare room. I just wanted to line some stuff up first so he might be able to get a place straightaway. I couldn't stand the idea of breaking up with someone then being forced to live in that emotion every day until someone moved out. Looking back, I also don't think I wanted another argument. I just wanted to plod along ignoring it all for as long as I could. But he was always so persuasive and managed to do this mixture of putting me down and building me up to keep me feeling like I might need him or something. Does that even make sense?'

Yianni's nodding but not in a polite general way, but like he actually understands the experience and examples. My feelings and thoughts seem to have shattered like glass, and I feel like I'm picking up small pieces of memories and feelings, cutting myself to tell Yianni what they are, and none of them link together. They're just there, laid out all higgledy-piggledy and I barely know what's about to slip out of my mouth, so I can't imagine how it is that Yianni seems to so fervently agree with me.

'My girlfriend, Angelika, she was like this too. Compliments that she would take back. She would say, *You try so hard, Yianni, I'm so proud of you. It is a shame you aren't better at math, I will help you, I am here.*' He puts on a stupid girl voice when talking as her and I have to giggle.

'Is it bad to say I'm glad you understand?'

'A little.' He laughs though, and sips his drink.

Thoughts creep over me like a cloud. How much do I really want to tell him about what happened with Jonathan?

Chapter 30

Then

This isn't where I wanted to be when it came out of me, but this is where it's going to happen. Here in the car, on our way home. I can feel it. It's creeping its way up my throat and sitting in my mouth lurking, waiting to be released.

I barely saw Jonathan at the party, which was a good thing. He worked the room. I could hear the laughter and chatter follow him around. The thing is, I saw him drinking. It's lucky that I did notice because there was me thinking, *It's my birthday gathering, I'll have a couple of glasses of wine, maybe a cheeky rum and Coke because Jonathan will be driving home.* Apparently, he had other plans.

Even when I went up and said, in front of my dad, 'I thought you were driving?'

'Oh shit, sorry! I totally forgot. Your dad got me this, couldn't say no, could I?'

Yes, actually, you could. I'm sure that Jonathan didn't pay

for one drink all night, and now he is drunk; not so drunk anyone else would know, but drunk enough for me to notice. He's being snide. Making comments that I was talking to Rob for too long – and he keeps it up when we get in the car to go home. I'm having to drive of course.

'Bloody hell, Jonathan, he's gay!'

'He's bi. I'm pretty fucking sure I saw him looking at your tits.'

'Yes, he did compliment my outfit. I'm sure in your mind that constitutes as staring at my tits.'

'I just don't trust him.'

Tension ripples over me as the ties that Jonathan has enforced on me begin to crush every muscle. I can't take it. I can't let him consume my life in this way anymore. It's drowning me and I can't live this way for a moment longer. He's still talking about some imaginary crap that he thinks he saw, or that he thinks I did.

'Shut up.' I grip the steering wheel of the car. The leather's still cold from the night air and my fingers are so cold they feel almost crisp.

'What did you say to me?'

I'm not looking at him. I'm looking at the road being swallowed by our headlights, the A14 disappearing underneath us.

Through gritted teeth I repeat myself. 'I said, shut up.'

Trees are rushing past us in the dark. The wipers automatically awake with a screech, as rain speckles the windscreen. I snatch a breath and speak without letting myself think about the words. I had some planned, but they're being washed away with the rain as it begins to increase.

'I can't do this anymore. It's over. I'm sorry, but look, I've worked it out and I can pay rent without you, so we don't have to worry about that, and I paid the deposit anyway. I've put together a list of places that are looking for flatmates. Before you dropped your job you could afford them all. Maybe if you ask for the job back it might work out.'

'Stop. This is how you break up with me after all these years? You're money-obsessed, Ruby. Listen to you, you heartless bitch. Is that all you care about after all this time? How much money I earn and if you can afford to live without me?'

I didn't mean for it to come out that way, but I've been storing this all up for so damn long that it comes out as a mixture of the thoughts that I've been processing and ironing out in my mind.

'You know that's not it. I just—'

'I only took that directing job on for you. Surely that proves I'm willing to do anything?'

'You quit!' My voice matches the sound of the wipers in tone and my head snaps to look at him.

He curls in on himself as if the rain outside is directly pummelling his skin and he holds his face in his hands. He's crying.

Waves of pain crash into me. I should have waited and told him at home. Got my words out right. Made it softer, more amicable.

'I can't believe you're being so heartless, selfish. Fuck sake. Just think about it for a minute, you can't do this to us. I can't live without you, Rubes. I'll do anything.'

He places his hand over mine on the wheel. His thumb gently glancing along my skin, thawing it. So comfortable. Then his words hit back into my brain, *You're money-obsessed, Ruby. Listen to you, you heartless bitch.* No, I'm not. I am, on the other hand, desperate to be free, desperate to not have someone draining my energy. If I'm obsessed with anything, it would be security and peace. I can't get that from him. There's no peace of mind, there's no security. On my own, I can have those things. With him it's all turmoil, a rollercoaster because each day I don't know what shit surprise will come next. Is there enough money to pay the bills today? Is he going to accuse me of something I haven't done? Well, no more.

'I don't believe you.' My words were meant to be soft, but they come out defiant, because I don't believe he will change or that he will do anything to keep me with him. I'm ready to step away from him and his delusions. Tears slip down my cheeks because I'm pushing away someone who was once my best friend. The person I've shared all of me with. The person I used to chat to until sunrise about dreams and ideas, the person I thought I would marry one day.

'Why are you doing this? Is there someone else? There is, isn't there? Is it that new waiter at work? Fucking tell me, Ruby!'

'No. You don't know me at all, do you?'

'If I can't have you, no one can!'

Jonathan's fingers crush mine and jerk down on the steering wheel. He is howling like a wild animal in my left ear. It's slow motion but it's somehow incredibly fast at the same time. Trees, grass, headlights only showing us a snippet of the world around us as the car dances along, almost gracefully. As though it's relaxed in contrast to my body, which is braced, tugging the steering wheel almost out of the column and pressing my feet to the pedals.

I awake from tormented dreams of pixies slicing up my skin and feasting on it. My head's pounding in time with the music in the distance. Where the hell is that coming from? My eyes flicker.

It's not music.

It's sirens creeping closer.

Everything stings and something's in my face.

Then the jagged memory of the car spinning off the road comes back to me.

'Jonathan?' My voice seems disembodied, searching in the dim light.

Something's clawing at my skin, pressing into my face.

A branch?

What the hell is a branch doing in the car? Focus is coming back to me. I can see an empty field stretching out that is being illuminated by my headlights. But inside, a branch is pressing into my face and my abdomen.

I try to turn my head to Jonathan, but I'm pinned in place.

'Jonathan? Are you okay?' At least I can hear him breathing next to me.

Engines and voices swirl around not far from the car. I try to call out, but it hurts. I try again. 'Help. We're over here,' I call. 'It's okay, Jonathan, help is here.'

Still no reply, only the sound of breathing. It's laboured, slow. The fingers of my left hand crawl along the rough bark of the branch and over to Jonathan. His side is wet. Really wet.

More light fills the space around us, and a man appears at the windscreen.

I'm squinting, but he seems relieved when he sees me make eye contact with him.

'Hello, I'm Byron. I'm a fireman.' He doesn't move around the car. He stands in front of the windscreen... Wait, there's no windscreen. Where's the damn windscreen? 'What's your name?'

'Ruby.'

'Hi, Ruby. What I need you to do for me is keep looking at my hand. Can you see my hand?'

He holds his hand up in front of the car and I nod.

'Don't nod, okay? Just answer me.'

'Yes.'

He keeps his hand in front of the car as he moves to the side.

'Keep looking forward, keep looking at my hand, okay?'

'Okay.'

A voice, noises, crowd the left side of the car.

He's still breathing.

We need to get him out now.

Get the cutting equipment.

We need to cut away the car, and the tree.

If we don't get him out soon...

'Ruby? Did you hear me? I said: can you tell me where it hurts?'

I squeeze my eyes shut and tears burn in cuts on my skin. 'Everywhere.'

Chapter 31

Now

I close my eyes. I can vividly recall the day Jonathan died but only in snapshots. Nothing's fluid. It's almost like a picture book. How we argued. How he pulled the wheel as hard as he could. How he sealed both of our fates. If he had lived, all the anger I felt would still be with me, but as it is, he died because of a stupid, angry reaction to news he didn't like. It was my fault. I shouldn't have told him in the car when he was drunk. I knew he had a temper, a flair for the dramatic. He always had. He seemed to be able to absorb other people's emotions and regurgitate them perfectly. He could store them up and let them out for stage and screen too. Each moment of extreme drama was something he felt every grain of and relished. I knew that. So, it was my fault. I may as well have been the one to turn the wheel. I did, I suppose, just with my words and not my hands.

But do I tell this to Yianni? I've never told anyone before.

That it was Jonathan who made us crash. I've never told anyone because I'm to blame anyway and I knew my silence would protect his reputation. It's the least I can do. There's a pull to Yianni though, like he might listen and take it in, but he is also far enough away from the situation to be objective, unlike everyone who met Jonathan and knew him... loved him. He never knew Jonathan, so I wouldn't be ruining his memory of him the way I would for everyone else. I don't know; I'm still not sure.

I remove my hand from underneath Yianni's where it had been quietly enjoying his touch and it retreats to my lap.

'I was driving my car in the rain back from a party. My birthday party. He, Jonathan, was in the passenger seat.'

'That is how you got your scars? It was that car accident?'

It's obvious, but I silently dip my head to acknowledge that he is correct. The last rum and Coke I made was a little stronger than I would normally pour. It's as though my skin is resonating like the cicadas and turning me lightly numb.

'I loved him, but I wasn't *in* love with him anymore. I miss him now and then. We were together so long and then he wasn't there anymore. Death is so final. That's a stupid thing to say. It's just— I'd prepared myself to not having him there every day, but death meant he left on his terms and I can't do a damn thing to change it.'

'It was an accident. He did not really leave on his terms.'

My eyes flick to Yianni. Perhaps it's the physical loosening that comes with the consumption of alcohol, even in small doses, or perhaps my mouth folded in on itself in a certain way, or the way I shifted my weight signalled something to him, but Yianni's frowning, leaning in towards me. His fingers stretch towards mine and he steals them from the security of my lap, placing my hand back on the table and lightly gripping it.

'Ruby?' That's it. That's all he says. It's not like my mum knocking on my door to check on me twice a day for months and asking me to talk to her about what happened. It's simple. His deep voice vibrates through me and the way he says my name rattles something loose inside me. I have to squeeze my eyes closed again.

'He grabbed the wheel. He pulled it down...' The words are barely audible. They don't even sound like they came from my lips, but I felt my lips move. I've never told anyone this part of the story – or even that we broke up right before the accident – and now the words are floating on the warm Greek breeze that sweeps in through the doors and I can't take them back. I'm too afraid to open my eyes to see Yianni's thoughts written all over his face.

I feel the fingers of his other hand curl under my chin, and his thumb skims my cheek.

'Ruby, this is not your fault. He tried to kill you. You are not to blame for this.'

My eyes are still closed, but I shake my head. My lung capacity seems to have ripped in half as I snatch in miniscule breaths that shrink with each inhale. Yianni pulls me in and wraps me in his arms. Our knees press together awkwardly under the table, but the hug is comforting, with the smell of his aftershave and the feel of his solid clavicle against my forehead. I bite back the thought of tears. I will not let them fall. There have been so many tears over Jonathan and so many people have treated me differently since it happened. It's taken a long time to get to this point, to one where I feel closer to myself and my dreams without the nightmare of our ending and his death constantly on my mind. Not that it's completely gone, it's always lingering nearby.

'You can talk to me, Ruby. I will not tell anyone your secrets. They are yours, and if you want to share them with me, I will keep them safe for you, locked inside my chest. You can trust me, I promise.'

'Thank you.' My voice is muffled against the soft fabric of his black shirt. I pull away slightly to look up at him. Our faces are so close together I can feel the warmth of his breath on my cheek and the sweet scent of vanilla from the rum lingers between us. I want to tell him that Jonathan wasn't trying to kill me, or himself. Maybe he was, but I like to think that it was more of an impulsive act. He had said many times he couldn't live without me, that he would die. Not exactly that he'd kill himself – like Yianni's ex – more that he would just stop living. Or that's what I thought he meant. I'd never believed him, he was always being overly dramatic. I still like to believe that if Jonathan had thought about it, there was no way he would have done what he did. But I can't say it. I can't say any of it. Instead, my lips edge towards his. I carefully press them to the side of his lips.

'Thank you,' I repeat. Then he turns and kisses my mouth fully. His right hand slips round to the back of my neck and his fingers get lost in my hair. *He's your cousin's brother* flashes into my head and I snatch myself away from him.

'I shouldn't have done that.' I touch my lips as though by removing the warmth of his mouth on mine, I've removed a layer of my skin. As though my lips are burning and stinging, knowing the only antidote is for him to kiss me again. To soothe me with the soft touch of his lips and the prickle of his stubble.

He doesn't say anything. Instead, he dips his face towards mine again and kisses the scar on my chin. The sensation makes me almost wince as though the scar is an open wound, and he is sprinkling it with salt.

'It is not your fault, Ruby.' He kisses along my jaw. 'You cannot punish yourself because of what he did to you. He was a man with his own freedom, and he nearly stole yours. You did nothing wrong.'

I pull away from him, but he catches my hands in his.

'That's not true. I shouldn't have told him it was over while we were in the car. That was a stupid thing to do.'

'You could not know he would do this.'

Yianni's fingers glance over my scar.

'It was stupid of me not to pick a better time. I was getting irritated at him, and I just let it all out and I didn't even let him down gently.' I snatch my hands from Yianni and go to twist the imaginary ring on my finger. But that's all it is now, imaginary. It's another lost part of my past, like a bad dream. That ring was my reminder to be kind, my reminder of how we once were, and my reminder to be cautious with my heart and my actions. But it was also my constant reminder of Jonathan. As though he was there watching every decision I've made since he died. Without his presence pressing into my skin and imprisoning my finger, maybe I can let myself be free to step out of his shadow.

I look up to see Yianni's eyes looking at the same spot on my lonely right ring finger.

He's squinting and I can almost see the words bubbling up towards his lips before he says, 'What is the real story about that ring?'

Chapter 32

Then

Sue keeps hugging me and crying. She keeps almost touching the stitches on my chin with her shoulder when she pulls me in. She apologises to me, then I apologise to her. Neither of us have anything to apologise for, but we both feel sorry. So, so sorry. I'm sorry she's lost her son, she's sorry I've lost my boyfriend. I said that now I'm out of hospital and back on my feet, she could come round and go through Jonathan's things with me. She'll want to keep things and I already know that I want almost nothing. It all hurts too much. I haven't told anyone he pulled the steering wheel from my hands. Everyone thinks it was an aquaplaning issue in the rain and I play dumb. The professionals say it's shock and injury. That loads of people can't remember the moments just before impact. To be fair, I can't remember the moments right before, only the sensation of Jonathan's fingers digging into mine on the steering wheel and pulling the car off course.

As far as Sue knows, it's all my fault that her son is dead. She hasn't blamed me though. I blame me instead. If I'd kept my mouth shut for even twenty more minutes that night, then it would be him packing up his things and moving out to carry on living. Now it's as though we both died in the accident. Everything feels irreparably shattered. Picking up the pieces of my life is like dropping a packet of glitter on the floor and trying to pick up every last piece. I can't. And even if I could, the glitter is pretty, and this mess is damn ugly. Even if I managed to pick up all the pieces of my broken life and try to stick them back together, the cracks would still show, and everyone would still be able to see how broken I am. So why am I even bothering to be alive?

The whole morning has consisted of blurred vision and tissues with every shirt pulled from our shared cupboard. I guess it's just my cupboard now. I sniff and pass Jonathan's backpack to Sue. There are a few scripts and headshots inside. I let her look through it while sitting on our bed. My bed. It's only me who lives here now.

I start opening my drawers too, to look for cufflinks that have been thrown in with my jewellery. I know there were some that had been his grandad's and I'm sure she'll want to keep them. I silently ask Jonathan how we let it all come to this. Why did he do this? I find the little silver discs. They're so simple, about the size of a penny, highly polished with a tiny ruby in the centre. He thought it was fate that we met, that his grandad had sent me to him. I rub along the red dot at the centre of one with my thumb. I wonder whether he's with his grandad now. Whether they're both blaming me. I blame me. I never met Jonathan's grandad, but I'm sure he would have hated me and there's no way he sent me to ruin

Jonathan's life. To accidently murder him. I'm still eyeing the cufflinks and I'm about to tell Sue I've found them when I hear the sharp inhale of horror in her lungs.

'Oh my god,' she adds on the exhale. It's as though the air has been completely snatched from her, making her words high-pitched. 'Ruby, I'm so sorry. I'm so sorry.' There's a new layer of grief hanging in her voice and I feel it in the cut along my stomach as though I've been freshly jousted by that damn tree. My whole body shudders and I press my hand to the healing wounds on my abdomen.

I turn to look at her and see she is holding a small green box in her nimble fingers. It's only as I step forwards that I understand what it is, and the fresh tears falling down her narrow face make sense.

An engagement ring.

He was preparing to marry me, as I was preparing to leave him.

No wonder he wanted me dead.

Chapter 33

Now

'His mum, Sue, she found the ring after he died. She wanted me to keep it, to wear it… to keep his spirit alive. I'm terrified to tell her I've lost it. Mum thinks it's best I don't tell her. For the past couple of years, she's wanted to see me on his birthday. Luckily, it's in a couple of weeks and I'll be here, so that breaks that painful tradition… unless of course she takes a holiday here just to see me. Honestly, I wouldn't put it past her. We got on well enough but only because I always kept my mouth shut and went along with things to maintain a peaceful life. Same way I did with Jonathan really.'

Yianni takes it all in, then he says, 'When Hazel told me it was your engagement ring, and you chose not to tell me that when it was lost, I thought I should step back. When I kissed you in the dark, you pulled away, but I understand why. You have been through so much.' Yianni's eyes somehow look more round, tinged with sadness.

'Do you know what I'm fed up of?' He arches his eyebrow at me, and I continue. 'I'm so fed up with everyone seeing me as broken. I liked not telling you everything because I didn't want you to feel sorry for me. I've always told myself I didn't tell people what he did to protect his memory, but maybe I was protecting me a little too. Think how they would look at me then. How you're looking at me now.'

Both of his fluffy eyebrows shoot up at this and his hand comes to his chest. 'Me?' he says, 'How am I looking at you?'

I gesture towards his face, 'You're all sorry for me because I'm the girl whose boyfriend tried to kill her and ended up killing himself. The last thing he said was, *If I can't have you, no one can.* And since then, it's like I've been cursed to live by his words with everyone keeping their distance. I'm damaged goods.'

Yianni starts to laugh and my eyebrows pull together at the sound of it. Folding my arms over my chest, I wait for him to calm a little.

'Do you want to know what *I* see, Ruby?'

I shrug, because even though I do want to know what he sees, I don't like that he's been laughing at my pathetic life for the past ten seconds. I'm not about to smile about it and tell him I'm desperate to find out every thought he has ever had about me.

'Not damaged goods. Not people keeping away. A girl who is loved by family and friends and people who come up to the bar at night. A girl who doesn't see her own face when she looks in the mirror. I see an independent thinker, a girl who doesn't share herself easily. You are guarded, but you are not afraid. You hide behind this past, but it does not have to *be* you. You do not have a curse on you. You are always trying to protect yourself. Hiding. But this *curse*... It doesn't change the way I feel when I'm near you. Am I sad this happened to you? Yes and no.' His fingers confidently lift my fringe to look for my scar there. It's the worse of the two but my makeup will be covering it in the dim light, I'm confident of that. I hold my face and body taut under his gaze. As his eyes meander over me, his smile deepens. 'I would never want anyone to feel such pain, but if this is why Hazel pushed you to come here and help when we did not need it, then I am glad.'

All my nerves tingle as though each and every one has been touched by his words. In all the time he has spent glancing at me at work, it's like he has seen more of me than I do. Maybe he is right in thinking I can't see my own face in the mirror. Sometimes I can't even understand who I've become. I don't dare to dwell on the emotions he's brought up from the depths of my chest. Instead I focus on the last part, about Hazel.

'She said someone left to go to uni.'

'Then she lied.'

'Proving that everyone pities me.'

'Good. It brought you here, and I will never be sad about this.'

'Do you know what I don't understand?'

Yianni tilts his head and crosses his arms over his chest to mirror me.

'Why Hazel didn't tell you sooner. I thought everyone knew. She's not the sort of person not to tell you all about it when it happened. She can keep a secret, but what happened wasn't a secret.'

'No, she did. Only, it was years ago and she kept talking

203

about this Jonathan guy. I don't know any Jonathan and I was at uni going through things with Angelika. I didn't realise her stories were about you. Somehow, I miss this part. Then when she is saying, *We need to be kind to Ruby, we need to be gentle with Ruby*, I thought you were some delicate princess now. I was foolish.'

'We all make mistakes.'

Yianni rolls his eyes to the ceiling and pushes his fingers through his wavy curls.

'You know, when I told Hazel about you losing your ring, she says to me how important that ring would be to you, it all made sense to realise *you* are the girl who lost her boyfriend. Hazel tells me you *lost the love of your life, no one can compete with that*.'

'She doesn't know what she's talking about. He wasn't the love of my life.' A breeze rolls in and against the warm night I shiver, and goosebumps explode across my skin.

As I say this, Yianni's face changes into something much more serious. Even the night air seems to shift again, and a cool breeze rolls around us, making my hair shimmy around my cheeks. He smooths it down then his fingers linger on my face again. My breathing starts to weigh me down and I'm much too aware of everything – the music still playing to itself, the gentle breeze, my heart screaming in my chest.

His face moves towards me, but I can't wait a moment more and I meet him halfway. Our lips collide, and his tongue finds mine and we melt together in the fiery night's heat. Or at least my body feels like it's alight as he presses into me. His right hand slips behind me on the bench to support his weight as his left hand tickles under my shirt and round my waist before it's his turn to pull away, but only a centimetre.

'You won't break my arm, will you?'

I laugh into his warm mouth, then pull away long enough to say, 'No, you're safe.'

Yianni pulls me harder towards him and slips his hand further up and along my ribs. I breathe into his mouth as I adjust myself to bring my right leg around him, pinning it between the wall and his side. Now his weight's lowering between my thighs and my head falls back as he kisses my jaw and the length of my neck. He skims the scar on my chin with his lips. I don't feel pain this time. Instead, everything inside me has shifted. He has seen it all, all my suffering, everything I've hidden from the world, and instead of walking away or pitying me, he laughed. It was the last thing I expected, but it was what I needed.

I can see straight out to the road. It's dimly lit in the restaurant with most of the lights out, and we are as far from the road as we can get, but I don't really like the idea of someone walking back late from of the bars and seeing us like this.

'Yianni?' I lift my head and shift my weight onto my elbow to sit up. 'Everything is open to the street, and you haven't even locked the bar.'

His head flops back down between my breasts. A moment later he bounces up and runs round closing the doors and turning the music off. While he finishes sorting things out, I go to the ladies' toilets. A knot forms as I think about what's unfolding. Every fibre is telling me this is a stupid idea. I should go say goodnight now and go back to the house. There's no way Hazel would be okay with me and Yianni, even if she did bring me here under false pretences. As I leave the toilets everything is dark except a stream of light like an

arrow leading towards Yianni's bedroom. I have no choice
but to go in.

Chapter 34

Now

The little reading lamp is on and the bed is neatly made; pale blue sheets tucked in perfectly in a way I can never quite achieve myself. Yianni has either put two glasses of water by the bed or two glasses of vodka, either way it's a clear liquid. As I enter, he switches off the screen to his phone and places it next to the lamp.

'Anyone interesting?' I consider closing the door behind me, but I don't because I know I should be walking straight back out of it. I shouldn't have even engaged in a question.

'Nico.'
'Messaging this late?'
Yianni shrugs and begins to shuffle towards the edge of the bed.
'You've got air con in here now!'
A little machine hums in the corner of the room. It's free-standing and only small, but it's enough to make the

room comfortable.

'It's for when I have guests,' he laughs and gets up to walk past me and closes the door. Perhaps he can sense my thoughts and my uncertainties, but as he steps towards me, he has no such hesitations. He tilts his head down towards me and his hand wraps around the back of my neck as his lips meet mine. My skin tingles all over and I let out an involuntary low sigh into his mouth making him smile against mine.

We hold on to each other, our hands skimming each other's bodies, our feet edging one by one towards the bed until we lower ourselves on to it. We fall onto our sides and he begins to slowly unbutton my shirt.

It's been so long since I've had someone's face and eyes so close to mine. Seeing me in close up, seeing into every part of me. When Yianni and I were last pressed together in this room it was dark and clumsy. It was nothing like this. Now it feels like I'm watching him under a magnifying glass as we press together. I pull away to see him more clearly, but my fingers linger, clinging to Yianni's shirt, looping my fingers in between two buttons. I don't want to pull away any further, but I also need a moment to think. Yianni's quietly gasping for air, my air, straight from my lips as our foreheads press together. A thought escapes my brain and falls from my lips.

'How can I trust you?'

He cups my face and his eyes search mine, from one to the other. In the shadowy room, his eyes look almost black, but even so, I can see the kindness that resides in them.

'We do not have to rush.' The corners of his lips tug upwards and he releases me from his grasp. 'In truth, I do not want to rush.'

I can't help but lower an eyebrow at him and pull on my

open blouse.

'I didn't say I don't want you, just that it's nice not to rush. We have all the time.'

Yianni's eyes linger on my abdomen now it's exposed.

'Do you have to stare at my scars?' I wrap my blouse back around my torso and hunch forwards over my knees and turn away from him. Outside of doctors, he's the only person to have seen them. I haven't shown them to anyone. Why would I? It's not the sort of thing anyone would ask to see. My mum helped me with them when they were wounds and I needed her to, but since then she hasn't seen them. A small part of me wants to put my hand over the jagged line where the branch of a tree tore into my skin. I fight the urge. This is me. I can't change my past. It's written all over me in silver lines, freckles, tan lines and I'm sure soon enough in laughter lines and age spots. They will never change, even if they have changed me. It's fixed. The past is fixed. The future isn't though. It's open and full of anything I want it to be.

'No, I like to stare at you though.' Yianni shuffles back in the single bed and presses his back against the wall, before he pulls his legs up to stop them dangling over the side. 'Hey, would you like to see my scar?' I twist to look at him, now that he's behind me. His fingers are in his hair and his elbow is resting on one knee. 'My stories are not so impressive, but...' His lips downturn in thought. 'Maybe you still like to see them?'

'Go on then, impress me.' Still clutching my blouse, I sit up and twist to face him. His cheeky face lights up ready for the show-and-tell session to commence.

His fingers dive deeper into his hair, and he tilts his head forwards.

'Here, look.' His finger jabs at a thick scar, thicker than any of mine and a good inch long.

'How the hell did you get that.'

'A good friend throws a rock at me. Not his fault—'

'How is that not his fault?'

'We were, what do you call it?' He folds his leg underneath himself then slices with his right arm.

'Oh, skimming stones?' I jump my finger along, acting out the motion in a similar way to Yianni. 'So they bounce.'

'Yes, I duck down to pick up a stone, he throws but I stand up too fast and his stone hits me. I shouldn't have gone in front of him, but there was a good stone.' He is grinning at the memory while rubbing his head. 'I got stitches.'

'But that's a nice story. Mine ends with a dead boyfriend and a tree in my side.' Yianni, stops laughing and his lips press together. 'Sorry, that was a bit... abrupt.' The air con unit next to the chair hums along under the silence I've caused.

Yianni says, 'You can tell me. You don't always have to be alone.'

I look about his box room. It's a lot tidier than last time I was in here. All the clothes have been put away, the bed is neat-freak perfect and even the items on the bedside have been organised in rows. I'm going to assume this effort is for me. Because he invited me to talk to him tonight. It's strangely comforting, the effort he has put in for me.

'I'm not sure I'm ready to give you all the gory details. It's been two years and it's stayed between me and Byron the whole time.'

'Byron?'

A smile crosses my lips at the memory of the fireman who talked to me – for what felt like days – while they cut the car and tree away from us and did their best to save Jonathan.

'Yeah, he's a fireman.'

'A sexy fireman?' Yianni almost looks jealous, that is until my face cracks and I burst into laughter.

'No! He was twice my age and reminded me of my dad. But, the Suffolk version.' My abdomen relaxes and I think back to that time. How hard the responders worked and it still ended with a funeral. 'Do you know what? There *is* something I can tell you.'

Yianni leans in a little bit ready to give me his full attention. To be honest, when I'm with Yianni, I always feel like I have his full attention. He never seems half-hearted. He's present with me. Not picking up his phone halfway through a conversation or looking off into the distance. Other than one time, when I was going to possibly tell him a little bit about Jonathan.

'No, wait, why did you look so distant that time I was going to tell you that Jonathan had died? You kind of brushed it under the carpet.'

'In the bar?'

I nod. Where else? We're always in the damn bar.

'I was,' he hesitates before continuing, 'jealous, maybe. You dwelling on a boyfriend. It's not what I was wanting to hear.'

I nibble my lip. Makes sense that he was different to his usual, focused self.

'What were you going to tell me?'

'At Jonathan's funeral, there was this girl I didn't recognise. A tiny little thing but held herself like she was a giant, you know? Shoulders pulled back, chin in the air like she was looking down at people but with a soft face that didn't match her body. Anyway, at the wake she comes up to me and does the usual *I'm so sorry for your loss* bit. I asked her how she knew Jonathan. She said that she was a performer and they used to work together. She heard about his passing through a friend and wanted to pay her respects. She tells me they even dated for a little while when they were touring around schools performing A Midsummer Night's Dream. I asked her when, but I knew when before she answered. We hadn't been together that long, and he was seeing her at the same time. I didn't tell her. I think she would have been mortified. The thing is, I just wanted to laugh. It all made sense, how controlling he was, how he would accuse me of cheating. That's because he was reflecting what he had done himself. In that moment I was kind of glad he was dead, but feeling that way burdened me with so much guilt. Just because he was controlling and cheated on me doesn't mean I wish him dead.'

'This Jonathan, he sounds lovely.'

I'd been looking at my fingers and the space where Jonathan's ring once gripped my finger, but Yianni's comment makes my head snap up so fast I'm surprised I don't have whiplash. Yianni's eyes are bulging in his head they're so wide, and he's baring his teeth is an exaggerated grimace. He looks like a maniac.

Laughter tickles my sides. It bubbles out until I flop back onto the bed. Yianni's laughing too, looking down at me. Then his face slowly falls serious. 'He did not deserve you.'

'No, perhaps not. We were young when we got together. I think I was a bit naive and, sort of star-struck with the actor boyfriend bit. He could be so charming and funny when he wanted to be. But, that's not enough, is it? Just to be pretty and charming. There was no care, no kindness... No that's not fair, there just wasn't enough. Not for me anyway. I'm sure he loved me, but only as much as a narcissist can love anyone other than the mirror.'

Yianni exhales through his teeth and hangs his head before sliding down next to me on the bed. He's still watching over me as he props himself on his elbow.

'You've changed. I guess he changed you. Or perhaps the accident changed you?'

'How do you know I've changed?' I screw my face up, but this only makes Yianni laugh and etch his finger along the creases I've formed in my forehead.

'I remember you. How could I not? This beautiful creature with long dark hair. Softly spoken and kind to everyone. My friend, who throws the rock at my head?' I nod as he says it like a question. 'Well, he was at Hazel and Papa's wedding too, everyone was at the wedding. We were, maybe eleven and you were, I don't know, maybe sixteen? To us you were a woman and we were nothing. But my friend, he is called Yianni too by the way, he says he will ask you to dance. I burned with anger at the idea that he will have his hands on you and I never could.'

'I don't remember anyone asking me to dance.'

'Oh no, he didn't ask. He was all bravado.'

'I find it weird to think of you as a kid watching me.' I brush my fringe out of my eyes to look up at him a little bit better.

'I'm Greek, I was born as a man. At that age I was helping in the restaurant, learning the family business.' He falters, looking towards the door. 'I thought I was a man, but I already knew you were too good for me.'

'I can't believe you've been harbouring feelings for me for all these years.' My fingers press to my lips and my head gently shakes at the thought of it, but it can't shake off the smile that's hidden under my fingertips. 'In what way have I changed?'

'You're more confident. At sixteen you didn't say much, or get involved in the dancing. You were a watcher. Now, not so much. Now you want to talk to people, you smile at them. Yes, sometimes I see you falling into your head full of thoughts, but you can get involved now too. And, of course now you can break a man's arm as well as his heart.'

My lips open to dispute this claim but before I can form words, he cuts across the sound.

'*Nai, nai, nai.* Yes, you can. Don't you pretend. I think you could break a man's arm.'

'Oh yeah, I'm sure I can. It's the *heart* part I'm laughing at.'

'I wouldn't be so sure.'

We lie smiling at each other for a moment before I tilt my chin up, signalling to him my intentions. He slides lower on the bed and kisses me slowly. His lips are firm yet delightfully smooth. His hands glide over my back to pull me in.

He snatches his lips away and breathes, 'I am still safe, yes? You won't break my hand?' His eyes glint in the reflection of the lamp and his face is taut with suppressed giggles.

'Honestly, with me, who knows?'

We are so close I can feel the vibration of his laughter in my own chest as though we exist in the same space and are already fusing together as our lips collide again, and we search each other for answers to questions we're too afraid to ask.

Chapter 35

Now

Five hours of sleep is better than no sleep. We kissed all night, well, until maybe four in the morning, maybe five. I'm not really sure anymore. It was like being in high school again, like we were both a little too nervous to take it any further than kissing. Our hands were everywhere, like shadows following each other's bodies from place to place.

We didn't discuss that we wouldn't take it any further. If we take this further, we can't undo it and we have no idea how the rest of the family will react. To them we are cousins and to us, we're just two people who really like each other. We weren't brought up together – we're not even really related – but it's still tricky to know what people will say. I didn't come to Corfu just to upset people and ruin their lives. I guess I came because I was looking for something I knew I wouldn't find on my doorstep. There were plenty of jobs I *could* have applied for, but I just kept finding reasons why they weren't good enough. I needed adventure on my terms, and this was right at my feet, waiting to be scooped up.

Yianni messages Hazel and Pericles to say that we had a late night and won't be in for the lunch shift, that Nico will be there instead. They don't mind. So now we are walking to get pancakes – or maybe waffles – from Silver Star. It's only a short walk down the road. Everyone who passes us says hello. I can't help but wonder whether they're questioning why we're together at nine in the morning. I'm sure they're not. I feel pretty grim in yesterday's clothes, but they're so plain, and I wear variations of the same every day so it's not obvious to anyone but me, I hope.

'I can't bare this. I'll meet you in there, okay?'

Yianni mumbles an 'okay' but looks puzzled as I begin to jog away.

I'm in my little ballet pumps. It's still a little painful on my foot to jog, so after a short distance I stick with very fast walking, going up the incline towards one of the clothes shops. I nip into the first one I come to. I've often admired the clothes in these places as I pass on my bike, but I haven't actually gone inside. There's a mixture of cotton dresses, children's toys and keepsakes all under one roof. I whip my fingers along the clothing, one item to the next, occasionally pulling something forward. I settle on a loose-fitting dress in a dark purple that's gathered at the bust. I'm making my way to the till when something else catches my eye. Like the pull of gravity, I move towards it without thinking or choosing. I pick it up from its resting place, and looking it over, I swallow hard and take a deep breath. *You are brave. You are strong.*

I come into Silver Star at the side entrance that's level with the street instead of walking around and climbing the stairs. After saying hello to the owners, I scan the terrace for Yianni. I can't see him so I keep moving around. There are only a few tables taken, and I start to think he's turned around and gone back to Greek Secret when I find him as far away from where I walked in as possible. Past all the round tables circled in wicker chairs and brightly coloured cushions, he's sitting on a long swing chair with cream cushions, and he's slowly rocking back and forth with his heels.

'I thought I lost you.' I stand over him as he lowers the menu he's hiding behind.

'I thought you ran away.' He looks me up and down. 'That's where you went. You look lovely.'

'Thank you.'

I want to sit next to him, but I'm not sure if that will look too coupley and cosy. I don't care. If I want to sit next to Yianni, then I'll sit next to Yianni.

I plonk myself down right next to him making the swing chair shoot backwards a little harder than I meant to. Yianni laughs and watches me from the corner of his eye.

'I cannot believe you put face wipes and makeup in your bag.' He passes me his menu to peruse.

'Don't be so shocked. You tidied your room and got air con. Anyway, after the last time, I just wanted to have them in my bag just in case. It's no big deal.'

Yianni makes a low growling noise in the back of his throat like he doesn't believe me. He shouldn't believe me. We all live in hope, I guess.

We order waffles with ice cream for breakfast and greedily scoff our way through it all. Mine has sticky chocolate sauce too with a few slices of tangy strawberries to top it off. Delicious.

When we're done, I don't want to rush back to the house for showers, although I don't think anyone will be there. I'm not ready to break this little bubble. We might not be holding hands or kissing, but being in Yianni's company is as warm as the Corfu sun.

'Can we go for a walk along the beach? Instead of straight back to the house?'

'Of course.'

We meander along the road, waving to everyone, smiling at everyone. Anywhere else it might feel like some sort of celebrity status. Not here. It's just saying hello to all your friends. More for Yianni, of course, and some of them are his family too. We walk all the way to the beach, talking about nothing and everything, enjoying the slow, delightful pace of life.

I lead us all the way to the water's edge and kick off my shoes to let the foam tickle my toes. In silence we look out to sea and the line that is the meeting of two entities. It's like the crux of where the past and present meet, and that almost-invisible line is the present. As soon as you focus in on it, it's already gone and melted into the past. All we have is now. Everything else is just the shades of blue that encase us on this planet.

We're standing close enough together that when I stretch my little finger in Yianni's direction, it glances his. My heart is like a drum so loud I feel it in my chest. The present is now. There's nothing else.

I turn to face him then take two steps past him, away from the sea and I remove my dress. In the shop, I also purchased a bikini, the first bikini I've worn since the accident. I subdue the urge to put my hands over my stomach and I turn towards the sea. Yianni doesn't look at my scars this time. He looks me in the eye and in a low voice says, 'I really want to kiss you.'

My lips press together in what I can only imagine looks like a nervous smile, because that's how I feel, tinged red with anxiety. But it's not enough to stop me. Not enough to worry or care. It is not so much that I needed anyone else's approval to get me to this place, but I needed to find someone I could tell the truth to before I could show the world the end result – the jagged scar of an injury, that, if it had been only an inch or so further, could have killed me. So I was told anyway. Lucky. Over and over I was told I was lucky, when I really didn't feel lucky at all. But I was. I'm here on this beautiful island surrounded by happy voices and the calm crawling of the sea along the sand. Then there's Yianni, someone I like. I don't want to think further than that. One step at a time. And that's exactly what I do, take one step at a time into the sea, into the all-encompassing blue. It's taken me two years, a ton of alone time, staring into space and trying to connect with something and reaffirming everything in my head to get me here. Jonathan took more than his life that day.

Yianni pulls off his top and throws it down with my dress. He's not wearing swim shorts, but they're sporty and breathable material. He doesn't even question it, he just strides into the sea behind me with his pants and shorts on. I have to laugh.

He says, 'What made you change?'

I don't know if he wants me to say that it was him. If he does, he'll be disappointed.

'That.' I point out to sea and into the distance.

Yianni squints, looking for something he'll never find. To him it's turquoise seas and cloudless skies. We continue walking into the sea until it's skimming along under my fingertips then past my scars above my belly button.

'Do you want me to explain?' I smile over at him. He has raised one hand to shade his eyes while he continues to look out into the wide open expanse of blue.

'It might help.'

'I've stood here looking out to sea for weeks now, and it's helped me to focus. It's helped to put everything I've been doing over the past few years into perspective. I haven't really been living. I've been existing somewhere between the past and the future, but never in the present. I'd be wrenching my neck in one direction or the other, but I'd never be seeing the now. Looking at the place where the sea and the sky come together, it's not really a line, I mean, it is, but the earth is a globe and the sky is all around us, so the line is this fleeting thing. I see it as the present, the here and now. The sea is a reflection, so it's like the past, it's who we were, and the sky is the future, wide and infinite. I sound stupid, don't I? Like I've spent way too long on my own.'

'Not stupid. Perhaps, alone to think. But I like this idea of the line, and if it helps you, this is no bad thing.'

'It has. It's made me want to live in the present. It's forced me to focus on it and what's important. Then there's you. You're the catalyst I didn't know I needed, but not how you might think. You were staring at my scars and it didn't make them hurt any more or any less. I didn't need a man – even one I really like – to tell me I look okay. Or even that they don't look okay. What I needed was someone to see them before I could walk around with them for the world to see, because

I needed to know that I would be alright. That I wouldn't fall apart at the thought of the accident. That people seeing my scar wouldn't make me instantly see Jonathan illuminated under artificial lights with the shadow of the tree over his face as his life slipped away. His head pressing against the tree, and—' I stop myself because the memory is much too gruesome. My wet hands are pressing to my head as I'm acting out the memory, but the water dripping over my face makes me think of the blood trickling over Jonathan's skin. I saw a lot before they could get a screen between us. He died soon after. There was no hope of him living, not really, but the firemen and women and the paramedics did everything they could anyway. They didn't want to give up, but it was too late.

Yianni's hands carefully wrap around my wrists and remove my hands from my face. My body's shivering like I've been in a bath too long and the water's gone cold. He brings me into him and my wet face sticks to the soft skin of his chest.

'You really like me. It's too late, you've said this now,' and with his words, we both begin to laugh. He brings the light back onto my skin again and it penetrates my soul, illuminating the pain, but letting it dissolve a little into the shadows. I don't give him the satisfaction of a response. Instead, I step back out of his embrace and splash him, before diving into the blue.

Chapter 36

Now

Of course, we had to get to work eventually. Although we did find time to kiss some more on my bed, that is, Yianni's bed at the house, until we heard the door swing open downstairs as Pericles called up to Yianni. We jumped apart so quickly that Yianni was out of the room and jogging down the stairs to speak to his dad in a nanosecond. I feel like my heart might never stop speeding. It's like being a teenager again. Even now, Yianni's actually looking at me less than normal. Usually, I catch him gawping at me all the time. Today it's the opposite, it's like he knows he can't look at me, because if he does look at me, it'll all fall apart, and everyone will see right through us.

Nico on the other hand has been toying with me. He hasn't actually said anything or asked what happened, but he's being very suggestive, which is designed to get me to a breaking point of snapping and saying something about Yianni without Nico having to ask. I have no intention of snapping, so it's a waiting game.

'Yianni looks very mutz happier today, no? Do you not think so?' Nico's pouring a glass of wine while watching Yianni. He's brimming with smiles at an elderly couple he's helping up from their table-for-two underneath the hanging vines. It's the time of evening where it all starts to thin out and people who are still here are moving on to desserts.

'You would have to ask him whether he's happy. I'm sure I couldn't comment.'

'Oh, so, you would not know any reason, or any events that might put smiles over his face?'

'Nothing I'm aware of. Although, he did get to see me in a bikini earlier.'

Nico makes a noise that sounds a little like a high-hat as a reproach to my comment.

'A bikini? Everyone is wearing a bikini. Some not even that. You went swimming with him before, what is so special about a bikini?' Nico laughs as he places the wine on a tray along with a bottle of beer and a glass. He turns to face me because I'm in the way. He stops to assess me.

'What's wrong?'

'Nothing. Just, it was a big deal actually. I haven't worn a bikini for quite some years. I was in a car accident, and I have some scars. It's silly really.'

'No, it is never silly to have scars. These accidents, they can change lives forever and leave you with pains worse than scars. But I am glad you're in a bikini again.' He brushes past me and continues, 'You should never hide who you are, especially when you have a body like yours.' He smirks and walks away. I know he said it for two reasons, one because he is the biggest damn flirt on the island, and two, because Yianni had appeared so he complimented my body in an exaggerated voice to try to get a rise out of him. It didn't work. Not this time.

'I almost thought Nico was going to be sensitive or mature then.' I do my best not to beam at Yianni coming over to chat to me.

'He is underneath it all. He just likes to hide it.' Yianni scans the room then turns back to me. 'It should start settling down in here soon.' He leans on the bar with both his forearms flat to the wood, leaving him looking up at me for a change.

'Correct. I was thinking of getting an early night.'

His face changes, and he stutters something about that being a good idea and it's important to get rest after a busy day.

'I'm kidding. Can I stay?'

'You're staying here again?' Hazel's voice appears at my elbow, and she comes to stand over the books next to the till.

'Only if it's alright with Yianni.'

Hazel pulls her glasses down off her head and onto her nose as she peers at the books in front of her. My eyes widen at Yianni because I feel a little trapped in this conversation. We haven't really been quizzed on the sleeping arrangements when I've stayed here, but I have a feeling it's about to come up.

'Well I'm glad he lets you sleep on the bed. You're a gentleman, aren't you Yianni?' Hazel reaches over the bar and pinches his chin.

'I do my best.' Yianni playfully rolls his eyes as she releases him.

'I hope you don't *really* sleep on the floor, though. Not when you have comfy chairs out here.'

'No, no. Not the floor.'

My palms feel clammy and it's not just the fact that there's no breeze tonight. I hope no one puts a drink order in or I might end up being the one to drop it on my foot this time.

'I can't believe it's my turn to check the receipts again. I hate this part of the job, don't you? I think we're due someone coming in to check though. It seems like ages since the last spot check.' Hazel glances between us, her eyes looking even wider under her glasses.

We both begin to agree. I don't mind too much; I like taking in everything there is to know about owning a restaurant anywhere in the world.

'I best get back to work,' Yianni taps the bar and begins to turn around, only Hazel starts to make a rhythmical *uh-uh* sound and looks at him over her glasses.

'You didn't answer the poor girl, Yianni. Can she kick you out of another one of your beds for the night? She's a cheeky one, isn't she?' Hazel's elbow finds my ribs. There's a funny tone about her and my clammy palms are no longer my biggest worry; my face is feeling hot. To make matters worse, I sort of snort at her little joke about me being cheeky.

'I wouldn't kick him out of his bed.'

'Oh really?' Her bright blue eyes shine their light on me and I wish I could go back and swallow my words. I'd probably only choke on them though.

'I mean, you know what I mean.'

From the corner of my eye, I can see Yianni cringing, and sweat is weaving down my spine as Hazel looks between us.

'Well, it's good to see you're getting on.'

Pericles strolls over and mildly berates Yianni in Greek.

225

I'm pretty sure Hazel speaks in his defence, maybe blaming herself for his pause in his duties. I'm going by body language alone. Pericles softens at Hazel's tone and Yianni moves away. Nico scoots behind Hazel and me and begins to clean down the bar. More people vacate the restaurant and another group leave their table in favour of bar stools.

I watch as Yianni disappears.

'I can do the books if you like,' I offer.

'Would you, dear?'

I bob my head and she cups my face. 'Are you happy here, Ruby? You seem happy.'

'I am.'

She pulls me in for a hug and I see Yianni watching us as he takes down a dessert order. As he walks away from the table, he gives me the briefest wink before pushing his hair off his face.

Hazel kisses my cheek. 'Right, looks like Yianni has some work for me. Thanks for doing the books tonight, sweetheart.'

'No worries.' I smile in her wake then turn around to Nico only a short distance away from me.

He says, 'Don't think I didn't see that wink. Were you telling Hazel her stepson is your new boyfriend?' His grin engulfs his whole face, but I ignore him. I have no interest in letting anyone else's excitement layer on top of my own. Yianni and I are still finding out who we are. I'm not going to start thinking about what we are, or what we could be. That's a little too much future, and not enough present.

Chapter 37

Now

As the night draws to a close, Nico takes too much satisfaction in hanging around and having a drink while everyone else is leaving. I don't mind particularly, I like Nico. Yianni seems to be amused by how amusing Nico finds himself to be too. It's a completely relaxed evening and the scent of honeysuckle floats on the air from a plant growing beside the restaurant. I've never noticed it much before, but tonight the sickly, sweet fragrance being carried in reminds me of my childhood. There was honeysuckle in my parents' garden and it was always smothered in butterflies. I wish I could tell my mum about Yianni and the bikini and how much I've pushed myself lately. I miss seeing my parents face to face. Even FaceTime isn't the same.

Yianni gets behind the bar and serves me and Nico as we take seats on the stools. He hasn't quite the finesse that Nico has when it comes to putting on a show with glasses and bottles, but he's still bloody good. Not like me. I flinch and close my eyes every time they juggle bottles and glasses near me, let alone trying it for myself. Yianni fills three glasses with chocolate tequila and slides two of them over to Nico and me.

'*Yamas*,' we all chime – not quite in unison – and knock back the smooth liquid.

'I'm not interrupting your alone time, am I?' Nico glances between us, his eye glinting.

'Piss off.' Yianni's glass knocks against the bar to punctuate his words. There's no malice though, only jest.

'When will you tell your parents?' Nico then turns to me, 'Sorry, sorry, your *theía* and *theíos*? What is it?' Nico snaps his fingers as though this will help him remember.

'Aunt and uncle,' Yianni and I both reply, this time in perfect unison.

'Nico, there really isn't anything to tell yet. We aren't thinking in those terms. Let's just see what life brings our way.' I do my best to give him a sweet smile, one that might soften him up and make him relent a little about Yianni and me.

'Fine, fine. I have mutz to do in the morning. I need to help my mother. Be good. *Kalinikta*.'

We both watch as Nico struts his way out of the bifold doors that are halfway shut.

As soon as he's gone, I lean my forearms onto the bar and Yianni does the same until our faces are only inches apart.

He removes the space between us with a lingering kiss that lands on my lips with a taste of chocolate.

'Would you like to go for a walk? Condor Bar has live music tonight,' Yianni says, but stays inches away from me.

228

'Nah, I'm good, thanks. I quite like the music here.' We both grin as the most cliché Greek music quietly chimes around us, with the traditional bouzouki taking pride of place.

'We could dance here,' Yianni says. 'Practice for next week.'

'Oh damn, I'd forgotten it was a special Greek Night next week.'

'Yes, for the height of season we will have our very own dancers and set menu once every two weeks.'

'Who are the dancers?'

'Are you sure you want to know?' His dark eyebrows lift but he lowers his chin.

My head bobs enthusiastically.

'Just some kids from Natalia's school. We join in too.'

'We? Who's we?' I'm suddenly giddy at the idea of Yianni dancing.

'Me, Nico, Papa. Then Natalia and Gaia sing.'

'What?' I pull myself up straight and press my fingers over my mouth. 'You have to be kidding. How did I not know this?'

Yianni shrugs and collects our shot glasses ready for washing.

'Seriously, you dance?'

'We all dance.'

'Teach me.'

As soon as I've said the words a niggle of regret fills my belly, but it's right there next to excitement. Living in the present has to include doing new things.

He looks over the bar at me with doubt written all over his face. Looking me up and down, he considers his options. Maybe he think's I'll be too rubbish. He's probably right, if that *is* what he's thinking. His hand swipes over the bar and he goes towards the little iPod behind it, which connects to the sound system of small speakers concealed in the vines and corners of the room. He changes the track, although the music is still Greek in style.

I move back from the bar waiting for instruction. Yianni looks at me with a serious expression from under his curls. His wrist starts to curl around itself and he clicks his fingers. I'm not really sure what to expect. The only Greek dancing I've seen has been groups of people walking in a circle and crossing over their legs as they go, or men kneeling and getting back up again. That's all I remember.

This is different. The air seems to shift and part of me wants to giggle while another part feels distinctly like I'm about to fall into something I'll never be able to escape from – a perfectly made spider's web with glittering threads that I'll never want to leave.

My fingers twitch by my sides as Yianni edges towards me, then moves to stand behind me. He places his hands on my hips and begins to move them in a rolling figure of eight motion.

'Lightly step your feet to the music. On the spot.' His voice trickles down from above my ear.

I step my feet lightly like a happy cat as my hips swirl. 'Like this?' I feel mildly ridiculous and intoxicated in equal measure.

'*Nai, nai.* That's it.'

His hands run along my waist, my ribs, then along the inside of my arms to lift them away from my sides. Then he stops touching me completely. He moves like a shadow only inches from my body, slowly weaving around me, so close, but as if we are magnets that can never meet. He moves in front of me with small steps, holding his arms out and somehow encasing me within them. His chin lowers, his face is right there above mine. I look up and our eyes meet as our hips twist in perfect synchronicity, so close but still not touching. He moves lower on my body, still without touching me. He licks his lower lips and all I want is for him to kiss me. Full lips edge a millimetre closer to my face and his heat fuses with mine.

Yianni's hips stop moving and his arms drop as he leans down and presses his lips to mine. He pulls me in, almost lifting me off my feet. Then that's exactly what he does. My legs wrap around his waist as we explore each other's mouths and cling to each other. He carries me like this all the way to his room and places me on his bed on my back.

His hair's so silky my fingers get lost in the curls, while his fingers masterfully unbutton my blouse. When it's completely unbuttoned, he presses his forehead to mine and looks across me and makes a soft sound of appreciation. I'm still aware of my scars, but it's like they've become invisible to him.

I press my lips hard to Yianni's, and hold him to me with my legs, wrapping them around his buttocks. In the small space of his bed, we twist around one another until I'm straddling him, and I undo his buttons at an even faster rate than he undid mine. Sitting straight on top of him, I make the same kind of sound that he did as I admire him. He laughs and I feel it in my thighs – and that's not all I can feel there. I bite my lip as we make eye contact. Is he too good to be true? He is not perfect, no one's perfect, I'm under no illusions there. But, from his smooth golden-brown skin to his handsome face and intense eyes, to his thoughtful soul, he seems as close as anyone could possibly get. Then the imperfection of the situation floods my brain. If we take this any further, there's no going back.

'We shouldn't be doing this.' My voice is wispy like smoke, fine and almost transparent.

He either doesn't hear me or he chooses to ignore me, sitting up to meet my mouth with his. He starts to kiss my neck while he carefully peels off my blouse, and undoes the clasp of my bra. The bra falls away to the floor, discarded along with my blouse. His tongue glides along my skin and his mouth covers my nipple. A ripple of pleasure nibbles all the way through my spine down to my toes, which curl with pleasurable tension. My mind completely empties of everything that exists outside of this moment. It's just me and Yianni. One of my hands continues to coil around his hair as my other hand grips his shoulder, firm and grounding.

'Yianni, how have we gone from you being such a grumpy shit to this?' My voice is still floating and fine like smoke.

Yianni looks up and laughs before murmuring, 'I was never this *grumpy shit*. It is much more complicated than this, and you know it. You would not be with me if you thought I was only a *grumpy shit*.' His tongue cautiously teases me again, then he adds, 'Or maybe it is because I thought you were here to torment me to show me all that I wanted but could never have.' His warm mouth finds me, making me gasp. 'Until now, perhaps.' He mumbles as his mouth moves over my body.

His hands push my fitted skirt up and now it's just a belt around my hips and waist. Every muscle in his body becomes solid under my touch. In one move he manages to place me on my back again and removes the last items of my clothing and more of his. I'm completely exposed, and even with my scars, I'm more confident than I was before them. This is who I am now. This is all of me and I'm not changing for anyone but me. Sitting over me, taking me in for a moment, Yianni's face glows with a wash of red and he licks his lips as his fingers slide and dance over my thighs, my hips, my breasts; making goosebumps appear in rebellion against my body heat.

'You are perfect, you know that?' He smooths my hair off my cheek where it has stuck to my burning skin. I grab his hand and hold it to my face for a moment more and close my eyes.

Opening my eyes, I look down at the area still covered in his tight, black boxers. 'Your turn.' My fingers stretch out, but he moves away.

'What was it you said to Hazel?' He is trying to suppress his laughter. 'Two adults can share a bed...?' He lowers one eyebrow with this reminder.

I roll my eyes and momentarily cover my face at the memory of it. I expect him to take off his boxers, but he doesn't. Instead, he places his hands either side of my waist and kisses me. He kisses all of me, every inch of me. I feel his lips like a branding iron hot on my skin, burning me with the need for more until I can feel my hips gently lifting, rising to him as he takes me. Sweat springs on my skin and my chest feels like it might explode as I gasp for air. It's all I can do to stop myself from screaming his name, until I don't stop myself, and I'm just saying it over and over.

My whole body trembles and I realise I'm holding fistfuls of the bed sheets.

'Oh my god,' is all I say, and it's like I've lost my entire vocabulary.

Yianni smiles. 'Yes, you may call me Zeus now.'

'I'm going to need a moment.' I put my finger up and that's

about all I can manage.

Yianni slides his arm under me and pulls me in to hold me close. I close my eyes against his chest. When my breath finally begins to steady itself, I let my fingers travel down his body, feeling the rise and fall of each individual muscle across his stomach, and his deep groan of pleasure vibrates in my ear. My mouth finds and nibbles his earlobe, then slips down his neck, enjoying the light salty taste and the smell of his citrus aftershave warming me, as I nuzzle my face around his collarbone. I let my fingers tease him, then I manoeuvre myself down his body and devour him in his entirety. His fingers find their way into my hair, and he's swearing in Greek – I know that because Nico taught me words and phrases. I laugh a little and the vibration spurs him on.

'Wait…' There's a rasp in his voice that doesn't usually belong there, but I do as he wants, and I make my way back along his perfectly tanned body and straddle him. He reaches across to his drawer and hunts out the protection. I take it from his hand and do it for him.

We move slowly, cautiously, as though we both know that this changes everything now. We can't go back to playing a game of chess around each other. We can't pretend we don't need or want each other anymore. It's officially gone too far. We sit up together, one of his arms is around my waist and the other is behind him holding his weight. His lips begin to caress my nipple, but I take his face in my hands and run my thumbs lightly over the stubble on his cheeks. We look into one another's eyes as we breathe each other in. We consume one another slowly. I can feel every sensation, every moment is vivid as though we were designed to be together. Our lips press together, but all too soon I can't catch my breath again.

I'm not used to feeling so out of control and so easily pushed to the edge of a cliff by anyone; yet here I am ready to fall all over again. His name is on my lips and his breath is in my lungs and then together we fall. Deeply, painfully, perfectly. We fall. Over and over again, we fall.

Chapter 38

Now

If I wasn't still tingling from the night before, I would be too exhausted to function. All I've had is two hours' sleep. Yianni and I stayed awake for hours talking, before deciding to relive our passion all over again. Now I'm dressed in yesterday's clothes waiting for him to bring me back a pain au chocolat from the bakery as well as a black coffee to keep me awake for the rest of the day.

During our long discussions, we agreed that we still aren't ready to tell anyone else yet, although Yianni did point out that Nico will be impossible about the situation – which I completely agree with. We both use Nico as a sounding board, and he just loves to use what he knows to wind us up. We decided to give ourselves a couple of weeks and then we will find a way to tell everyone. Underneath it all, I feel sure about us, and I know he does too. There's something here, something real. Yianni said he felt sure about us too, enough to tell people now, but he agreed that waiting was probably the right choice because we need to figure out how to word it. Plus, I'm only here for the summer, and then what happens? There's a lot to figure out, and since my last relationship still haunts me, we are going to do our best to stay in that impossible place – the present.

My phone vibrates from his bedside. I've got it on charge there. Leaning up onto my elbow, I can see it's a message from Amara.

How's life in paradise? It's shit here. I just broke it off with Si. Don't worry. I'll still pay your rent. Call when you can. Miss you. <3

'Oh my god,' I say out loud to my phone screen. I hit the screen to call her right away.

Without bothering with *hello,* I'm asking questions. 'What happened? How're you feeling? I thought it was all going so well?'

'It was.' I can tell she's been crying. There's a wobble in her voice. It's tiny, but it's there, almost like an echo of recent pain becoming audible all over again.

'I don't know, I just got so fed up and I wasn't very well at all last week and he was barely sympathetic. He got me chocolates.' Her voice is incredulous at the idea.

'So? Isn't that a nice thing to do?'

'No,' she snaps, 'not if someone is feeling sicky. How will chocolate help with that? And dairy always makes my migraines worse.'

Jumping up, I start pacing around Yianni's small room. Two

paces then turn, two paces then turn. I must look like one of those big cats that are shut in zoos, going round and round all day.

'Sorry,' I begin. 'It's hard to gauge. It's not like I'm there to see it all and assess it all.'

'Wish you were.'

Yianni carefully opens the door and I instantly smile at him. A white plastic bag hangs from his wrist, and he has a takeaway cup in each hand. He passes me one of the cups and stoops to kiss my neck while Amara continues. She explains how she felt like she was snapping at Si every day and that he begged her to change her mind, but she was feeling much too miserable around him.

'What's the time there?' Amara cuts herself off with a question to me.

'Nine-ish, I think.'

'It's still early here. I've said I would meet the girls from work for breakfast. They wanted to cheer me up. Wish you were coming.'

'Me too.'

'No, you don't.'

I don't. I really don't. I wish Amara could appear in Corfu for me to comfort her, but if I'm being completely honest, I don't want to leave Greece any time soon.

'I do wish you were here though.'

'Me too. I best go. Call me later?'

'Of course.'

'Ciao.'

'Call me anytime. *Salut.* Bye.'

Then she's gone and it's just Yianni and me.

We chat over our breakfast, but we both know we need to

get back to the house to shower and we have to hope that we don't get quizzed when we're there.

Back at the house everything's normal. We are normal. Our past normal anyway. Other than turning up at the same time which has only happened once before. In front of Hazel and Pericles, I thank Yianni for a lovely evening – and I'm pretty sure it comes off a lot more stilted than I intended. In passing I tell them that we stayed up chatting and Yianni adds with a scowl that I ended up taking over his bed again. I have to nip my tongue with my teeth to suppress my laughter. It's like I'm a kid again. But they don't seem to notice; they're on their way out the door to do everyday chores and Natalia is already at her boyfriend's house for the morning.

No sooner are we in the door than we're alone again. The last words from Hazel were, 'See you at the restaurant.' Which will probably be in a couple of hours at least. I follow Yianni up the stairs. He turns in to my room then stops in the doorway.

'Sorry. I'm forgetting—'

'It's okay. It is technically your room.'

We edge around each other in the doorway, our bodies so close but like the wrong side of two magnets again, we make sure we don't actually touch each other. We already agreed we should be *normal* in the house. We need to get ourselves ready for work. That's all. He leaves and I close the door and go straight for the bathroom to shower.

I don't even make eye contact with myself in the mirror. My head is down and I get myself ready for the day. I need to call my mum at some point. She tried to call while I was on the bike, and now I have two missed calls from her. Steam

239

fills the room and my body drips with sweat that muddles with the water. The taste of Yianni's skin is on the tip of my tongue and his fingers searching my body for answers plays in my memory.

I *really* like him. There's no way I would do anything that might rock the boat with Hazel unless it was worth it, and I know in the pit of my stomach that Yianni is worth it. He is the first person since Jonathan that I like. I've been asked out a few times by men who seemed nice enough, but I wasn't interested in even giving them a chance. Not until Yianni. The spark there isn't something I can explain, it's just there. Burning embers that won't quit. It doesn't really matter that I didn't bloody well want to like him this way. There's no choice in the matter now. Every fibre of my body decided on it without my brain and even when my brain caught up, I just liked him more.

Dread seeps in as I lather my hair. I know I'm trying to live in the inches of now, but some questions can't be ignored, not when they're screaming at the back of my head. How will we tell Hazel, Pericles, my mum and dad – Natalia? Shit, she's going to think I'm dreadful. She adores her big brother and she's included me like a sister. My eyes clamp shut at the thought of it and I do my best to move away from that thought.

Do I want to move to Corfu? I'd miss my parents and Amara and a couple of other friends. It's mostly my parents though. Since Jonathan died, I've been talking to my mum almost every other day and seeing them at least once a week, and sometimes more. I can't see Yianni moving to England, in fact, I can't see it being possible at all.

I turn the shower off and step out to grab my towel, wrapping myself up in its fluffy white cotton threads. Stepping into my room, steam lifts off my skin. A quiet knock sounds at the door. It can only be Yianni. I hesitate, wondering whether I should try to get dressed before answering, but I'm soaking wet still. There isn't much choice but to let him in; it is his room after all.

'Come in.'

The door creaks and Yianni is standing there with one towel around his waist and one rolled-up towel around his shoulder catching the drips from his thick mop of hair. He looks me over and I'm aware how short my towel is, grazing my thighs.

'I have been thinking. Maybe we break one rule? It is only one.'

He walks into the room and stands an inch or so away from me.

'It depends which one, I suppose.' I want to touch him, but I refrain.

'The one that says I can't touch you in this house. This is my bedroom after all.'

He hooks my chin with his index finger and lifts it up towards him, pulling me into him. Our towels melt away to the floor.

'You're all wet.'

I laugh into his mouth, and he makes a little noise of acknowledgement as though he hadn't realised what he was saying when he said it.

We flop back onto the bed in our heated embrace and our flesh is sticking, fusing together, but we know we shouldn't take it further. We just enjoy each other's hands and mouths before we really *do* have to get ready for work.

Chapter 39

Now

We spend the next couple of days staying up most nights talking – and touching of course. I don't drink though; I ride my bike back to the house every night so that no one questions us. Nico sometimes passes comments and winks but never within earshot of anyone else. He's actually been tamer than I gave him credit for.

Traditional bouzouki music is blaring out of the speakers at a volume I haven't heard at Greek Secret before, and Yianni's little bedroom has a bunch of boys from Natalia and Gaia's school in there, including their boyfriends. I've only met Natalia's boyfriend a couple of times. He doesn't speak English – not to me anyway – and my Greek is mostly rude words, thanks to Nico.

Everyone's smiling and the taverna vibrates with clapping hands as the lads, all dressed in black with white sashes around the waist, exit the little side room and dance in a circle. Yianni and Nico sit out this round of side-stepping and circling. Then one boy, who I think might be Gaia's boyfriend, steps forwards to do a little solo that consists of impressive kicks and dropping to his knees a fair amount. Gaia's parents and family have booked a table and they stand up to clap until their little baby cries and has to be joggled about just outside of the restaurant.

Yianni comes to the bar to place an order for another round of drinks and I see Gaia bring out plates of food, but really, she wants to see her boyfriend's big finale. As soon as the plates of food leave her hands, she's frantically clapping him.

'When's it your turn?'

'Not long, another dance in ten minutes perhaps.' He looks at an invisible watch on his wrist then laughs at himself before giving me the slightest wink and moving back to help with the serving of food and general running of the place.

Drinks orders flow easier than the wine itself and soon the music kicks up a notch and it's Yianni, Nico and Pericles who step forwards for their turn on the floor. More stepping and stamping ensues, and Pericles even smothers the floor in lighter fluid, igniting it in front of them. I'm clapping along so hard my palms sting and my cheeks ache from giggling. Yianni glances at me a couple of times, but he's a good little performer, they all are. I guess they've been doing it long enough.

Just as they're really going for it, I hear – and feel – my phone in the back pocket of my shorts. I pull it out and glance at the screen. Amara. I hesitate over the answer button. She'll call back, she probably forgot the time difference, she's all over the place at the moment, but even if I answered her, I don't think I'd hear her over the music filling the room. As soon as the ringing stops, I place the phone back into my pocket and continue to enjoy the dancing.

When they finish, whooping and clapping from the tables takes over, but Yianni isn't taking it in, he isn't even bothered. He's pulled Nico close to whisper in his ear. Nico's forehead collapses into a frown but he bobs his head in some kind of agreement. Yianni then does the same to his dad as Nico jogs towards the bar.

'All done?' I inquire as Nico gropes for the little iPod.

He doesn't answer me, but there's a lingering smile as he hits play. I recognise the song just as he grabs my wrist.

'No, Nico, no, please,' I hiss. I try to look calm because I don't want people to know how much I don't want to be pulled forwards into the clearing they've made for the event. Nico passes me to Yianni as Pericles pulls Hazel forwards, who has basically been pushed out of the kitchen behind me by the looks of it. She delicately pushes her glasses on top of her head and tucks loose strands of hair behind her ears as she spies the people watching us.

Nico steps forwards and points to a woman not too far in front and invites her up to dance with him. She looks thrilled to get involved and they take centre stage with Yianni and me framing one side and Hazel with Pericles framing the other.

Yianni moves around me and I do my best to steady my pulse, because I can feel my hands shaking. It's impossible to hide with my arms out at the sides.

'It is just me and you,' Yianni whispers in my ear as he glances around me. I look up at him and for a moment I can almost believe him from the way he's looking at me. It's so intense. Our hips sway but we never touch, not even a graze. I'm losing myself to him and this island. Maybe this is him telling me he wants everyone to know about us? Maybe I want that too.

My phone blares out in my pocket again and I physically jump at the sensation of it vibrating. We try to continue to awkwardly dance in spite of it as Nico and his audience partner repeatedly glance in our direction until it stops. Then moments later it starts again, and this time I can't ignore it.

'I have to answer it, I'm sorry.'

I break from the bubble and let my hand glance Yianni's stubbled cheek before running off to answer the phone. I glance back to catch a glimpse of Yianni's hurt eyes watching me before he turns to merge with the people watching the sensual dancing from the others.

'Can you hear me, Amara?'

I weave my way into the kitchen for some quiet. One of the cooks who works alongside Hazel nods as I come in, but carries on with what she's doing.

Amara's sobbing. I can almost see her soaked face with hair all stuck to it through the phone call.

'Christ, Amara, what's happened?' I start to march forwards and backwards wanting to sit and concentrate but with no way to do so. My body fills up with electricity in the form of anxiety.

'I'm pregnant.' Amara's voice crackles and she sniffs then lets out a huge moaning sound into the phone. 'I don't know what to do, Ruby. I can't have a baby. I just can't. I'd be a useless mum and I don't want that. I just can't.' Then there's more words, but I can't understand them through the sound of snot and tears.

Amara isn't close to her parents. She speaks to her dad but not very often and her mum less than that. She's the type of person who has a million acquaintances and only a few real friends. Those friends are people who truly bother with her. I am the closest friend she has because I have endless calm and patience for her antics, and she stuck around even when Jonathan was slowly penning me off from my other friends. There's no way I could leave her alone to deal with this.

'Have you told Si?'

'Hell no! I've taken a test. Cried. Taken another test. Cried some more. Called you. That's it.'

My back slumps against the kitchen wall as I lean against it for support. I know what I have to do. There's no choice in the matter.

'I'll book a flight home. You won't be alone in this. I'm here for you.'

'Don't be insane. You can't come home. Hazel needs you there.'

'Don't worry about that. I think she only brought me here because of Jonathan in truth. I'll work it out.'

We talk for maybe five more minutes before we hang up. Hazel is back to working and Natalia and Gaia are in and out with trays of dessert. I can see Hazel watching me as I lower the phone and my head simultaneously.

She moves towards me and holds my upper arms.

'What's happened?'

'I have to go back to Suffolk. It's Amara. She's pregnant and she doesn't have anyone to help her… to decide what to do about it.'

Hazel's lips form a sombre line. I know she understands, it's Yianni I don't want to tell.

Natalia appears in the kitchen swinging an empty tray at her side.

'You look like you've done this dance before. You and Yianni looked good together. You should do it next time.'

I swallow the sudden urge to cry and smile instead. 'No, thank you. I was terrified. I'll leave the performing to you lot.'

I briefly squeeze her shoulder and make my way back through the staggered corridor and out towards the bar.

'You've broken Yianni,' Nico laughs, as I slip behind the bar. He glances at me then back towards the draft beer he's pouring. 'Can you do two house white?'

'Of course.' I sound like a robot and then move like one around him.

The night drags on, although hearing Natalia and Gaia sing together still manages to bring a smile to my face. Outside of that, I skulk around. Yianni catches my elbow when he can and asks whether I'm okay. I do my best to smile and tell him I'll explain later, but that's all I can manage.

The night goes from completely banging to dying off surprisingly quickly. I think the set menu and set time to turn up for the entertainment helped to bring the evening to an end earlier than usual.

As Hazel and Natalia exit the kitchen, I'm stifling a yawn and suppressing the urge to rub my eyes.

'Are you coming home now, Ruby mou?' Hazel comes all the way behind the bar and squeezes me.

'I think I'll stay for a bit.' She releases me halfway but keeps my hands.

'When do you think you'll leave?'

Her question is poorly timed as Yianni arrives next to the bar with a tray of empties just in time to clatter them down on the bar. Hazel shoots him a pained look.

'I'm not sure. I'll look at flights tonight and let you know.'

Natalia has clearly been updated by Hazel as she clings to me and whispers out from her hair, *'Kalinikta.* Make sure you come back.'

Yianni says nothing. His eyes are glass but sadly nothing like windows to the soul, because I've been blocked out and I can't see a thing.

Chapter 40

Now

Yianni sits on the floor opposite the side of the bed where I'm sitting. His back is pressing into the wall and arms resting on his knees.

'You are leaving.' His chin is still lowered but he looks up at me under his hooded eyes. They look so dark, like lumps of freshly split coal.

'Yeah. She's pregnant. Amara, I mean. She doesn't have anyone else to turn to. I'm going to go with her to the appointments.'

Yianni presses his lips together in an attempted smile – or I think that's what he was attempting – but it comes off as sad either way. I slide myself off the bed and curl up between his legs. We hold each other in silence for a moment.

'Will you come back?'
'Of course, I will.'
'Promise?'

'Promise.' It takes a lot for me to break a promise. I'm glad he made me promise, that he wants that from me. 'How about, when I'm home I tell my parents about us? That way my mum might be able to help me work out how to tell Hazel without causing too much trauma.'

His arms squeeze me that little bit tighter and a smile pushes out of my lips.

'Now this is a good idea. It almost makes me happy you are going.'

'Will you miss me?'

'Yes. I have not wanted to think about you leaving, and that was before, when it was months away.'

Yianni plants a lingering kiss on the top of my head.

'Come on, you can help me book a flight.' I wiggle free of his grasp and look up at him before reaching for my phone on the edge of the bed.

'How long will you stay?'

I shrug. I really don't know. I don't know how long she'll need me.

'You will book a return flight? *Nai?*'

'I can't. I don't know how long she'll need me.'

Yianni slowly nods his head, then leaves it bowed towards me before kissing my forehead right where my scar is.

'At least you have promised to return.'

The next day I speak to Hazel about it in more detail and she confirms what I already know, that they can manage perfectly well without me. Although she does make sure to add that my help has been very useful, ultimately she agrees that Amara needs me more, and I don't want to let her down anyway.

My flight is booked for tomorrow, but the restaurant really

is too busy for any of them to take me to the airport and risk not being back in time for the rush. I've booked a transfer with the help of San Stefanos Travel. They were so helpful and accommodating and managed to find me a way to the airport at short notice.

I need to leave early-ish in the morning and it's easier to leave from San Stefanos, and not the village where Hazel and Pericles live, which gives me the perfect excuse for one last night with Yianni. When Hazel, Pericles and Natalia say goodnight, I get a little tearful. It's been such a long time since I've lived as a little family, I know I'll miss them terribly even if I do intend to be back to help in a few weeks' time. We all embrace, and kiss cheeks and Hazel tells me to have a safe journey while she squeezes my hands then my face. She says at least six times how she feels terrible for not taking me to the airport. It's okay though, they have so much to do every minute of every single day in the summer, that I would almost be annoyed if they did ask to take me to the airport. Even Pericles squeezes me so tightly I think I might pop and Natalia demands I come back as soon as I'm able.

By the time they've gone, and Nico leaves with a hug and a kiss on the cheek, I'm willing everyone who is still drinking cocktails and wine to leave too, so that Yianni and I can be alone together. I feel bad but I can't help myself. He's even trying to skim past me and touch me without them noticing and it's making the heat of the Corfu evening even more intense. By the time the last people do wave goodbye, he is pulling the door across so quickly they're barely on the street, and it's all he can do to not pull my clothes off in the restaurant.

We are stumbling along undoing each other's buttons as

251

though this is it. As though this is the last time, and we only have minutes before everything disintegrates. He manages to undo all of my buttons first and he tugs the shirt from my shoulders and down my arms as we edge into his room, our lips still pressing together, determined not to separate. I pull at his shirt and the last button rips off completely making a tiny tinny sound as it bounces to the floor. Neither of us care. I don't even apologise.

His right hand is unclasping my bra as his left disappears into the left cup before that item of clothing joins my shirt and his button on the floor. It's not long until our mouths are everywhere. Then I pull away and step back. Then another step. For a moment he's confused. His eyebrows knit together so tightly they almost join before he sees what I'm doing. I want to take all of him in. To imprint him on my memory in this moment. His dark eyes, strong cheekbones, thick curly hair, firm muscular frame, dark tan. At first, he shifts his weight from one foot to the next, but then he decides to watch me too.

My chest heaves at the sight of him and I don't want to spend another second not pressed against him. I almost lunge at him and nearly knock him off his feet. We laugh and kiss and fall onto the bed together and spend most of the night awake, knotted together.

Chapter 41

Now

When my alarm goes off Yianni is already awake and gently stroking the scar on my abdomen.

'How long have you been awake?' I croak. He only shrugs in response.

My fists gravitate to my eyes to rub away the blur before I open them again to marvel at how handsome he is, even with almost no sleep inside him. My fingers run along his stubbled face. It's as though his beard never grows; it's always just perfectly trimmed to a millimetre or two.

Stretching over Yianni, I grab my phone and turn off the alarm that's still making a high-pitched tinkling noise next to Yianni's head.

'*Merde*! I set the wrong time! *Merde*!' I'm up and rushing about. I'd set my alarm an hour later than I meant to.

Yianni jumps up too and grabs pants and shorts. 'How long before they are here?'

'Twenty minutes maybe? Shit.'

There's no time to think. I just grab the day's clothes and sprint towards the loos. I hear Yianni call after me, but I don't catch what he says. Then he repeats it, shouting it towards me.

'I'll go get you breakfast. You must eat.'

Then he's gone and I'm already halfway to ready.

Six minutes later and I'm washed, dressed and I've dragged my suitcases out towards the car park. I'm sitting on a bar stool doing my makeup waiting for Yianni's return. I hear tugging on the unlocked door.

'Don't rush off like that again, Yianni. I missed you.'

When there's no reply, I look up from my compact to see the silhouette of a girl standing in the doorway. Her head is tilted and she seems to be watching me.

'Oh, *kalimera*. Can I help you?'

'You mutz be... Rubay? Cousin? Err, is Yianni?' She flicks her heavy, black hair over her shoulder as her eyes dart past me. It's not even nine in the morning, but she's perfectly put together in silver pumps and a short but very baggy black dress. She walks towards me and smiles. Her accent is very strong and her English is slow but understandable.

'Yes, I'm Ruby. Hazel's niece.' I do my best to keep my words a little slower than normal. Her eyes narrow and she tilts her head again searching for understanding. I reword my meaning and tap my hand on my chest, 'I'm Natalia's cousin.'

'*Nai, Nai*, Natalia and Yianni cousin.'

I physically recoil when she says I'm Yianni's cousin, and I have to correct her immediately.

'Natalia's cousin.'

She smiles and says, 'Daphne', and touches her chest.

There's a pause and I feel the need to fill it. I'm not usually sucked into feeling awkward in a pause, but her eyes are almost unblinking as she comes to stand next to me at the bar.

'So, Daphne, why are you here so early?'

'I am early. *Nai*. Yes. Mutz of the time. Today, I have the, the good news for Yianni.' She leans in and lowers her voice. 'I am having baby.' A wide grin shows a mouthful of small gapped teeth. 'Yianni baby. He will be very please. Very happy.'

Behind her head, I can see my car pulling up. My entire mouth is dry and I have no words. That's when it hits me. I recognise her. She was here early once before. I saw her being let out by Yianni on my first morning here.

'Yianni baby?' I repeat, and point at her stomach.

'*Nai*, yes. I tell Yianni about *my* Yianni baby.'

'So,' I stutter over my words as my tongue feels twice its normal size, 'Yianni is going to be a dad, a papa?'

'*Nai*, my Yianni. My Yianni baby.'

While I'm scooping up my makeup, I manage to say congratulations, because what else do you say when someone says they're pregnant with the man you love's child? Shit. I love him. I hadn't wanted to admit that to myself, but as I'm walking past the girl and dragging bags to the car and greeting the driver, I know that's how I feel. As I slip into the car, I'm sure I hear Yianni call my name. It doesn't stop me. The car door slams behind me and the vehicle pulls slowly away out of the dusty car park. My eyes start to sting, but I hold it together, because if there is one thing I'm good at, it's keeping everything locked up inside.

It's only when I get halfway to the airport that I realise I've left my phone in Yianni's bedroom. There's nothing I can do about it now. Luckily Hazel printed out my boarding pass because she doesn't *trust all these apps*. I'd laughed at her, but now I'm grateful for her organisation. I was due an upgrade on my phone anyway and it'll still be there when I return. A stab of pain nearly splits me open from my belly button to my teeth. I promised I would go back, but what would I be going back to? No wonder he so happily agreed that no one should know about us. He hadn't wanted anyone to know about us. Our strange family entanglement made it easy to cheat on his girlfriend – or whoever she is. I'm such an idiot. I swallow it back. Maybe I'm wrong. Maybe I've somehow got it all wrong. I don't usually let myself be vulnerable and rash, but asking questions is hard too. It's easier to put up the wall of silence. This time though, I'll ask Hazel. I shouldn't have run off. I should have spoken to Yianni. It's too late for that now and I have to know what's really going on. But for now, I'll have to wait until I can use Mum or Dad's phone.

The flight gets delayed by two hours and my luggage is the last off the belt. By the time I round the doors at Gatwick, my nails have never been shorter and my hair is a tangled mess from constantly pushing it off my face.

When my eyes meet Mum and Dad, they look elated and concerned in equal measure. Instead of hello, my dad's first words are, 'Bad flight?'

'Something like that. I left my phone in Corfu.'

'Don't worry about that now,' Mum coos. 'You're here safe and sound and I've missed you terribly.'

'Not just your mum, me too,' Dad adds, as he kisses the top of my head. Mum then squeezes me until I can feel my cheeks flushing red.

We chat as we walk to the car, but my mind isn't listening. The words are going in my ears and other words are coming out my mouth, but my brain isn't engaged. I'm wondering at what point I can borrow a phone and call Hazel. I wait until we are settled into the car to bring it up.

'Can I borrow your phone to call Aunt Hazel and tell her I'm here? With the delay she'll probably be worrying.'

'Of course.' Mum digs in her fat pink handbag for what feels like twenty years as the car's air conditioning cools off my sweaty nerves. 'Here.'

She passes the phone to me over her shoulder and I scroll the names to find Hazel. As soon as the phone presses to my ear, acid burns at my insides and I remember I still haven't had anything to eat all day.

'Fern? Is everything alright with Ruby? Yianni says she left her phone behind.'

'It's me, I'm fine. The flight was delayed, but I'm in the car with Mum and Dad. I just wanted to let you know I'm safe.'

'Oh, thank goodness. Thank you for letting me know.'

'That's alright.' I hesitate as I try to formulate a way of asking this naturally. 'I heard about Daphne's baby. Please say another congratulations for me, won't you?'

'Well, good news really does travel fast! How did you know? Oh, I suppose you were here this morning. We couldn't be more pleased for them.'

'What did Yianni say?'

'Oh, he was thrilled. How could he not be? He adores Daphne. We all do. She and Yianni are such a beautiful couple too. Have you seen them together?'

'No, no I haven't.' My voice is a shadow.

'Sorry, Ruby, I've got to go. I'll make sure to pass on good wishes. Natalia's got a big dinner order for me. Love you, sweetheart. Bye.'

'Love you too.'

I hang up.

I pass the phone to my mum.

I bite my cheeks hard enough to taste metal to stop the tears from welling in my eyes and the lump swelling inside me, making it hard to breathe. Only my lump isn't a child, it's the death of another relationship.

Chapter 42

Now

All I've done is think about Yianni for the past week. Mostly with flaming anger burning me. There's no stalking him on socials, he's not on there. I don't like to ask Hazel more questions about him, unless I can come up with a legitimate reason, which I haven't. I'm meant to book a flight and head back to Corfu once Amara has had her abortion.

So far, I've been to an appointment with Amara. It's early enough to take a few pills and that will be enough. It seems such a simple way to put out a life. They make it sound so easy, but Amara keeps reading horror stories about how much it can hurt some people. She's booked in with Colchester Hospital to collect what she needs in five days' time. Currently, I'm doing my best impersonation of a broken record.

'Please talk to Si.' We are in our pyjamas eating our way

through a tub of chocolate and caramel ice cream... each.

Amara's shaking her head even as her spoon makes its way back in her mouth.

'I've told you. No point.'

'Can I tell him?'

'No!' Her spoon slaps down on her tub and the scowl is convincing enough to make me think that if I'm not careful, I'll be the next one to be hit by her spoon. 'Can't we both just admit that poorly timed babies have ruined our lives and then move on?'

'Actually, it could have saved me from making a big mistake. Now at least I know who he is.' I stare into my half-empty tub and mutter, 'Even if I still can't damn well believe it.'

Digging out another chunk of gooey caramel from the ice cream tub, I shovel it into my mouth. The sugar helps to soothe my mind at least in the moment. It's a bit like putting a plaster on a bullet wound though.

'Si texted me yesterday. Begging to come back. Saying he still doesn't know why I pushed him away.'

'Poor guy.'

'Poor guy? He knocked me up.' Her spoon is waving about again and I can't help but flinch.

'And he doesn't even know it! It's completely unfair. You only ditched him because you're a hormonal mess. You might regret this forever and you can't undo it. Please at least meet up with him, even if you're not going to tell him about the baby. You might realise that you still want him. You were bloody brilliant together. Don't just bin it because you accidently got pregnant. How did you feel about him before all this?'

Amara sucks on her spoon while staring into space. Her hair is so long and wild it's like a crazy blanket when it's loose.

It's pretty much waist-length frizz that she sometimes hides behind. Not in an afraid sort of way, more to intimidate people who can't figure her out.

'I accept. I'll text him and say we can meet up. Tomorrow after the lunch rush. Why don't you pop into work with me tomorrow too? Everyone has been asking about you and how you got on in Corfu. Oh, just so you know, I lied and said you were back because your nan had a health scare.'

'My nan's dead.'

'That's quite the health scare. I also meant to tell you, Rob was in yesterday asking after you.'

'Rob?'

'Rob Murray, who introduced us.'

'I thought he was in France?'

'He is. He's on holiday in sunny Suffolk and he thought you still worked at ours. He said he would be in at lunch tomorrow and to tell you to come and say hi.'

'Well, I suppose I did say to Charles I'd come back in for coq au vin at some point. Might as well be tomorrow. It's not like my diary is full, is it? Unless you count moping about the house being pissed off at Yianni and how I'm such an idiot.'

'I don't count that.'

'I guess I'm heading back to the restaurant then.'

Nothing has changed. I'm not really sure why I thought it might have in the past few months since I'd last been in. Maybe it's because I've changed. After opening up to Yianni about everything with Jonathan, it's as though I'm free to live again. As though he helped me to rip away the last shackles of Jonathan's death that held me trapped like a mammoth in tar. If only he hadn't then shat all over me, the world would be a much better place. As it is, it's a rainy August day in the heart of Ipswich, and the town has never looked more grey. I've been and bought myself a book from the local bookshop and now I'm reading it while I wait for my hearty lunch. It's good to keep my hands busy. My new phone arrived this morning and I so want to text Hazel and ask for Yianni's number, but I can't think of a reason to ask for it without sounding shady. From her point of view, I was closer to Nico and just used Yianni's room to stay in when I'd had a drink a handful of times. Plus, if I message, she'll ask when I'm coming back. I could ask Nico for the number, but I already know I don't want to hear his thoughts on the matter. What would Yianni be able to say to make me feel any better anyway? Sorry, it was an accident? I'm being ridiculous.

My mind is running along the same old stuff when Rob pulls out the chair opposite mine and floats down into it.

'Long time no see, *ma chérie.*'

My eyes flick up from my book. When he pulled the chair out my heart had fluttered at the screeching sound, but I didn't want him to know his bold entrance had made me flinch because I know him well enough to know that's exactly what he wants.

'Sad but true.' I slam my book shut and sit back in my chair. 'Have you had your lips done?'

He angles his face from left to right. 'You like them? I just gave them a photo of you to work from.'

'Then they're perfect.' For a moment we pout at each other before breaking into giggles.

'How's Rouen?' I say as I shimmy off the fine cotton blouse I have on over my crop top. It might still be drizzling outside, but inside the restaurant it's starting to remember it's still

August.

'Well, that's why I came in to find you actually.' I lower one of my eyebrows in response and almost cut in with a question, but he continues before I can. 'I heard you were working here, but it seems my information is a little past tense, but that's good for me and bad for Charley-boy.'

I shudder as I can almost hear Jonathan in the back of my head calling him Charley-boy in the same tone as Rob.

If I could press my eyebrow further down I would, because now I'm really confused.

'I need a good maître d' in Rouen. I've gone through two girls and one guy in the past six months and they've all been useless. It's a busy position all year round and we need someone who can keep everything running smoothly. I know you're meant to be in Corfu with your aunt, Amara told me the whole thing, but would you—?'

'I'm in.'

Chapter 43

Now

Hazel understood I couldn't give up this wonderful opportunity to work with Rob. In fact, when I spoke to her, she sounded like she could burst. She squealed and told everyone then and there while she was on the phone. Natalia had snatched it off her to congratulate me herself and to tell me how sad she was that I wouldn't be back right away. Yianni was there too. I had to ask who was in earshot. He didn't snatch the phone. He didn't say anything that I knew of, other than Hazel saying *everyone says congratulations.*

Amara spoke to Si and ended up telling him everything about the baby. He wanted to keep it and proposed to her then and there. I've never seen anyone cry so much while trying to tell me a story. She was completely conflicted, but I knew that underneath it all she wanted the baby. She says she would be a bad mother, because she had dreadful parents, but her grandparents on her dad's side were always wonderful. I told her to just do what she wanted. It's her body. Even the fact she needed me with her so badly told me she wasn't clear about her choice. She isn't normally one to cry and ask for help. Amara's always travelled from place to place knowing what she wanted or letting the world guide her. This felt different. It was the day of the abortion and she went with Si to the clinic in the end. When she came home, I had a massive box of chocolates and extra ice cream ready for her, but she couldn't do it. She decided to keep the baby and they've asked me to be a godparent – unofficially though as neither of them is religious. Of course, I said yes. They're back to living in my house and I'm renting a room in an apartment in Rouen. I was lucky that Rob had a friend who wanted to let the room. So, here I am in a little white box room riddled with beautiful dark wooden beams, and furniture that rests at all angles on uneven floorboards. I'm often on my own too, as my flatmate, Pierre, is almost always away for work.

The building itself is beautiful. Although the front looks modern, it hides what I assume is the original entrance. The tiny walkway makes me think of a tunnel into history. It even smells musty and old, but how I imagine it smelt when it was new too, as though the smell is caught in a capsule along with the thick beams and peeling paint. It feels like a place where I can go back in time, long before my time. Long before I caused myself misery by being a poor picker of men.

I've heard nothing from Yianni and I don't ask about him when I speak to Hazel. We don't talk that often anyway. Maybe we message once a month to check all is well in the world. I often catch myself wondering how far along the girl, Daphne, is. As Yianni didn't know yet and therefore hadn't seen a change in her body, it must have been early. Maybe as far along as Amara.

I settle into my job, get to know Rob's fiancé Hugo, try to make friends in the city, which is almost impossible, particularly when working most nights. When I'm not working, I walk. Rouen is a beautiful city, one of my favourites. It's filled with narrow streets and crooked buildings. Being on my feet and working is what I need. It stops me dwelling on my situation too much. I follow Nico on socials and we have spoken via message a little bit, here and there, but we never mention Yianni. It's like our relationship never happened, as though it was just a dream. I saw a photo of the two of them out at one of the clubs. Dark with piercing lights refracting here and there. Their eyes were creased in the corners and both had their mouths opened in laughter. I could almost hear the two of them. I didn't go on social media for a week after that.

And now, instead of staring into the impossible line that is the curve of the earth, and seeing it as the elusive present, I lie in bed in the morning and stare at the point where my white wall meets my white ceiling. It really isn't the same as having warm, wet sand cocooning my toes and the breeze moving through my hair as the sun drenches my soul and tans my skin. I don't always wear foundation now. My freckles are getting a well-deserved airing. So far, no one has asked about my scar.

One of the deals I made with Rob before agreeing to work in Rouen was that when I needed to, I could visit Amara when she had her baby. I wanted at least a month off to be in England. He accepted my terms, partly because what other choice did he have? I'm an asset he wanted. I can train up a junior, and I'm bilingual even though I play it down. Amara's baby shower is tomorrow, and she is due in two weeks' time. Today the deal begins, and I'm travelling back to the UK after living in Rouen for seven months.

I didn't bother bringing a car with me to France. As with most cities, there's nowhere to park and nowhere I couldn't get to easily on the metro. Which now means I'm hauling about a massive suitcase on public transport to get to Paris to get my Eurostar train back to England where my dad is picking me up. Although I saw my parents over Christmas, it feels like forever since we've all been together. They have visited me on two separate weekends, but it's been brief and I've still had to work. I can't wait to be back with them both for a full month.

The journey seems to take forever, even though everything runs perfectly on time and the trains are much faster than I'm used to back home. When I'm finally in England, and I see my dad's face glowing over his waving hands, I nearly burst into tears. He scoops me up like he did when I was a child, and everything about him is a comfort. The smell of clean laundry and his daily cigarette makes me grin. We kiss cheeks and chat away in French. Mum had an appointment, apparently, so Dad came on his own to get me. It's natural to talk to him in French, especially after living there for the first time in my life.

On the journey back to Suffolk, I catch him up on all restaurant-related items, and he tells me about his work and about how much he and Mum have been missing me and how much Mum is looking forward to me staying at their house for a change. Everything feels exciting and settled all at once. Maybe I'm actually starting to let go of the idea of Yianni.

That is until I remember that Yianni's baby is probably due about now too, and that thought rolls around my head until I feel queasy.

When we do arrive home, Mum's at the door. I think she must be psychic, but she's probably been tracking our every move on her phone. She totters along the drive in her slippers and opens my door before the engine has a chance to cut out.

'Ruby!'

I step into her arms.

'I'm so happy you're home. I've made a special lunch, all English things that I'm sure you'll have missed. It's an afternoon tea, with finger sandwiches and mini pork pies and even cream cakes.'

'Sounds great, Mum.' She's leading me indoors by my elbow and I can hear the low laughter of my dad behind us as he gets my suitcase out of the boot.

I've barely managed to go for a wee and step out of the loo when Mum is bringing me to sit at the oval table in the dining room. It's been laid with a white linen cloth and adorned with sachets of tea, a silver tower packed with savoury treats and another one lined with cakes.

'Blimey Mum, how many people are coming for lunch?'

A grin spreads across her face and she looks like an over inflated pink balloon as she puts her index finger up and disappears from the room. Dad comes back down the stairs from putting my bags in my old bedroom. I crinkle my face in confusion and shrug.

'Indulge her.' He smiles as he goes through the dining room and into the kitchen.

'Surprise!'

Chapter 44

Now

Voices echo as Mum, Hazel and Natalia jump in the doorway. I physically jump even though their punch of noise didn't surprise me in itself. I jumped when I saw them jump around into the doorway. All the memories of last year catch in my throat and create a rock, stopping words from passing my lips. They don't notice though. They grab me and kiss me. Hazel strokes my hair, and tells me I look good, and France must have treated me well, while Natalia hops from foot to foot completely giddy.

Eventually I manage words, but they're probably not very well fitted. 'How are you here?' My voice is so thin it sounds like my grandmother just before she died. 'Isn't it Easter in a couple of days?'

My head swings to my mum and dad then back to Hazel who's laughing.

'Oh yes, we might love you, but we won't be missing a Greek

Easter. It's later there than here, so we will be back in time for it. When your mum said you would be here for Amara's baby and Easter, we booked to be here at the same time. It's only for a week then we have to get back to prepare for our Easter. We just missed you.'

She pulls me in and it's almost like I can smell Corfu on her skin, because her clothes smell like her house and like Yianni's clothes. It feels suffocating. So much time has passed, seven months of it – the best part of a year – but the smell of Hazel takes me back and everything is as raw as ever. There's part of me that wants to tell them all exactly what happened with Yianni, to get him in trouble for breaking my heart and for having a baby and a life with someone else. He was leading me on. Do they know he's like that? An utter shit to women? Seemingly thoughtful and lovely but with one plan in his mind? No one warned me away from him the way he warned Nico away from me. I suppose they thought we would act as cousins, and we didn't because we aren't and because I didn't mean to, but I fell in love with the lying shitbag.

We seat ourselves at the table. Hazel and Mum are almost talking over each other, layering the room with sound, telling me how they planned it all and how Hazel and Natalia had only arrived a matter of hours before me. I nod along under a peaceful façade and wonder when they'll tell me about Yianni and his baby. Or that the baby is due any day now. Something. Anything. We make it all the way through the sandwiches, without so much as mentioning his name. I only manage to eat one cucumber finger sandwich and half a mini pork pie when Mum quizzes me.

'Why aren't you eating?' She looks hurt, so I quickly snatch up one of the last salmon and cream cheese sandwiches near to me and put it on my plate.

'I am. I'm just saving myself for those cream cakes.'

This brings the glow back into her cheeks.

'Well, I'm sure it won't be as good as anything from the patisseries near you in Rouen, but I did my best.' She smooths her hands along the tablecloth as though removing an invisible wrinkle.

'It's all lovely, Mum.'

'Thank you, sweet pea.'

Hazel cuts in and changes the subject. 'Are you looking forward to the baby shower tomorrow?'

I rapidly bob my head as I fill my mouth with smoked salmon with a hint of lemon and cream cheese. This forced pause gives me the moment of clarity I need to align myself, and perhaps get some answers. I swallow.

'I really am. And how's Yianni? And his baby?'

Hazel tilts her head towards her shoulder in question, 'Oh you mean Yianni and Daphne? Yes, well, I think. They had the baby last week actually. It's a little girl. Natalia, what's her name again? I haven't seen her yet, but Natalia has.'

'Zoe.'

'You haven't seen Yianni's baby yet?'

'No dreadful I know. I was getting ready for coming here and I just haven't had a chance. I must pop round when we're back. That's an idea, maybe we could get them a little something for the baby while we're here? Something English-y?.' Hazel looks completely blasé about it.

'What? You haven't, but Natalia has?'

'Yeah, Daphne came in early, and I wasn't there. Why?'

'I'm sorry, I'm confused.' My temples throb as I collect my thoughts. 'Why haven't you gone to see the baby? Surely

Pericles is excited to be a grandfather?'

The room becomes a vacuum. No noise is permitted, the vacuum sucks up all thoughts and feelings and only leaves confusion. In a cartoon this is where a cricket noise would follow, but for a moment it's like everyone's completely frozen. That is until I hear the thud at the front door of post being delivered.

Hazel crosses her arms over her chest, and says, 'What?'

I notice that Natalia still hasn't closed her mouth yet and her eyes are almost crossed in confusion. I glance from one person to the next and it's as though I've shrunk under the pressure of the looks that are being bestowed on me. My whole face feels like it's back in the burning sun of Corfu and I've burnt to a crisp in minutes.

'Yianni's girlfriend had a baby. Surely Pericles at least would be excited, and you would go with him? I'm so confused.' I bite my lip waiting for answers, but I have a dreadful feeling I know what's coming next.

Hazel laughs. Natalia laughs. My mum is smiling but looks pretty confused too and my dad picks up a cream cake and takes a mouthful while he watches my life unravel.

'Daphne is Maria's daughter. You've met Maria many times.'

I had. She is the cleaner at Greek Secret, an older woman who speaks almost no English at all. She would smile at me and wave if she saw me. She was in five nights a week to empty the bins in the loos and clean the kitchen and such. I didn't know she had a daughter.

'Daphne's husband is called Yianni. She comes in two mornings a week to give her mum two nights off. So, when she told you she was pregnant you thought—?'

'I thought it was Yianni's baby. She said it was Yianni's

baby.' My words are whispered and although I'm finishing Hazel's sentence my eyes aren't focused on her, or anyone, or anything. For seven months I've let myself believe that he was a cheating shit and in reality he had done nothing wrong.

My mouth is completely dry, and my insides feel hollow. As the laughter dies out around me something touches my hand. My eyes snap down to where it sits on the table and it's my dad's fingers that are lightly resting over mine.

'Ruby? What's wrong? It was a misunderstanding, nothing to fret about. *Tu peut m'en parler.*' *You can talk to me.* He can read me well enough to know I'm hiding something and by going into French, a language my mum can only speak in basic terms and no one else speaks at all, he hopes to help me. It's what we've always done. When I was at a party and I felt unsafe or I wanted to leave early we would chat in French.

I try to swallow to gain some traction for words, but no one is laughing anymore.

'*J'ai fait une grosse erreur. Je suis tellement conne.*' I don't want to say more than that I've made a mistake and that I'm a goddamn idiot. I can't say more. Even that felt like it was ripped out like a thorn.

'I understood that.' My mum's eyes narrow to mine. Damn her for also knowing all the swear words. 'Honey, you're really pale. Do you need to have a lie-down? It was only a silly mistake.' My mum pulls her glasses off the top of her head and looks at me through them, inspecting me for some previously unseen issue that only glasses could uncover. She's so similar to Hazel it's uncanny at times.

I want to tell them all the truth, but how can I? I have no idea if Yianni has moved on. He must hate me. I promised him I would come back and as far as he knows I took a job in France and forgot about him. He doesn't even know why. Vomit threatens to emerge unpredictably.

'I'm fine. I just feel like an idiot, that's all.'

'Don't be silly.' Hazel flaps a hand in my direction. 'I can't wait to tell Yianni and Pericles this. They'll think it's so funny. We never know when Yianni has girlfriends, not since he was at uni with that dreadful girl. I only met her once, but I didn't take to her at all. Since then, we never hear about anyone. I thought he had someone last year. He seemed to be chirpier. Did he tell you he had a girlfriend? Is that why you thought it was his baby?'

I don't want to lie. I want to hold onto something because even sitting down I feel off-kilter. Instead, I do my best to pull myself straighter in my chair. It's time to be honest.

'Yeah. He had a girlfriend. I just don't think he was ready to tell anyone about her.'

Natalia rolls her eyes. 'He always wants to be mysterious. I do not know why he thinks he is so interesting.'

Her reaction snaps me out of my pain momentarily and a smile comes to my lips.

'Did you meet her?' Hazel leans forwards in her chair.

'I really don't want to say. It's—' I nearly say it's not my place but that would be a lie. It is my place. I am the girl in question. 'I think it should be left up to him to decide what he tells you.'

'You're a good friend, Ruby.' Hazel looks truly appreciative of this, and it makes me want to leave the room in some kind of shameful stupor. I don't enjoy manipulating the truth, but I hate lying even more.

'Speaking of Yianni, he gave your phone to Natalia.' Hazel turns to Natalia as my mum points to the cakes, physically interrupting the conversation instead of doing so verbally. Dad's hand leaves mine to take a second cake, and I can feel the heat of her scowl on him, but she lightens as Natalia takes one. I'd forgotten his hand was even there, supporting me silently.

'You have it with you, don't you?' Hazel continues.

Natalia hovers the cake next to her mouth, debating whether to bite or answer. 'It's in my bag upstairs. Do you want me to get it now?'

Yes, of course, I want to say, but I remain silent. Natalia starts to put her cake back on her plate as though she is going to go now and my palms begin to sweat.

'No. I have a new phone now anyway. It's not important this minute. Thanks for bringing it with you though. You enjoy the cake.'

'We know you've got a new one, how else would we have messaged you in France,' Hazel smiles as she studies me under her glasses, 'but it's yours still. You might want to sell it.'

'Natalia, did you want to keep it? The phone I mean? It's newer than the one you've got, and I've got no need for it now.'

'Seriously?'

'Sure. I don't need it anymore and I don't need the money. I'd rather you had it.'

Natalia beams, 'Thank you, Ruby.'

Hazel touches my arm and adds to Natalia's sentiments, 'That's very kind of you.'

'Honestly, it's nothing. I wish I'd thought of it sooner then you could've had it months ago. Let me look over to make sure I've got everything off it, then you can have it when I'm done.'

I am desperate to get my hands on that phone and to see if Yianni has somehow left his imprint on it. It's unlikely, I know. But while we all chat over the cakes all I want to do is get my old phone out of Natalia's bag and scroll through it.

Chapter 45

Now

It was just before going to bed that I got my phone back from Natalia. Now I'm charging it and waiting for it to turn on. As the screen comes alive my heart flutters. It takes it a moment to sort itself out and then I see seven missed calls and a voicemail.

Three missed calls are from Yianni, and the rest are from Hazel or my mum. All from last year. I pull a deep breath into my lungs and hiss it out my teeth before clicking to listen to the voicemail. I can't believe I'm shaking as I lift the phone to my ear.

Before I hear any words, there's the sound of Yianni's feet hitting the ground and heavy breathing. I recognise that heavy breathing, intimate in my ear. Goosebumps wave along my legs. Then his voice is there and it's like it never left me. As though his voice has been floating around my soul since the moment we met, wrapping itself around me until his fibres became a part of my own, and even moving to a new country and starting again wasn't enough to escape the mark he's left on me.

Ruby, what are you doing? Why did you go like this? I... Call me back, please.

Based on the sounds in the background, he left the message after he called out my name as I got in the car to take me to the airport.

Once, when I was a child, I got stung by a jelly fish. Right now, I feel like my entire body is wrapped in jelly fish tendrils and the venom is burning my skin. Tears stream down my cheeks and I silently let my body flatten onto my bed to try to suppress any sound.

I don't feel like I can talk to anyone. That's not true. I can talk to Amara about it, but it's her baby shower tomorrow and I don't want to monopolise it with tales of my stupidity. I should message him now. Better to message than call. That way if he does reject me, I only have to read it. I start writing out a message:

Yianni, sorry I left in such a hurry and didn't contact you I thought

DELETE

I've just found out I made a massive mistake I thought you had got Daphne pregnant... Crazy right? Please forgive me

DELETE

Yianni, I'm so sorry. Can I see you?

DELETE

Then I delete another ten or more messages and everything I write sounds ridiculous, because it is. If I had spoken to him, and not Hazel, this might not have happened. I remind myself I didn't have his number, so how could I? But my brain seems to be stuck on a roundabout and nothing I can think of could have made me realise my error any sooner than this. Eventually, I try to sleep but it doesn't come easily, and when it does, all I hear is Yianni's voice calling my name.

Chapter 46

Now

I feel bad that I have done absolutely nothing to organise Amara's baby shower apart from bringing pin the dummy on the baby. That's it. There's about a dozen or so of us and a room has been hired in an old pub full of beams and uneven walls. It reminds me of my flat in Rouen, only much bigger. There would have been more of us, but as most of our friends work in the same industry, mealtimes together tend to be harder to coordinate. It's impressive that this many people have managed to make it.

Mum, Aunt Hazel and Natalia have come along. Amara had already known more than a month before that Hazel and Natalia were going to make a surprise visit. I manage to switch chairs with one of the other girls after the meal to be next to Amara for a bit, as previously I was sitting next to my mum at the other end of the long wooden table.

'Are you enjoying celebrating?' I say as I take my seat.

'It's dinner followed by as much cake as I can eat – what do you think?' Amara pushes back her dark, unruly mane then her hands come to rest on the roundness of her stomach.

I gaze at her full belly for a moment, thinking how close that little baby nearly came to not being here at all.

'Stop thinking,' Amara says.

My eyes switch back towards her mouth and I see her round lips are pulled tightly together. 'Sorry. I'm just really pleased you didn't let your past hold you back.'

'And I will always be grateful that you literally forced me to see Si.' Her eyes gravitate to the emerald engagement ring adorning her left hand.

'That ring is so you.'

'Yep.' She can't help but smile. 'Now Little Miss Face of Anxiety, what's going on with you? It can't just be the worry of people not pinning the dummy in the correct place on the baby. You've been fidgety. Why?'

'Bloody hell, Amara, not much gets past you.' Just the word fidget makes me want to rock a little in my chair and adjust my miniskirt, but I'm afraid if I do, she'll soon lift an eyebrow at me or purse her lips. I stay as still as possible as we talk, restraining from even using my hands to emphasise words.

'I'm fine. We can talk about it tomorrow. This is your day, and I don't want to ruin it.'

'Ruin it?' She attempts to lean into me, but her belly is sticking out a bit too far, so she settles on jutting her chin a little in my direction.

I shouldn't have used the word *ruin*. 'That's more dramatic than I intended. I just mean... I don't want to monopolise your day talking rubbish about my life. Honestly, everything is fine.'

'Why do people always say honestly when they're lying?'

'I'm not lying! Bloody cheek.'

She doesn't return with a rebuttal. She doesn't need to. Her face says she doesn't believe me. Her hands say it, her body says it. Every fibre of her is telling me *yeah, whatever,* and it's highly frustrating.

I hold my position, but in the end, she holds hers better and I break with a sigh, letting my body crumple back into the tough wooden chair. It does have padding, but they might as well not have bothered.

In a low monotone voice, and as quickly as I can say it, I update her. 'I am fine. But it turns out Yianni *didn't* have a baby. Annoyingly, Yianni is one of the most popular Greek names and everyone was talking about a different Yianni. I'm a fucking idiot.'

'What?' Amara almost shouts and the room – previously filled with the clinking of plates and the chatter of voices – completely freezes. People are stockstill mid-sentence and with drinks halfway to their mouths. My mum gives me a quizzical look and Hazel looks concerned under her glasses. 'Sorry,' Amara says, 'please carry on.' She puts on her work smile and the mildly sarcastic tone she usually reserves for Charles when he's being a pain. Slowly everyone in the room continues with what they were doing, but Mum and Hazel's eyes linger on me. I mouth *don't worry* at them, with a laugh on my cheeks, and in perfect unison they nod, then pull their lips into a faux smile and in that moment they look like bookends with Natalia sandwiched in the middle.

Amara glances about the room once more at people eating cake, and seeing that everyone has got settled again, she shuffles her chair closer to mine and says in a hushed tone,

'What did you say?'

'Yeah. No baby. The cleaner's daughter's husband is called Yianni. It's their baby. A girl apparently. She and *Yianni*-Yianni, *my* Yianni...' Why did I have to call him my Yianni? That's a painful wording. 'They're friends. But, yeah. No baby. Well, not one that's his anyway.'

'So why the hell are you here?'

'Because it's your baby shower.'

'So? When we used to chat on the phone when you were with Yianni in Corfu, I have never heard so much light in your voice. You were so happy. Happier than you ever were with Jonathan. Is it okay to say that? He was a good guy, but if I'm being completely honest, I didn't see you being with him forever.'

This is it. The opening to be honest with someone else. Someone I know and who also knew Jonathan. I can feel the lump of my heart beating in my throat and the sadness that makes my fingertips tingle.

'Ruby, you've gone really pale. Eat some cake.' Amara goes to reach across me for more cake, but I catch her hand.

'I broke up with him.'

'Yianni?'

'No. Jonathan. I broke up with him, and he grabbed the wheel and pulled the car off the road.' I have to keep my mouth open to breathe or I might not be able to take in enough air to survive telling her this. 'I'm so sorry, telling you this now. Let's talk about it tomorrow. Just enjoy the baby shower. I shouldn't have said anything.'

'Yes, you should.' She's almost growling at me. 'Okay, maybe you should have said, I don't know, maybe two years ago. But we all know your secrets are as easy to find as lost pirate treasure at the bottom of the sea. The fact this has floated to the surface is damn astonishing. Does your mum know this?'

I shake my head and lower my chin so my fringe covers my eyes enough for people not to see them beginning to fill with tears. Why in the hell did I tell her now? But if I hadn't said it now, I probably never would have. Slowly I take in a few deep breaths to steady myself and I look at my right hand, bare, without Jonathan's ring there to remind me of what I caused every day.

'You need to tell her.'

'I told Yianni.'

'You told Yianni?' Amara almost spits at me. I can't help but laugh a little. This brings some brightness to her cheeks too. 'Wow. If he managed to crack your shell *that* much, you can't give up on him, Rubes.'

'I'm not interrupting, am I?' It's Samantha, a waitress from Charles's restaurant, who helped to organise the event. 'I think it's time to play the last game.'

'Yes, great,' Amara says. Then she turns back to me and whispers. 'Not for you though. No more games for you. It's time to face the truth.'

I tell my mum. I tell her everything. What happened with Jonathan. What happened with Yianni. It's past midnight when I'm done telling her, because I had to wait for Hazel and Natalia to go to bed and then I had to sneak to my parents' door, quietly knock and ask her to chat with me in the dining room, because it's the least likely place for anyone to hear us talk.

She has spent half the time leaning forward to put her arm around me and the other half with her hand covering her mouth. Now she has deep lines accumulating on her forehead and around her pursed lips. Finally, she says, 'So what now? Do you want to see if Yianni still likes you?'

'I think so. But I don't want to hurt Hazel or Pericles or Natalia. And I might have hurt him too much. I just left, Mum. And he has no idea why. Well, he might now if Hazel had a good laugh with Pericles about it.' A moan bursts out of me as my head falls onto my folded arms on the dining room table. 'I've ruined the best thing that ever bloody well happened to me. *Merde, Merde, merde!*'

'Please don't talk like that.' Her fingers lightly tap my arm. I twist my face to look at her, but keep my tired head resting on my arms before I let loose a wild yawn. 'Telling the truth is exhausting.'

'You make it sound like you're always telling me lies.' Mum shifts in her chair and stifles a yawn herself behind her hand.

'You know what I mean. I didn't lie, I just withheld the truth because it was too hard to explain.'

'You've been the same since you were small. I remember when you were a tot at play group. You came home with grazed knees and hands. When I asked you what had happened, you refused to tell me.' I exhale a small laugh, recalling the story, although it's been a while since I've heard it. 'I already knew what had happened. I was told as I came in to get you, but you didn't know that. You were trying to protect your little friend who had accidentally bumped into you and knocked you over. You keep everything in. And always think you're protecting someone else. That's how you end up hurting yourself. It's brilliant if someone has a secret – you're the best person to tell – but sometimes you hurt yourself by keeping things locked inside.'

The old house feels so cool that I shiver and sit up straight. Mum places her hand on my cheeks and tilts her head to assess me.

'Love you,' she says, before continuing. 'You know, I'm not happy Jonathan died. That would be cruel. But I'm glad you let go of him. I never did like him much. He was too full of himself. And now I know it was his fault – he almost killed you on purpose – if he had survived, I would go and bloody kill him myself.'

I'm not used to this tone from my mum. She's more likely to bake a cake to make someone happy than threaten to hurt them. In fact, this is probably the first time I've ever heard her say she would kill someone. It's not the sort of thing she would even joke about, and the steely look in her blue eyes says that this isn't a joke. Her eyes close and when she opens them the death fog seems to have cleared.

'Why don't you go back to Corfu with Hazel and Natalia. Tell them you want to see a Greek Easter, that they've made it sound so good, you've always wanted to see one and can you come and stay.'

'I can't do that. Yianni will be back in his room.'

She starts to shake her head. 'No. He moved out.'

'When?' My voice sounds like I'm accusing my mum of some kind of cheating.

The fact things are happening in his life and I don't know about them makes me nervous. What else has changed? His feelings? Why would he have any interest in me now? Mum's mouth opens to answer, but I cut in again before she can.

'No. Don't tell me. I don't want to know. I can't go to Corfu anyway, I'm here in case Amara needs me and to meet that beautiful baby of hers and it's not due for another week. I need sleep.' I scoot my chair back along the floor. 'Love you, Mum.'

She stands and kisses me on the forehead in the same way she always has, before wrapping me up in her slender arms.

'Love you, Ruby. Thank you for talking to me.' Then she says, 'Even if it has taken your whole life.'

A comforting laugh shudders through us. This needs to be a turning point. I might not be able to change completely, but I recognise the importance of talking to someone about pain. I hope never to see such pain again, but if I do, then I'll do my best to be more open.

Chapter 47

Now

Amara cancels our lunch. That's not accurate – I got a breathy phone call from Si saying that Amara is having contractions and she can't come to lunch. She snatched the phone off him to qualify that she is actually fine, and it'll probably be ages before anything happens, but she doesn't want her waters breaking while she is out and about. I offered to come over, but she swept the offer under the carpet, which leads me to believe she is in more pain than she was letting on.

Tomorrow is Good Friday and my plans have now adjusted to make a trip to the Abbey Gardens in Bury St Edmunds. The sun is illuminating the ruins of the Abbey so the flint almost looks silver in places, and the grass is dark and fresh in a way that only comes after lots of rain followed by the first day of sun. It's a beautiful place filled with manicured gardens leading to the ruins. I haven't been there in so long, not since I was a kid.

We've brought a blanket, so we plonk ourselves down in the sun and we all have to peel off our cardigans because it's too warm for them. We haven't been there long before Mum is throwing me in the deep end. She says to Hazel, 'Ruby mentioned to me about going to Corfu for a Greek Easter. I think she wants to experience all the food and such, don't you Ruby?'

Although she takes me by surprise, I manage to stifle a scowl and do my best to change it into thoughtful reflection.

Natalia bounces a little on her knees. '*Nai*! Ruby! Come and stay again. It would be so nice to have you back, even for a small time.' She grins and looks so much like Hazel. I'm grateful she doesn't look like Yianni. I would find that much too creepy. I shouldn't, but I would. Instead, Yianni looks like Pericles and his mother and Natalia is like a darker and smaller version of Hazel, without the glasses.

'It would be lovely, but I don't know how possible it is. I'll be back in France.'

Hazel says, 'You can get a flight from France to Corfu this time of year. We would love to have you. Easter is for family.' She turns to my mum. 'Why don't you come too? It's been much too long since you've visited us. Although, if you want to come for Easter, it's not until May this year.'

My mum doesn't take long mulling this idea over.

'We were going to visit when Ruby was in Corfu, but then she came home. Do you know what? Yes. I think we can make this happen. Marco can pay for us all.' Mum gives my knee three sharp taps. 'How exciting!'

'Mum...' I can't control my face any longer. If my eyes could form daggers, I would be sending very deadly ones over to her.

She deflects my gaze as though I'm not even looking at her. A white butterfly dances past and a group of teens cut through our conversation, cheering as a goal is scored between posts made of coats.

'Ruby, I know you're busy,' she begins, 'but family comes first.'

'Of course it does, and I would love to,' I turn to Natalia and Hazel, 'of course I would. But I can't right now. Not after taking all this time off to see Amara's baby.' They both press their lips together and nod sympathetically.

Mum gets Dad to agree to the whole Corfu thing. This means the public booking of their tickets around the dining room table after roast lamb on Easter Sunday. My stomach is in knots, because I do want to go but I can't just turn up in a months time out of the blue. My mum glances at me and gives me a look as if to ask whether I'm sure. I am. But that leads me to be sure of something else too. I need to do something. When everyone is in bed, I'm going to call Yianni.

Chapter 48

Now

Perched on the edge of my bed, I hover over my old phone screen looking at his name. I close my eyes and picture his face. Then it hits me – there's a few photos of us on this phone. I'd completely forgotten. Instead of calling him, I go into the pictures and skip to one of him from the night he took me to Manthos for dinner. I had wanted a photo in their swinging seat. I'd pushed Yianni down into the seat and taken a couple of photos. That's before we were together. Were we ever really together? Was it all a fling and the rest was just in my head? No. It was real. I take one last look at the laughter and surprise on his face as his hair whips in all directions. There's no way to suppress my smile as I look at the expression on his face.

I exit the photo and hit call instead. I press the phone into my ear. The thumb of my other hand gravitates to my mouth as I nibble the edge of my nail, something I've rarely done since my teens. The sound of the phone ringing in my ear makes my heart seem to flutter in the same awkward rhythm. It rings and rings then clicks over to voicemail. I hadn't prepared to leave a message, I just assumed he would answer. What's the time there? It's past midnight. He might be asleep.

'Hi, it's me. Ruby. Erm, I thought... it doesn't matter what I thought. I made a mistake. I'll call again in the morning. Night.' Then I hang up the phone. All I can do is hope he doesn't hate me for being such an idiot.

It's early on bank holiday Monday; it has to be because I feel as though I've barely slept. That or the constant dreams of Yianni and Corfu beach have left me more exhausted than when I started. My phone buzzes somewhere outside of my dream's reach. Groping around with blurry eyes, I knock it off the bedside table. The thump of it on the wooden floor snaps me out of my dream world and I abruptly sit up, flinging myself off the bed to find it.

'Hello? I'm here!'

'It's a girl!' Amara's voice sings down the line. I pull the phone from my ear and look at the screen. It's my new phone I'm holding, not my old one, and it's Si's name not Yianni's in front of me. Although it was definitely Amara's voice. My tired mind still can't understand how it isn't Yianni on the other end of the call. It's not. I replay what I just heard before realising what the information means.

'Congratulations!' I spend a moment squealing on her behalf before asking how she is. 'And how's the baby? What's her name?'

'I'm not telling you until you meet her. It went well ... that's not true. It was shit. Episiotomy level of shit. They said I'll get to leave once they've seen her latch on well to my boob. Then home. Can you come round? I forgot—'

'I'll be there. You couldn't stop me. Tell me what you need.'

'We left the baby's damn car seat at home. I thought we were so organised with the bag and all the other crap that was on the list. But no car seat, and they've said we can't leave unless they see her in it. Can you pop to our house now and bring it here?'

'Of course. Do you need anything else?'

'Not that I can think of. Thanks so much.'

'I'll be there soon. Give that gorgeous baby of yours a kiss from me. And send a photo, so I can confirm she is as gorgeous as I'm sure she is.'

'I'll think about it.' She laughs and I know she wouldn't be so mean as to not send one. 'My tea has arrived. I'll see you in a bit. Just head to the maternity ward.'

'Shall do. Congratulations, Amara.'

'*Ciao.*'

'*À bientôt.*' See you soon. And with that statement I jump up and rush around to get to her as quickly as I can. I wake up the whole house to announce the arrival of my god-daughter.

'You'll be back before we leave for our flight, right?' Natalia tracks me as I gather up my keys and thrust them in my bag.

'I can't see why not. You leave this afternoon, right? What time?'

Natalia tugs her coral dressing gown tight around her body then turns to Hazel before she steps forwards and kisses my cheek.

'Just after lunch.' Hazel's voice is warm in my ear. 'Drive safe and give her baby a kiss from us.'

Thoughts of Yianni melt away in the excitement of getting to meet my god-daughter. Going into my old house to get the car seat feels a little bizarre. I have to go all the way into the spare room to find it. The house is now officially Amara and Si's since we organised with the landlord to switch the lease. They've painted the living room purple and the spare bedroom is now white instead of blue. It has a cot, and bunches of stuffed toys as well. I've brought a little soft pink bunny to add to the collection.

As soon as I get to the hospital and find my way through the maze of white walls and the clouds of antiseptic, all my focus is on what's in front of me. Amara's always-wild hair looks like it'll turn to braids if she doesn't brush it soon, and Si looks like he hasn't slept, possibly ever. I kiss his stubbled cheek and he apologises for not having managed to wash as he smooths his hand over his soft Afro hair. He leaves to get us some hot chocolate as requested by Amara.

'Meet Lola,' Amara coos as I step towards her. She's still in the hospital bed with the curtain pulled around to give some flimsy privacy from other crying newborns.

I look over to see a squishy red face wrapped in a pink fluffy blanket. Lola's eyes are tightly shut. She's perfect.

Amara tells me her birth story which might be the tonic to put anyone off having children ever. She admits to being overjoyed and overwhelmed in equal measure, and I'm envious of her ability to always be honest about her feelings.

'How do you do that?'

'What?' She isn't looking at me; she's watching Lola and slowly rocking.

'Be so open about how you feel? It took me months to say to Jonathan that I loved him and even longer to tell him I didn't anymore. I couldn't even tell you or Mum what *actually* happened in the end until this week.'

Amara looks up at me and smiles. 'It's simple. You just open your mouth and say what's in your head. It's not a big deal. If you let go of hurting yourself or the people around you, you can pretty much say anything you like.'

I make a *tsk* sound. She's right, but it's completely unhelpful. It's just not that easy for me. It leaves everything too open. Although I do think Jonathan made me even more guarded, there's no way to magically change that now. It's going to be hard going.

'Here.' Amara passes me Lola and I'm suddenly over-whelmed with the fear of dropping her. I've never held a brand-new baby before. As I scoop her out of Amara's arms, she chuckles at me. 'I didn't know your eyes could get that big. She's a baby not a rabid dog.' I glance at her but only for a second. I'm too afraid to take my eyes off the creature in my arms. She barely weighs as much as a doll. Her eyes stay closed and her mouth puckers into a tiny O. Carefully I sit on the chair next to the hospital bed. Amara shifts her weight, and groans in doing so. 'When are you going to see Yianni?'

I match her groan. She doesn't know about my mum's attempted intervention and I'm loathe to tell her, even though I know I should, because I'm trying to be more open. It's a short explanation, but she is giddy by the end of it. As I glance from her to Lola, Amara looks like she could squeeze out tears of laughter with very little effort, other than not wanting to because of her stitches, and moaning at me for making her want to laugh.

'I'm not going with them.'

My words completely stop her in her tracks.

'What? Why?' she snaps at a louder volume than the rest of our conversation and baby Lola disapprovingly exhales and wriggles in my arms.

'I called him last night. He didn't answer. It was late, which I guess might be why. I left a message asking him to call me back. He must know the mistake I made by now. Bloody hell, Aunt Hazel was almost suffocating herself with laughter over it.'

'I'm still in shock you called him. Well done, I think you might actually be starting to own your feelings.'

The ticking clock in the corner of the room taunts me, letting me know that everything is catching up with me. The past is colliding with my present again and the future is an impossible task with too much possibility for trauma. The tiny wailing of a baby screeches out somewhere in the maternity ward and sets off another baby nearby.

'He hasn't exactly called back, though.'

'It doesn't matter. At the baby shower you said you were pleased I hadn't let my past hold me back. I'm proud you're starting to break away from your past too.'

'Sorry it took so long.' Si steps in from the other side of the curtain holding three paper cups of hot chocolate. 'The queue was crazy big.'

With that I manage to change the subject back to Lola and when they'll be allowed to take her home.

Chapter 49

Now

I left in plenty of time to get back so I could say goodbye to Hazel and Natalia. Plenty of time. Amara, Si and Lola were given the go-ahead to leave and we said our goodbyes and went our separate ways. Now I'm sitting in traffic and time is slipping away. I haven't moved more than an inch in twenty minutes. My phone rings through the car speakers and there's my mum's voice consuming the space in the car.

'Hello, sweet pea. Will you be back soon?'
'I'm stuck in traffic. I haven't moved in ages.'
'We have to leave in less than an hour to get to the airport.'
'Hopefully I'll get moving again soon. I'll let you know.'
'Alright, honey. Let me know.'

On the local news later that night I find out that a lorry full of livestock had jack-knifed. By some miracle no one was hurt, but it took ages for the freed pigs to stop causing mayhem on the road. Then, to top it off, someone had an accident on the nearest slip road while trying to avoid hitting one of the pigs. Again, no one was hurt, but it was enough to cause a complete standstill and for me to miss seeing off Hazel and Natalia.

Hazel called me before they left and I said goodbye over the phone. I spoke to Mum too. She wanted to check that it was alright for Natalia to take my old phone from my room. I asked whether there were any missed calls or texts. But there was nothing. Yianni obviously couldn't get over my stupidity. I'd hurt him too much and that was that. I don't blame him. I shouldn't have run away. I should've spoken to him, not Hazel. Instead, I let the inbuilt distrust I had acquired from my past with Jonathan spill over into my present. It's too late to dwell on it now, though. I hurt Yianni. Of course he doesn't want to speak to me. One minute I'm there wrapped in his arms promising I'll return, and the next I'm leaving without even saying goodbye. If it were the other way round, I wouldn't want to speak to him either. He must think I'm the worst kind of bitch.

Before agreeing that Natalia can, of course, have the phone, I ask Mum to wipe my stuff off it. *Restore to factory settings.* I wish I could restore *my* factory settings and move on from the ingrained ideas from the past. The notion that people can easily lie to me and cheat on me and hurt me. Forgetting that I can cause pain too simply by doing what I've trained my mind to do. Closing down and walking away.

In the days that follow I spend as much time with my god-daughter as I can before heading back to Rouen. Amara doesn't make a fuss about Yianni; she knows me better than that. She asks questions and I answer honestly. She reassures me that it's all good. My first steps towards dating. That I can move on now. Automatically my head bobs, but inside it feels like an impossible thought. In some ways this is worse than when Jonathan killed himself. When that happened, I had the trauma and loss to recover from, but I had known that I didn't want to spend my life with him. I'll always carry it with me. It's not something that will ever go away, but time changes everything. With Yianni, my pathetic misunderstanding cost me my own happiness. A raw, unadulterated happiness that I then spoiled by mixing in the part of me that's held me back for so long... Fear. And now time has changed the way he feels about me. I guess I just have to hope it'll do the same for me. Right now I can't imagine ever not wanting to see his face.

Yianni was kind, supportive and honest, everything that Jonathan wasn't, and I lost him all because I didn't have faith in him. I want to say all of this to Amara, but the words catch in my chest. My ribcage squeezes them back down and then Lola squeaks for a feed, saving me from my torment. Knowing I need to speak up when things hurt doesn't make it any easier. It's still like pulling out fingernails to me.

After that the topic was left well alone. Maybe Amara doesn't want to push me when she knows how hard I'm trying. I focus all my efforts on being there for her and Si when they need anything or want anything.

Back at home even Mum doesn't ask any more questions. I catch her looking at me and occasionally she squeezes my hand in a certain way that makes me yearn to be alone in my room in Rouen. Dad isn't oblivious, but he knows better than to ask questions. Instead, he just ruffles my hair more than normal.

My bags are packed and in Dad's boot. Tomorrow I leave for Rouen. For home. It's maybe half an hour since saying goodnight to my parents. I wanted to get an early night, but as I can't seem to sleep, I pick up a book from the shelf. It's my old copy of *Rebecca*. The pages are yellow, and the corners are dog-eared and bent out of shape. I still love the book though. As soon as I pick it up, I'm engrossed.

A light tap on the door rouses me from the pages.

'Come in.' I barely have time to look up before my mum steps inside the door.

'I was hoping we could have a little chat,' she begins, before noticing the book in my hand. 'Oh gosh, how many times have you read that?'

My shoulders rise and fall. I can't even guess. 'What did you want to talk about?'

I scoot over a bit and she perches on the edge of the bed. It's as though I'm ten years old. Every movement we've made feels almost rehearsed, not because it's stilted or somehow fake, but because it's comfy and familiar. Mum would often sit and talk to me at night. Dad would too sometimes, but more often than not it would be Mum stroking the hair from my face and giving my cheek one last soft kiss for the day.

'I keep thinking about Sue and Jonathan.' She exhales, and clasps her hands firmly together. 'You didn't say much about how it was seeing her today. All you said over dinner was that she was very good about you losing the ring. I take it you didn't tell her what Jonathan did?'

I quickly shake my head to confirm that I hadn't – and wouldn't – tell her that particular truth. I think back to my lunch with Sue, Jonathan's mum. She had found out I was back from France and was desperate to see me. Up until then

I'd managed to avoid her and so had dodged telling her about the lost engagement ring. I didn't want to cause her more pain. None of it's her fault. Sue's eyes had glistened and she squeezed my hand with its missing ring before she reassured me.

'She said she thought it was Jonathan's way of telling me it was time to move on.'

Silence lingers in the air as I stare up at the blank ceiling above me.

Eventually Mum's gentle voice escapes her lips. 'That was a kind thing for her to say.'

'Was it?'

Although I know it was meant with the best of intentions, it felt like she was telling me that Jonathan was still making decisions for me. That I should be deferring to a ghost to organise my future.

'Wasn't it?' Mum says. Her forehead is lined with confusion.

'Yeah, I guess. I know Sue meant well. It was her son, her *perfect* son. I just… I don't want to think about him like he still has something over me.'

Mum nods before straightening herself out. 'Well, that brings me nicely to what I wanted to say. Which is rather handy as I had no idea how I was going to say it before. I think I wanted to say, or should I say ask, whether you think Jonathan is still affecting you? Not just the big dramatic end to it all, but the way he treated you before he died. Sadly, I'm sure you won't be telling me the half of it, but what I do know is you spoke to me less and less while he was alive, and you seemed to shrink away behind him. Before Jonathan you were always laughing, and you loved the social aspect to hospitality. You were so good at it. Then somewhere along the way you lost your spark, as though hospitality was the best way to avoid real connections, and the antisocial hours made it even easier for you to hide. If he ever put you down or told you—'

'Mum—' I need her to stop, because she's cutting way too close to the truth of it all.

'No, let me finish. If he ever put you down, he was only doing it to make himself feel bigger and better. Not because you weren't good enough, but because he knew he would never be. Slowly making you feel bad about yourself was his way of controlling you. I know the type, Ruby. I've seen it before.'

I don't need words to ask what she means. Folding my arms over the duvet and tilting my head on the pillow is enough for Mum to understand I'll need a little more explanation than that. She looks away and twiddles her fingers, running them over each other before turning back to me.

'Hazel, and her first husband. I didn't like to admit it to myself, but I could see a bit of Jonathan being a bit like Hazel's first husband. I don't know how much you remember about him. We didn't spend all that much time with him. He was always full of smiles when people were around. I was fooled too for a long time. Stupidly, I thought he was bloody brilliant in fact. He was such a charmer.'

I shuffle to roll on my side, giving Mum more room to move further onto the bed.

'What made you realise he wasn't?'

Mum lowers her eyes and her fingers begin twisting around each other again.

'One New Year's Eve, he had too much to drink when we were all out at a friend's party in this big country house. Anyway, it was almost midnight and I went to find them, him and Hazel I mean. They didn't know I was coming up behind them, so he didn't know I could hear him. He was pointing his beer towards some woman, and I heard him say something like, *you used to look that good. You still could if you put some effort in.* It was something like that. There was more to it all, but it made me see him differently. It made me open my eyes to how much Hazel was shrinking away. She was heartbroken when he left, but honestly, I was relieved.'

I can't imagine Hazel putting up with anyone like that. She always seems so put together and strong. She might be behind the scenes in the kitchen of Greek Secret, but she's a big part of its driving force. Plus, Pericles is so loving. That's not to say I haven't seen them have the odd heated debate, but the way he looks at her says it all. It's the same way Yianni would look at me. Watching me from across the room with a contented curl on his lips. I swallow back the thought and the image in my head.

'I can't imagine Hazel letting anyone talk to her like that.'

'These people wear you down so you don't notice it happen. You can start off as the strongest oak tree, but they can whittle you down to a toothpick and you won't even notice it happening or remember being rooted to the ground as they toss you about. I think you need to find your roots again, Ruby.'

Words don't come easily to me in response to this outpouring. I want to open up and tell her I agree and she's right. That that's exactly what Jonathan did to me, with constant back-handed compliments and his rollercoaster of emotions.

'It's okay, Ruby. You don't have to say anything if you don't want to. I'm always here for you. You know your dad and I would drop everything if you needed us to. Just think about

303

who you want to be and what you want. Start holding that beautiful head of yours up again. I know you can be that oak tree again. It's all still inside you and I don't want your confidence to be defined by anyone but you. Or your ability to trust people, including me.'

I look up to make eye contact with her. There is one thing I know she'll understand and that'll make her smile.

'I wore a bikini in Corfu for the first time since the accident.' I can feel my cheeks lift at the memory. Mum's face does the same, little wrinkles in the corners of her eyes deepening with the tender smile on her face. Her fingers move over my cheek as she smooths the hair from my eyes.

'I know that's a big step, showing people your scars. I'm so proud of you, Ruby.'

'Thanks, Mum.'

Chapter 50

Now

I've been back in Rouen for a few weeks. It's Monday and we don't open for lunch on a Monday or at all on a Sunday. I've been trudging around the very few shops that are open on a Monday morning. It's a massive city, but it's not like being in England. The French live at a completely different pace. They eat later, live slower, and that's something I admire wholeheartedly. Except when it's Sunday or Monday morning and I have nothing to do but spend my hard-earned euros and everything is closed. But luckily, Maison Vatelier is open, a patisserie that I adore. They have award-winning brioches, but that's not why I go there. I'm in it for the giant raspberry macaroons with a petal on top. I don't allow myself to go there often, because it's not cheap, but when I do go, it's worth every penny.

Once my treat is in its box in a pale pink paper bag, I make my way towards the cathedral. I like sitting outside the imposing structure while contemplating all the mistakes I've made that have brought me to this point – sitting alone on a stone step in the cold, eating giant macaroons. Yes, macaroons, because today I bought two. I settle into my daydreaming while studying the rows and rows of statues that decorate the facade of the cathedral. They all look down their stone noses at me, as though they know the truth about me – that I am a coward. I've always been a coward. I should have told Jonathan straightaway it wasn't right, and I should have asked Yianni outright when I thought he had got another girl pregnant. I've spent my whole life running away from my feelings. It's so easy to see in hindsight. As though it's all so bloody simple.

I scoop the first macaroon out of the box and inhale the fresh tang of the raspberries and the vanilla in the centre. As I take a deep lungful of the delicious scent, I notice a man watching me. He is also sitting on the steps not far from the cathedral and he's sprinkling little crumbs from what looks like a brioche for the birds near his feet. He's holding the same pink bag from the same shop as I am.

'*Bien choisi.*' Good choice. He gestures towards the pink bag by my feet.

He's good-looking with character to his face – wide lips, tidy hair, and he's well dressed in a smart overcoat. I smile and nod.

'Do you speak French?' he asks in heavily accented English.

I suppose I must look confused. Or perhaps sitting around sniffing macaroons is more of a tourist pastime. Who knows?

'*Oui,*' I say, and look out across the empty square in front of us, wondering how many of those little wooden huts they will manage to squeeze in for the Christmas market.

The man scoots closer to me and asks me if I live far from here.

I glance away from him as he shuffles nearer, and then I stiffen. '*Merde*,' I say under my breath. My heart suddenly feels like it's stopped, because I can't quite believe what I'm seeing in the square. 'What the hell?' I blurt out.

The stranger begins to apologise.

'No, not you.' I wave a hand towards him, then repeat in French. '*Non, pas vous.*'

The next word that falls out of my mouth is more like a scream. 'Yianni?!'

Although the man walking in the square looks like Yianni, even as his name screeches out of me, I don't really believe that it is him. I've never seen him in a coat and for some reason that makes the person I'm gazing at particularly implausible. He turns to look at the screeching woman on the steps. But, then, everyone has turned to face me. People walking dogs and meandering towards the cathedral look at me like I've gone mad, and two armed police officers have reacted to my outburst. '*Désolée*', I mouth in their direction. Sorry. They scowl, but they keep moving.

My face turns back to the man. Not the one next to me talking nonsense about my rudeness as he slowly edges away, the one walking in front of the cathedral. He is the only person to keep his eyes on me. He doesn't smile.

It's not him.

He has the same build, the same hair. But it's not him. It's not Yianni.

The image of the setting Corfu sun, disappearing as if it's been doused by the sea, flashes through my mind. It's as though my heart is the sun and without Yianni it's being extinguished. Drowning. My drowned heart. I'm drowning. Ever since Jonathan committed suicide – or whatever it is that he did – I've put up a wall to protect myself, but that's not really what I was doing. I've been hiding and avoiding living because simply existing is so much easier. Yianni, Amara, Mum… They've all been trying to tell me, trying to help me. It's just hard to accept. Yianni was right; I'm not sure I see who I really am when I look in the mirror. All that's been left is a shadow. Is this who I always was? I know I've always found it hard to open up to people – I'm secretive with my feelings and thoughts – but this is different. Mum was right. I didn't really want to admit that Jonathan had a lasting effect on me beyond the way that he ended it all. For years now, I've told myself it was the way he died that I was hiding from. I needed space and time to get over that, and I did, of course. I look at my hand still clasping the fat macaroon with a bite taken out of it. No ring on my finger, but Jonathan has left scars that lattice my soul. More trust issues, more pain. I'm still doing it. Still being defined by my past. Still letting it hold me back.

But not anymore. I can't let it define me. Someone else's behaviour shouldn't be what defines me. It's in the past. It shouldn't stop me going for what I want.

The way I felt like I was going to catch fire when I caught sight of that man in the square, believing he was Yianni, because I so desperately wanted it to be him.

I stand up, macaroon still in hand and my back as straight as it will go. With my other hand I scoop my phone out of my pocket to call Rob. I just hope he doesn't hate me for what I'm about to say.

Chapter 51

Now

From the moment I got off the phone to Rob and proceeded to swallow the last of my second macaroon, up until right now, my insides have been tangled. The entire time I've felt as though I've been breathing measured breaths with my mouth open, because it's like there's not enough oxygen in my lungs to sustain me. I guess the tangle is that strange place where excitement and fear collide and knot together. The emotions become inseparable and it feels hard to breathe.

Rob is the only person I have told about my trip to Corfu. Not Mum or Dad or Amara. This is about me grabbing life by the scruff of its neck and taking a risk I want to take. No matter what Yianni says, at least I'll have put myself out there. I'm taking a risk on something I want. I want him. I want to feel how I felt with him last year, wrapped in the bubble of his love. From the glances under his thick black lashes to the sensation of his hot skin against mine under the stars. I want all of it. To roll my eyes at him, to feel irritated, to feel excited, to feel loved. I want all of it with him. The knot weighs heavy in my stomach knowing he might not want me and he might have moved on. It's a strong possibility. The most likely one. But that's not going to stop me from trying.

Corfu. I'm back at long last. I've hired a little car from the airport and can almost taste the synthetic scent of pine needles hanging from the air freshener on the mirror. As I drive along the winding roads, I'm consumed by the real trees and vivid greens that carpet the rolling landscape. Passing through villages with terracotta-and-white houses and jutting balconies, the hot-pink bougainvillea in full bloom, it hits me: what if Yianni wants to give it a go? Then what? Would I move to Corfu? It's completely idyllic here. It's crazy to think this could be my home. Another wave of adrenaline pulses under my skin.

It's mid-afternoon by the time I pull up outside the taverna and park next to Yianni's car. It's almost exactly a year since I first arrived at Greek Secret with him. So much has happened. I've lived here in Corfu and been happier than I can ever remember, then France where I was lonelier than I could've imagined. And, of course, I became a godmother to beautiful Lola this year too. The past year has changed me for the better. It was something I needed rather than something I wanted.

My body tingles and my heart hammers in my chest as I make my way through the dusty carpark. The restaurant looks empty but the sign to say it's closed isn't up at the entrance. Plus, his car is here, although he could have walked down into the village. It's as though nothing has changed. The vines still beautifully weave along the terrace and the chairs and tables are all perfectly laid. As I take it all in, I know this is the place that feels most like home to me. It's where I want to be.

'*Kalimera*? Is anyone here?' I call out.

'One moment.'

Hearing his voice again makes me doubt it all. It's coming from the side room, the one he used as a bedroom while I was staying in his room at Hazel and Pericles's house.

Footsteps come echoing from the hall to the kitchen and Natalia appears.

'Ruby?' Her chocolate eyes shine as she bounds towards me. 'How are you here?' She grabs my arms and bounces before hugging me. That's when Yianni appears in his doorway. Nothing has outwardly changed him in the past year. Still in his black fitted short-sleeve shirt and tight trousers. As I eye him, his face gives nothing away, only perhaps the briefest note of surprise. I clutch Natalia's slim frame against my own, more to steady myself than anything else. All I want to do is run into Yianni's arms and tell him I'm sorry for being so ridiculous and not returning to Corfu for so long. I want to tell him I'm sorry for hurting him, for leaving him. But I can't, not with Natalia here. Maybe it's good that she's here. It delays me finding out whether he has moved on without me. The thought causes stomach acid to burn the back of my throat. If he turns me away, I need to hold it together. I swallow back the stinging sensation and try to stay focused.

Natalia releases me from her grasp. 'Look, Yianni, it's Ruby!'

'*Kalimera*, Ruby.' His tone is stone cold. At best I could call it neutral I suppose. His arms knit together over his broad chest, and he politely smiles, but I swear it's only because Natalia's beaming.

'Where is everyone?' I glance at the empty restaurant in an attempt to seem natural. To seem calm. Nothing feels natural or calm right now. I can even feel my pulse in my fingertips. I nip at the sides of my skirt to give my hands something to do.

'Mama and Papa left after the last customers,' Natalia says. 'Yianni promised to take me into Sidari to meet friends. I can call and cancel, and we can all go to the house.'

'No, no. Please don't cancel for me. I'll be staying for at least a week. We'll have plenty of time to catch up. I'll go to the house and surprise your mum and dad.'

'At least come in the car with us. I have so much to tell you. Please?' Natalia momentarily reminds me of her younger self back when she was ten and she followed me about and wanted to do anything I did.

I take a breath and look back at Yianni who has kept his distance in the doorway of his room. If it still is his room. 'It's up to Yianni. He might have things to do after dropping you off.'

'Oh yes, he has big plans to be helping Papa in the garden. So, he can take you there after taking me to Sidari. Let me get my bag.' Natalia bounds back towards the kitchen leaving Yianni and me alone.

'Yianni, I…'

But before I can even start, Natalia is back from the kitchen and marching us off towards Yianni's car.

Chapter 52

Now

'So how come you're so early?' Natalia quizzes me in the car.

'Early?' I look back at her, twisting in my seat. She had politely insisted I sit in the front of the car next to Yianni. Now he's backing the car out into the road, sitting only inches from me. Heat burns from my pores so hot it might mix with the air conditioning and cause a cyclone. Does he feel it too? So far he won't even look at me, avoiding my gaze as though I'm Medusa.

'Yes, *theia* Fern and *theios* Marco are coming to visit for Easter. You said you couldn't come, but you're here two days early. I'm so happy you changed your mind.'

Easter. I'd got it in my head that my mum and dad weren't leaving for another week or so. I knew they'd booked and I knew they were going to Corfu, but for some reason it seemed further away than it is. Two days and my mum and dad will both be here. If this doesn't work out, I'll then have to put up with sideways looks from my mum laden with pity. The thought of it makes me bite my cheek.

'Oh yeah, I'd forgotten they were coming.'

'Forgotten? Isn't that why you are here?' It's the most Yianni has said to me. His eyes dart towards me then back at the road.

I swallow hard, knowing I need to be honest, but I don't really want to include Natalia in the conversation.

'No, actually, it's not.' I openly study Yianni's reaction. The twitch of his fingers on the steering wheel and the way he sucks in his top lip in concentration. I've missed watching him, being near him, breathing in the same air as him. The car bounces over a pothole and I look away.

It's Natalia who breaks the moment of silence, clearly oblivious to any tension between me and Yianni.

'If not for Easter, then why? Not that I'm unhappy. It is always good to have you to stay.'

Fixing my eyes back on Yianni, I say, 'Because I made a promise to return.'

It's only a fifteen-minute drive to Sidari. In that time, Natalia tells me about the plan for Easter and hopes I'll be about to enjoy it all. She asks if I'll be staying at the house and I explain that I've booked a room at Perros Hotel for the week. It's not far from Greek Secret.

Then we're alone. Yianni and I driving along in his car. The air con is freezing and my throat is completely dry when I try to speak.

'I made a mistake,' I croak.

'Yes. You thought I was having a child.' There's a laugh in Yianni's voice that helps to ease the twisting emotions I've been feeling. 'Why didn't you talk to me?'

That's the question. It's like asking me why I'm a stupid idiot. I've asked myself that question so often since finding out my mistake.

'Jonathan. He's why. I was so used to being lied to and manipulated, and that girl told me she was having your baby—'

'No, she told you she was having her husband's baby.'

I bury my face in my hands as the memory rolls over me.

Yianni drives out of town and out into the bloom of Corfu. He pulls the car over in a layby next to high grasses and reeds. The engine abruptly shuts off and he gets out of the car. I follow suit and watch as Yianni looks up at the sparse clouds like froth in the sky.

'Why are you here, Ruby? You leave and I don't hear from you. You find out you were wrong and still I don't hear from you.'

'I called you.'

'When?'

'Before Hazel and Natalia left. I left a message and everything.'

'What did it say?'

'I don't know.' Yianni begins to walk down a narrow side road and I follow alongside him. 'Something about being wrong and that I'd call you again in the morning.'

'Ah.' Yianni pulls his phone from his pocket and passes it to me. The screen is a spiderweb of cracks and lines. I pass back his broken phone. 'I can answer calls and I can make calls, but that is it. I wouldn't know who is trying to call or message. I can't see the screen well enough. In fact...' Yianni talks to his phone in Greek then listens to his voicemail. He begins to laugh.

'There is one from Papa telling me I'm late.'

My palms are clammy, and not just because the late April sun is beating down on me, but because there's hope. He didn't know I'd called. He wasn't intentionally ignoring me. Then, there it is, my voicemail.

Hi, it's me. Ruby. Erm, I thought... it doesn't matter what I thought. I made a mistake. I'll call again in the morning. Night.

'Did you call again? In the morning?' Yianni glances at me before fixing his eyes back on the dirt track.

I shake my head. 'Amara had her baby and by the time I got home Natalia had left with my old phone and everything on it.' I stop walking and press my hands to my hips. Yianni turns to face me and looks me up and down. 'I know that everything that happened with Jonathan messed me up, but I don't want that. I don't want what happened in the past to define who I am now and ruin what we had.' I snatch a breath trying to figure out my words, before realising that it's simple. 'I've missed you.'

Yianni's eyes narrow on mine and he pushes a thick curl out of his face and behind his ear before mirroring my body language by placing his hands on his hips.

'You need to talk to *me* if we can work this out. No running away'

'I'm not good at talking about everything I think and feel, but I am better with you. And, I can promise I'll try to be better, and I won't leave without telling you why first.'

'You can leave without telling me, to the shops or the beach, but not to another country. *Nai?*'

'I think I can manage that.'

'If I remember,' he cuts the space between us in half, now our bodies are almost touching, 'you want your own restaurant.' Now his hands are slipping around my waist. My breath and my heart feel like a skipping record. I'm sure that my palpitations must be visible in my throat as I tilt my head further back to keep my eyes on his. 'Will Greek Secret do for now?'

All I manage to say is *mmmhmm* as his mouth descends towards mine, warm and inviting. The months we were apart were a gaping void, but in his arms I have found someone I can talk to, someone I want to be with. Someone I love. Yianni pulls me in even closer and I'm on my tiptoes to meet him. We hold each other so tightly I think our cells might fuse together as his aftershave fills my lungs.

Yianni pulls away from our kiss and looks down at me, gently shaking his head. His hand comes to rest on the line of my jaw.

'You know we have to tell everyone now. How do you think they will take it?'

We still have so much to work out, more than just telling Hazel, Pericles and Natalia. *I* have so much to work through to stop myself falling into the traps that Jonathan laid for me. But I'm determined to be a stronger person, and that starts with surrounding myself with better people, like Yianni. Like the supportive family I'm so lucky to have.

'My mum already knows. Which probably means Hazel knows. She's a lot better at keeping a secret than my mum.'

Yianni's eyebrows shoot up before relaxing again as his fingers trace a line down my neck. He says, 'Natalia also knows.'

'What?' Now my eyebrows shoot up to mimic Yianni's.

'You gave a fifteen-year-old girl your phone without

317

deleting anything. What did you think would happen? The same day she was knocking at my door asking question, question, question. A thousand questions.'

'Oh, bloody hell. I told Mum to delete everything.' I squeeze my eyes tightly shut to suppress the thought of Natalia reading texts that Yianni and I had sent one another.

'It does not matter. I love you, and it doesn't matter what anyone thinks of it. Just no more running and no more secrets.'

I weave my fingers into the curls around Yianni's neck, 'Not even a Greek Secret?' I let a cheeky grin spread across my face. Yianni groans and rolls his eyes before pulling me into his chest and pressing his lips to mine.

Epilogue

The Future Now

It all needs to be perfect. Every napkin needs to be just right, every glass. Everything's white and fresh from the wedding dress itself to the chairs. The only pop of colour is the bougainvillea over the curve of the arch. There will be nothing else to distract from the view of golden sand and the setting sun over the sea when the time comes. Right now, the sun is still high in the sky as it blazes into mid-afternoon.

I move frantically from table to table, cleaning knives, adjusting the well-placed linen swans until they're perfect, and picking up wedding favours only to put them back down again in the same position.

My heart pounds in my chest and adrenaline pulses, crashing over me like sea on rocks. I smooth my hands along my dress and step back. It's all ready. I turn and glance around only to remember I'm alone and my phone is nowhere to be seen for me to take a photo of it all. Soon the whole place will throb with people and napkins will be moved and placed on laps. There'll be no trace of the hard work that went into it all. It's worth it though. I couldn't be more excited for this moment. It's as though everything has been leading me here.

'It is perfect. Like you.' Yianni's voice carries on the sea breeze and a smile touches my lips. Turning back towards the entrance, I catch sight of him. White linen trousers and matching shirt unbuttoned just enough to see more of his silky tanned skin. The only embellishment of sorts is the sprig of gypsophila for his buttonhole. His dark curls dance around the smile on his face.

'You're not meant to be here. Not yet.'

I do my best to purse my lips. He isn't fazed. He strolls towards me and pulls me in.

'Something arrived, and I thought it was important to bring it before the guests arrive.'

'It's here? They finished in time?'

My fingers dig into the thick muscles on his upper arms and I almost hop with anticipation. A laugh pulses from his chest as he nods.

'Show me. No, wait, I need to take a photo before a breeze comes and changes everything. I can't find my phone though.'

'Ah.' He slips his hand into a back pocket, and his hand reappears with my phone in it. 'You left it at home on charge. Five years and you don't change.'

'Do you want me to change?'

He passes me the phone but doesn't let go of it when I try to take it. Instead, he pulls me in. Instinctively my chin tilts up for a lingering kiss, enjoying his soft lips and the graze of his stubble on my chin. It's the perfect moment of peace before the inevitable madness descends.

Yianni's mouth leaves mine and he studies my face before saying, 'No. It's too late for that now. I'm used to picking up after you.' He grins then snaps away as I swat at him.

'*Espèce de–*'

'Oh, yes? You know I know this one now. I'm some kind of…? What?' I narrow my eyes at him, but he's still there with a broad smile plastered on his face. 'It is alright. I forgive you. You take your picture and stay there. I will soon have a smile back on your face.'

'Be careful you don't get dirty,' I call as Yianni moves away, his feet padding back towards the entrance and out onto the beach beyond. I begin to snap photos of the neatly laid tables stretching out in front of me.

In the corner of my eye, I'm aware of Yianni putting out a stepladder and I listen as he begins banging about at the entrance. It isn't long before I can't wait a moment more. I march over, ducking under where he is working to watch him make the final adjustments. Stepping back into the sand, I look up and watch as he hangs the hand-painted and sculpted sign we commissioned only a month ago. We spent so long struggling to pick a name for our new venture I thought there wasn't going to be one.

'It's beautiful, just how I imagined. And just in time too. The caterers and staff will be here soon.' I press my thumbs to my temples. 'God. You know, I think I'm more stressed about this than *our* wedding. In fact, I'm a lot more stressed about it.'

Yianni and I had our beach wedding last year. Our wedding reception was at Manthos in San Stefanos, where we had our first unofficial date. It was such a wonderful day, bursting with happy faces, family and love. When it was all over, I knew that I wanted to organise more weddings. I'd enjoyed discussing every detail of ours so much. We both loved organising it all. It's the ultimate in hospitality. But at the same time, there was no way I wanted to give up working at Greek Secret either. I've loved every minute of working there every summer since first coming to Corfu, and enjoyed travelling with Yianni in the winter months. Then, only about a month after our honeymoon, Yianni came home with a story about a little lonely beach taverna for sale in another part of Corfu. It was tiny and falling apart. It had mostly been used for local families and even then, not for some time, not since the head of the family died and no one wanted to take it on. It needed everything done and there wasn't much else nearby so it hadn't turned a profit in a long time. The family just wanted it gone. Yianni knew I'd want it, knew the potential it had for events. It would mean that we could organise weddings and catering and have our own business just like I'd always wanted, while still working with Hazel, Pericles and Natalia. So, we've put everything we had into it. Every last penny of savings, every spare moment of time fixing things and building it up from scratch.

Today is the day. The first wedding reception. Amara and Si's wedding reception, no less. I check the time on my phone. I need to get back to have my makeup done. Amara has given me strict instructions not to be late getting my bridesmaid dress on. She knows I will be checking every detail of the reception up until the last moment. She knows I just want everything to be right for her. When she heard we were buying this place, she asked straight away whether theirs could be the first wedding for us to organise.

It's a dream venue, nestled back into the curve of a little

alcove of rocks and sand, with no one nearby. The guests will be able to dance all night if they want to. I want the whole reception to be a dream for Amara, and Si too. They have three kids now, a girl and two boys. They deserve to have this big family celebration of their love.

'Only you could get married then one year later be organising someone else's wedding. And anyway, it's Amara. She would forgive us if we get it all wrong.' Yianni edges the sign a little to the left as he speaks.

'*I* wouldn't.'

Yianni laughs as he studies the sign again from his vantage point on the stepladder. He says, 'I am very proud of you.'

With my thumb I spin the white-gold rings encrusted with diamonds on my left hand and smile. 'I'm proud of us.' I continue to look up at him as he steadily aligns the sign, taking as much care as I had with the tables. '*We've* done this. All of it. And there's going to be so many more.'

Yianni jumps off his stepladder and down into the soft golden sand.

'There,' he says, 'now we are ready.'

Yianni's arm wraps around me and he squeezes me in, tucking me into the curve of his arms before pressing a kiss onto the top of my head.

Over the entrance and under the swathe of sweet pink bougainvillea, our whitewashed sign reads "Secret Love". Only, it's not much of a secret anymore.

A note from the author…

Thank you for reading *Greek Secret*. I loved writing Ruby and Yianni's journey to happiness. It's always wonderful to take myself back to Corfu, but these characters really sucked me into their world with their flaws and heartfelt emotions. I really hope you felt the same.

I love to read what you think about my work. So please remember to review (reviews change lives - trust me - and I would be so grateful for you to review this book) and come and have a chat with me on my social pages.

Instagram & Facebook: @FrancescaCatlowOfficial
Twitter & TikTok: @FrancescaCatlow
You can also hit follow on amazon for updates with book releases.

Francesca x

Made in the USA
Coppell, TX
15 March 2024

9359R00194